Gilt

KATHERINE LONGSHORE

VIKING
An Imprint of Penguin Group (USA) Inc.

VIKING
Published by Penguin Group
Penguin Group (USA) Inc., 345 Hudson Street, New York, New York 10014, U.S.A.
Penguin Group (Canada), 90 Eglinton Avenue East, Suite 700, Toronto, Ontario, Canada M4P 2Y3
(a division of Pearson Penguin Canada Inc.)
Penguin Books Ltd, 80 Strand, London WC2R 0RL, England
Penguin Ireland, 25 St Stephen's Green, Dublin 2, Ireland (a division of Penguin Books Ltd)
Penguin Group (Australia), 250 Camberwell Road, Camberwell, Victoria 3124, Australia (a division
of Pearson Australia Group Pty Ltd)
Penguin Books India Pvt Ltd, 11 Community Centre, Panchsheel Park, New Delhi – 110 017, India
Penguin Group (NZ), 67 Apollo Drive, Rosedale, Auckland 0632, New Zealand (a division of
Pearson New Zealand Ltd.)
Penguin Books (South Africa) (Pty) Ltd, 24 Sturdee Avenue, Rosebank, Johannesburg 2196, South
Africa

Penguin Books Ltd, Registered Offices: 80 Strand, London WC2R 0RL, England

First published in 2012 by Viking, a member of Penguin Group (USA) Inc.

10 9 8 7 6 5 4 3 2

LIBRARY OF CONGRESS CATALOGING-IN-PUBLICATION DATA
Longshore, Katherine.
Gilt / by Katherine Longshore.
p. cm.
Summary: In 1539, Kitty Tylney and her best friend Cat Howard—the audacious, self-proclaimed
"Queen of Misrule"—both servants to the Duchess of Norfolk, move to the court of King Henry
VIII, who fancies Cat, and when Cat becomes queen Kitty must learn to navigate the complexities
and dangers of the royal court.
ISBN 978-0-670-01399-9 (hardcover)
1. Catharine Howard, Queen, consort of Henry VIII, King of England, d. 1542—Juvenile fiction.
[1. Catharine Howard, Queen, consort of Henry VIII, King of England, d. 1542—Fiction. 2. Kings,
queens, rulers, etc.—Fiction. 3. Court and courtiers—Fiction. 4. Henry VIII, King of England, 1491–
1547—Fiction. 5. Great Britain—History—Henry VIII, 1509–1547—Fiction.] I. Title.
PZ7.L864Gi 2012   [Fic]—dc23   2011028214

Printed in U.S.A.   Set in ITC Legacy Serif Std   Book design by Kate Renner

For my dad, who never let me feel unloved

Gilt

1539

"You're not going to steal anything."

I left the question—*Are you?*—off the end of the sentence. But Cat heard it anyway.

"Of course not." She paused to look at me, shadows eclipsing half her face, blue eyes glittering in the moonlight from the tall, narrow windows of the upper gallery. "I could be flogged. Or pilloried. Or have a hand cut off."

A drunken roar of laughter vented up through the beams of the great hall below us.

"Or executed," I muttered.

"We're just going to look. They can't hang us for that," she said, pulling me into a room congested with luxury. Arras tapestries mantled the walls, depicting knights on horseback charging to distant crusades. A silver goblet sat on a table by the fire between two chairs that were cushioned in velvet and tassled in gold.

"Consider it inventory," Cat explained, trailing her finger along the gold thread in a tapestry. "We're doing the duchess a favor."

"Right," I said. "Explain to me how Agnes Howard, née Tylney, the Dowager Duchess of Norfolk, most esteemed noblewoman in England, will think it a favor when she discovers two of her protégées riffling through her clothes."

"The duchess has gowns and furs and rings and pendants that she only wears on state occasions, and God knows we haven't had one of those since Queen Jane died. Someone has to appreciate her things."

"Without her realizing it."

"She's downstairs," Cat said. "Feasting with the duke. Nothing interrupts her when her stepson comes to visit. They closet themselves away and scheme until dawn."

She sat and laid her childlike hands over the lions' heads on the arms of the chair.

"Not like our wobbly old stools," she said, caressing the golden mane.

"Or splintery benches," I agreed, risking a seat in the other chair. I stretched my ragged slippers toward the fire.

Few had access to the duchess's chambers. Close to two hundred nieces, nephews, cousins, and staff lived at Norfolk House. Only select family members and the duchess's most trusted servants were allowed into her apartments. The rest of us did our best to stay out of her way. I stared up at the ceiling and wondered how it felt to have people care enough about you to avoid your presence.

"I could get used to this," Cat murmured. "Like being at court. Like a throne."

"Just like old times," I said, resting my head against the heraldic images carved on the back of the chair.

Cat laughed.

"You still remember that?" she said. "How we used to play that we were at court?"

"Used to?" I said. "We never stopped."

The game had just changed—from little girls playing princesses to a more grown-up and complicated hierarchy of status and favor.

Cat leaped up and mashed her face close to mine, a mischievous smile flickering over it.

"Onward," she said, widening her eyes. She spun around and marched to the next door. The door to the duchess's most private place: her bedchamber.

I pulled myself from the chair and stepped forward, the thrill of what we were about to do making my fingers tingle.

Cat stood to attention like the duchess's steward, staring straight ahead, eyes blank and unemotional. Even drawn up, she stood a full head shorter than me, and I slouched self-consciously to redress the balance.

She flicked the latch—the sound loud as a cannon shot—and pushed the door open with a grunt and a flourish. The room beyond lay draped in moonlight.

"After you."

Cat kept up her gallant pantomime until I came abreast of her. Then she threw back her auburn curls and danced through the door ahead of me.

"Glass in the windows!" she crowed, pressing her nose to the glazing. Our room had nothing but leaky shutters that

remained closed in the worst weather, forcing us to live out the winters in Gothic gloom.

Outside, the twisted and massacred topiary shambled to the banks of the Thames. Slightly downriver on the opposite bank, the abbey and palace of Westminster glowed ghostly, their hollows etched in shadow.

The heavy bed loomed like a giant, crouching toad in the center of the room, shrouded in velvet and redolent of sleep. The duchess had a down mattress and two real pillows and I desperately wanted to know what it felt like to lay my head on one of them.

Cat skipped right past the bed and into the narrow robing chamber, so I followed. The windowless room reeked of cedar and silk. I stood in the doorway, stunned by the number of chests and the potential opulence they might contain. But Cat threw them open, one by one, turfing out bell sleeves lined with fur, bodices trimmed with pearls, overskirts shot through with gold thread.

"Look at this!" she hooted, and held up the steel cage of an undergarment. "The duchess wears a corset! To lift those sagging, pendulous breasts!"

"And to trim her thickening middle," I reminded her.

Cat cackled and dove into another chest.

"This would look stunning on you," she said, pulling out a French hood, its buckram crown covered in deep green velvet, edged with a twisted tissue of gold and studded with pearls. "Bring out the color of your eyes."

My eyes were my best feature. That is, they were the one thing about my appearance that I liked, sea green and edged with gold, like the hood.

Cat tossed the hood at me and I snatched it out of the air, not wanting it to fall to the floor. I wrestled my straw-like hair into the black velvet veil and fitted the jeweled coronet over my head.

"Then again," Cat said, holding up a pink brocade bodice fronted by a crimson velvet stomacher, "perhaps your eyes are not something you want to call attention to."

"What do you mean?" I asked, my self-image purling away like leaves on the river.

She scrutinized me, head cocked to one side, the red-breasted gown completing the look of a robin about to catch a worm.

"Your eyes are too knowing," she said. "Men will think you see more than they wish you to understand. They want to surprise you. You look at them and they want to slink away."

"Thanks," I grumbled, pulling the hood over my face. "Better?"

But I wondered if my eyes were the reason no boy had ever visited me at our midnight parties. Or if it was some other lamentable feature—my hair, my height, or my face itself.

"What are friends for?" Cat smoothed her hair beneath a red velvet caul networked with gold braid and pearls that the duchess had probably worn for a royal coronation. "I tell you these things so you can attend to them in the future. You should practice looking more demure. Less judgmental."

Cat was a firm believer in practice. She had invented the way she walked, smiled, laid her fingers on a man's arm—even the way she turned her face to catch the light. She wasn't a stunning beauty, a brilliant musician, or a quick wit, but she could get a man's attention merely by entering the room.

And I was the perfect mirror. I helped her refine every performance—echoing and casting back at her all the things I couldn't be myself. She took me with her everywhere. We complemented each other. Completed each other. I was the Kitty to her Cat.

Being a reflection was better than being nothing at all.

"Why doesn't she do anything with this stuff?" Cat asked, pulling on crimson brocade sleeves lined with pink silk and trimmed with ermine. Their heavy bells dipped in the pool of the rosy train at her feet. Other people's clothes always looked ridiculously large on Cat.

"Maybe she doesn't want to wear it out," I said, swirling an overskirt the color of goldenrod. I thought of my own gowns, already worn out by two sisters I never saw and barely knew. Castoffs that fulfilled family duty, if not affection. The livery of the unloved.

"Humph." Cat dropped the duchess's gown to the floor, revealing her own frayed kirtle. Pink. The color brought out the roses in Cat's cheeks, and she insisted we all wear it every Tuesday and Saturday, despite the fact that it made me look sallow. "When I am rich and well-married, I shall wear something different every day, then give all my castoffs to the poor."

"The poor hardly have need of pearl-encrusted gable hoods."

"Oh, I'll take the pearls off first," she said. "And nothing could ever compel me to wear a gable, the most eye-gougingly ugly fashion accessory ever created."

"Well, that's all right, then," I muttered, but she didn't hear me. Something by the head of the duchess's bed had caught her eye and she crept out of the robing chamber to get a closer look.

It was a gilt coffer of wood and leather, covered in tiny romantic illustrations—*Tristan and Iseult* and *Orlando Innamorato*.

"No, Cat," I warned.

She ignored me and reached out cautiously, as though afraid it might scream like a magical box in a fairy story. But it opened silently, the leather and metal smooth beneath her fingers.

Cat let out a sigh that was half giggle, half moan.

"Come here," she said, her voice rich with awe.

"I really don't think we should be looking in there."

"Oh, come on," she coaxed. "I know you want to."

And she was right.

Tumbled within the smooth-sided box were pearls, rubies, emeralds. A diamond the size of a wren's egg dangled from a thick enameled collar. Cat stroked a gold letter *A* from which swung a single teardrop pearl.

"It's a good thing it's not a C," she said. "Or I might have to go back on my promise not to steal anything."

Coins sifted to the silk lining at the bottom of the box, gold sovereigns and angels, silver groats and pennies. Among them

lay papers folded and creased, the wax that once sealed them broken, smudged, or completely missing.

Cat picked up a roll of lace. It was a narrow series of white embroidery squares worked on white linen, the threads of the fabric cut and drawn out to leave behind nothing but air.

"Isn't this yours?" she asked. "Unoriginal. But pretty."

Ever since the dissolution of the monasteries, nun-made lace was hard to come by, and importing it from Italy was expensive. So the duchess had set all the girls on a program of learning how to make reticella and cutwork. Unfortunately, most failed miserably at the tiny stitches and intricate, repetitive knots. I surprised myself—and Cat—by excelling at it. It was the only thing I could do better than she.

"The duchess requisitioned it," I said. Not my best work. The pattern twisted crookedly, pulling the squares into oblongs.

I picked up a corner, and it unwound like a startled snake. A heavy iron key dropped to the floor. The sound reverberated through the quiet room, and we both stiffened, mirror images of horror.

"No one heard." Cat recovered quickly. She snatched the lace from me, wrenching it further out of kilter. She scooped up the key and paused, examining it.

"What's the matter?" I asked.

"Look at the scrollwork," she said, an edge of disgust creeping into her voice. "It matches the lock to our room."

The maidens' chamber was a dormitory crammed with

wooden plank beds, pallets on the floor, and twenty unwanted daughters. Cat and I had laid our heads on the same piece of timber in that room for eight years.

"Why is it in there?" I asked, pointing at the coffer, the money, and jewels.

"Because we are part of her fortune," Cat said, wrapping the key in the lace and stuffing it beneath a slurry of papers and coins. "We're a host of servants she never has to pay. Not to mention wardships and perhaps even a percentage of a dowry when we're sold into marriage."

She closed the lid and laid a finger on the engraving there. Sir Gawain bowed his head before the raised ax of the Green Knight, Lady Bertilak voluptuous and partially clothed in the background.

"Perhaps it's time we left," Cat said. "I no longer feel like playing dress-up. In fact"—she pointed at Lady Bertilak—"*un*dressing is a much more appealing prospect."

"Francis?" I asked, though I needn't have. He had shared our bed repeatedly for more than a year.

"Mmmm," she hummed through a seductive smile.

I turned back to the robing chamber. The cedar chests gaped like the mouths of benighted fish. Hoods and kirtles, sleeves and lacings lay strewn all over the floor. A single loose pearl scrolled out in front of me as I moved to put them away.

"I don't remember where they all go!" I smoothed a velvet hood and placed it on top of the bulging corset.

"It doesn't matter," Cat said, stuffing a fur-lined muff on top of a green silk sleeve.

"She'll know someone's been in here." I knew my voice was edged with panic, but I couldn't stop it. I matched a pair of sleeves to a bodice and laid them carefully on top of a similarly colored skirt.

"We'll blame it on a servant," Cat retorted, whipping the sleeves out from under my hands. "Or that weaselly Mary Lascelles. The duchess probably never checks on this stuff any-way." She crumpled each sleeve into a different chest.

"Why wouldn't she?"

Cat whirled on me.

"When you have this much money and this much power, you don't have to check on anything. You can have two chairs in your withdrawing room, gowns you'll never wear, and jewels you can't even count, and it's there because you *believe* it's there. Because it always has been and it always will be, and there's nothing anybody can do to change that."

She slammed the lid on the last chest, a reverberating bang that shuddered the floor beneath us, quenching the current of voices and laughter from the great hall. Then she laughed, grabbed my hand, and ran.

We fled back along the narrow, stuffy, unused upper gallery at the back of Norfolk House to the tightly packed living quarters of the lesser members of the household. And straight into Alice Restwold.

Whip-thin, blonde, and blandly pretty, Alice collected

secrets the way the rest of us collected ribbons. Joan Bulmer stood behind her, eyes wide and lips pressed together, her expression one of permanent confusion caused by eavesdropping on partial conversations.

"Where have you been?" Alice asked in a scandalized whisper. "The duchess was looking for you."

2

"Nowhere." Cat pushed past them into the maidens' chamber.

Alice's nose twitched beneath her particularly ugly magenta gable hood. She had married the previous summer and as a result could no longer wear her hair loose. However, her husband had left for Calais within weeks of their marriage and never returned, relegating Alice and her hood to the maidens' chamber. Cat called her a "once-again virgin."

"What did she want?" I asked.

"We don't know," Joan reported, tugging off her own hood, more orange than pink, though Cat didn't mention it. Joan's husband was also long absent and easily forgettable, her hood the only reminder he existed. "But when she asked about you, Mary Lascelles answered, 'Look in the company of Francis Dereham, for they are always together.'"

"That little . . ." Cat puffed up like her namesake, ready to spit.

"But Francis was right there in the room," Alice cut in, obviously not wanting the best part of the story to be told without her.

"Behind the duchess's chair!" Joan brayed, mirth shaking

her coif loose. Her unruly frizz of dark hair flew about her head like bees around a hive.

"Well, obviously what my *step*grandmother doesn't know can't hurt her."

As we talked, the room filled and crowded. The beds fitted together on the floor like a puzzle. A girl could walk between them, but not if another stood in the way. Our roommates climbed up on beds, had mock disagreements and danced aside, giggling and pushing. Gowns came off, hung on wooden pegs hammered into chinks between the stones in the walls. Cedar chests scraped the floors, pulled from beneath the beds and stirring the two-week-old rushes that moldered on the floor—no woven matting for us, just dried marsh-grass and herbs, loosely strewn. Chests opened to accept sleeves, hoods, shifts, and kirtles. Farthingales, their willow cane hoops creaking and clacking together like teeth, were shaken out and piled in the corner. Bedmates brushed and braided each other's hair in preparation for sleep.

Or not. At this moment, sleep was the last thing on most of the girls' minds.

"I shall be queen tonight," Cat said. No one disputed her. No one ever did. Cat ruled the maidens' chamber.

She sat enthroned on our bed, a coronet fashioned from yellow embroidery silk on her hair. Her nightdress, worn to the point of near transparency, slipped from one shoulder. I sat beside her, reflecting majesty. Elevated by proximity.

After dark, after the duchess and the dusty and decayed

members of the household had gone to bed, the doors of the maidens' chamber were thrown open and the room was invaded by boys. Each had received a personal invitation. Some were gentleman pensioners, dressed in the livery of the Duke of Norfolk. One, Lord William Howard, was the duchess's married son. Two were related to the duchess's steward, who, in turn, was related to the duchess herself. None were anything less patrician than the younger sons of landed gentry, making their way in a world that favored the firstborn.

The room was barely large enough to contain the girls who slept there. When boys entered, mayhem ensued.

"Ah, the Queen of Misrule," Francis Dereham declared as he strode up to our bed.

"Do you not bow before your sovereign?" Cat asked.

Francis cocked an eyebrow, and then extravagantly lowered his head over his bent knee.

"You may rise," Cat pronounced.

"My head?" he asked, straightening. "Or my . . ." His voice trailed off and he indicated his codpiece. I stifled a giggle.

"I brought wine." Francis produced a leather jug with a flourish. "Gascon. I bribed the wine steward."

The other men followed suit, and each deposited his pilfered offering at the foot of Cat's bed, like pilgrims at a shrine: marzipan that inspired Joan Bulmer to squeal, new apples from an orchard in Kent, spiced wafers so thin and crisp they dissolved with one snap of the teeth.

Cat bestowed on Francis a benedictory kiss that quickly became more heated. Cat and Francis could kiss forever. Their clandestine meetings in the chapel or unused galleries often concluded with their mouths puffy and red, their hair disheveled and clothing askew. Over Francis's ear, Cat gave me The Look. I would not rest my head on my own timber pillow that night.

Bedmates swapped and bickered and jostled for occupation. Four in a bed was not uncommon: half sitting, half lying, limbs cast out in the aisles.

The wine moved quickly, everyone taking a drink or two and passing it on. The sweetness overpowered the sharp tang of grape skins and soothed the burn of alcohol in my throat. I gazed hopefully about the room, though I knew none of the boys was there for me.

Joan pulled Edward Waldegrave, bearer of marzipan, to his feet, and hummed an almain, slightly off-key. Another girl giggled, but joined in, her gentleman offering a baritone harmony. They danced between the beds, tripping over feet and discarded clothing.

Alice perched precariously on the edge of her bed, as if ready to bolt the moment Joan and Edward returned for the rest of the evening's festivities.

"Come, Alice," I said to her. "Let's start something a little more lively."

I interrupted the monotonous hum with my own version of a galliard tune and coaxed Alice into a volta. My height put me

in the right position to play the man, but when I tried the first lift, I nearly dropped her.

The boys heckled and jeered, grabbing their girls to demonstrate proper form. Edward clasped Joan around the waist, and despite the fact that they probably weighed the same, lifted her up and buried his face between her unbound breasts, making her giggle uncontrollably. They collapsed together on the nearest bed, a tangle of limbs and laughter.

Suddenly the door banged open and the duchess herself stood framed by torches behind her, looking for all the world like an avenging angel come to hammer the light of righteousness into us.

"Out!" the duchess shrieked. Her long gray hair spilled from her head in wicked wisps. Her fur-trimmed velvet dressing gown churned with wrath. Her dark eyes scoured the room from furrowed sockets.

The men scampered to attention, straightening doublets and hunting for shoes. Girls bolted to their feet, arms held like breastplates over the thin fabric of their nightclothes. Francis looked bewildered as he tried to focus on his patroness.

"Francis Dereham," she spat at him. "You disappoint me."

Francis cringed. His chivalrous demeanor had always endeared him to the duchess.

"How dare you abuse my good nature and tarnish my name!" she shouted. She swept into the room, pushing and clouting as she went. The men hastened out the door like whipped dogs, shielding their faces and whimpering apologies.

Francis ducked a blind swipe of her bejeweled hand, but didn't fail to bow before fleeing down the stairs.

The duchess reached Cat, wrestled her to her feet, and then knocked her to the floor with a backhanded slap.

Cat sprawled in the rushes spitting lavender.

"Where do you think you are?" the duchess ranted. "The court of Henry the Eighth?"

She grabbed Joan, frozen nearby, and slapped her, too, for good measure.

"You think you can dissemble and cozen me? That I won't notice corruption and debauchery in my own household?"

Cat propped herself up on an elbow and laid a hand on her cheek. A red mark bloomed beneath it, a ring-shaped welt on her jawbone. She turned wide, brimming eyes to the duchess, who stopped screaming.

Joan knelt by Cat's side, but Cat took no notice. She stared only at the duchess.

A single drop welled in Cat's eye and spilled out over her fingers.

This was something we practiced together. I acted as Cat's mirror as she perfected ways to encourage emotional responses in her audience. *Tears bring sympathy,* she told me. Now I found that she was right. Cat's tears caused the duchess to pause and look about the room like someone who has forgotten her purpose.

"You know I would do nothing to vex you, *grandmère*," Cat said, her voice high and sweet, as if laced with honey.

The duchess appeared to be considering whether or not the pretty, delicate girl weeping at her feet was really capable of deception.

"And yet you invite men to a room meant for virginal maids," the duchess countered. I suppressed a snort of laughter. Cat hung her head, a picture of abject remorse.

"Which one came to your bed?" the duchess continued. "Francis Dereham? I've treated him as a favorite, but he doesn't befit you. You are a Howard. You are meant for better things."

"Yes, *grandmère*." Cat knew very little French, but exercised it liberally around the duchess. It made an impression.

"I never want to see you with him again," the duchess said, brushing her skirts as if to remove the detritus of scandal. "If I see the two of you together again, even kneeling in prayer, I will have both of you thrown out of this house so quickly you will never return to polite society."

Cat's face was hidden from the duchess by a shower of hair, but I saw it harden, the jaw clench and the eyes kindle and spark. Then it smoothed to an image of gratitude and she looked up at the old woman.

"Yes, *grandmère*."

"Who let them in?" the duchess said. "Who suggested this bedchamber farce?"

She scanned all of our faces, her own drawn down with age and anger like a melting candle.

"Joan?" she asked. But Joan just gaped at her.

"Alice?" But Alice never parted with information without something in return.

"Kitty?" She turned her trenchant gaze on me, but capitulated immediately. "I should know better," she scowled. "Loyal to the grave, that one."

She turned wearily, her shoulders hunched.

"This is best forgotten." The duchess waved away our stares. "From tonight onward, a curfew will be set, and the door to this chamber will be locked. There will be no repeat performance. Go to bed. All of you."

She parted the torchbearers like the Red Sea and hauled them down the gallery in her wake. Girls crept to their beds, thankful to have escaped the duchess's ire. Only Joan, Alice, and I remained standing.

Cat rose from the debris on the floor.

"Forgotten?" she said. "I'm unlikely to forget any of it. I'll make her life miserable."

"Cat," I warned.

"You can wipe that sanctimonious look right off your face, Kitty Tylney."

I kept silent. When Cat's anger gathered momentum, it was best to stand back and stay quiet, for fear of getting flayed alive by words or fingernails.

"Besides," she sneered, "I wasn't talking about the duchess. I was talking about Mary Lascelles."

Mary was one of the few girls even less connected than I

was, her only family a bully of a brother who had dumped her unceremoniously in the duchess's lap when he decided Mary needed "elevating." I looked at Mary's bed. Her bedmate sat in the middle of it, shocked by our stares. Mary was nowhere to be seen.

"You mean you didn't see her? She was right behind the duchess! Smirking away as if she deserved a medal. She'll be sleeping on the duchess's floor tonight, not because she's favored but because she's afraid of retaliation. She'd better never set foot in this room again."

Despite the annoyance I felt toward Mary for informing on us, I felt a little sorry for her, too. The remainder of her life in Norfolk House would be miserable. The punishment for snitching was to be shunned by all the girls. She would be pinched in chapel and thumped at dinner. Mary would be black and blue by the end of the week. And for the rest of her days.

"Did you hear the duchess?" Cat returned to her rant. "*Just where do you think you are, the court of Henry the Eighth*? As if I'd confuse this dreary, boring, hypocritical place with the dazzling circle the king has around him."

"What do you think she meant?" Joan asked.

Cat sighed and enunciated slowly as if speaking to the village idiot.

"Joan, at court people are always making secret assignations. It's *de rigueur*. It's expected. The duchess finds it morally reprehensible."

"If the king allows it, why doesn't she?" I wondered.

"Because she's a *Howard*. Ha! She's not even that. She's a *Tylney*." Cat spat the name as she would a bitter seed.

I willed myself not to react. My side of the family was so far removed from the duchess that our name—Tylney—felt like the only indication we were related at all. If the duchess was inferior, what did that make me?

"She's not even my real grandmother," Cat said. "Just some grasper who saw a hole in the Howard family and filled it."

We waited while Cat's anger spun itself out.

"One day she'll be sorry. One day she'll have to scrape and bow to me."

I failed to picture a time when the highest noblewoman in the country would fall so low as to look up to Catherine Howard, forgotten daughter of the forgotten third son of the man who had once been Duke of Norfolk. But I said nothing.

"I'll find a way to see Francis. She can't keep us apart."

"We could get them in through the window," I suggested.

"He tried that, remember?" Cat shot me a withering glare that brought heat surging to my cheeks.

True. The spring before, in a fit of romantic valor, Francis had attempted to scale the outside wall to the second-floor window with a rose between his teeth, but proved unequal to the task.

"Could we bribe one of the servants to unlock the door?" Joan asked, looking for approval.

"I don't trust any of them," Cat said.

We lapsed into silence, waiting for her to speak. Cat always thought of a solution.

"We'll just have to steal the key," she announced.

"Simple," I muttered, unsure if I wanted her to hear. Cat didn't take criticism well.

"It is, actually." Cat stared hard at me. "The steward has his own set of keys. The duchess's copy isn't used. She'll never know it's gone."

"It's brilliant, Cat," I said. "But who's going to do it?"

Whoever it was would have to be very well connected or very brave—or very stupid.

"Why, Kitty," Cat said. "You are."

WORDS CAN KILL. AS SURELY AS SWORD OR AX OR DAGGER. THEY CAN prostrate the subject and render the speaker voiceless. Words may not fracture bone, but they can wound with devastating precision.

"Me?"

"She'll never know," Cat said.

"She'll never know because I'll never do it." I couldn't let Cat convince me. It was suicide. And I was the last person who should be doing it. Tall, gawky, slightly clumsy, I was a questionable covert agent.

"But Kitty, don't you see? You are the perfect candidate."

"How so?"

"You have no suitor," she said with a sticky smile.

"Thanks for reminding me." My sarcasm fell flat. "But how does that help?"

"You have no motive. No one will suspect you."

She had a point. I had no reason to keep the midnight revelries going. No reason except it alleviated the boredom of the day-to-day existence in Lambeth. It gave us a taste of what real court life might be, with the wine and delicacies stolen from the duchess's kitchen. With whispered songs and barefoot dancing across the lavender-and-rosemary-strewn floor. Even if my only partner was Alice.

If I stole the key and got caught, I could be sent home, a god-forsaken hole on the far side of nowhere. My parents had leapt at the chance to disencumber themselves of their unwanted youngest daughter when I was eight. Cat discovered me on my first day, crying alone in the garden and told me they weren't worth my tears. I'd never looked back.

"Also," Cat continued, "you have little family and no one who really wants you. You have no motive, but you have everything to lose."

The words cut like thin blades. Cat understood the grief and terror lodged deep within me. She knew my fear that ultimately, the rest of the world would treat me as my parents had and abandon me to my own inept facilities.

If I didn't steal the key, I would forfeit my place at Cat's side, as forsaken and friendless as if I had gone home. Because Cat's favor was everything at Norfolk House—more important than money, men, or family influence. She was the one who set the standard, guided the aimless, and judged the unworthy.

But stealing?

"I can't." I hadn't the breath to speak louder than a whisper.

Cat narrowed her eyes.

"Can't? Or won't?"

Refusing Cat was like refusing the king. No one did it. No one knew where it could lead. To disfavor? Or beheading? But

the panic-inducing thought of returning to the frigid bosom of my family forced me to risk it.

"Won't."

Cat stiffened into silence, and I felt the breath quake in my chest.

"Joan?" Cat said sweetly.

Surely I couldn't get off that lightly? Joan couldn't say no to anyone.

"Joan, darling, you'd do anything for me, wouldn't you?"

"Of course, Cat," Joan said, her glance flicking from me to Cat and back again. Jittery. She could feel it, too. The same disquiet that wouldn't leave my limbs.

"Anything for the good of all the girls here, right?" Cat said.

She aimed all her words directly at me. I knew that she wouldn't ask Joan to steal from the duchess's coffer.

"Of course, Cat," Joan repeated. "You girls are my family."

I wanted to close my ears to her toadying. Didn't she know when to be quiet?

Cat linked her arm with Joan's. They were almost the same height, but where Cat was all curves, like a perfectly proportioned miniature, Joan was round, almost doughy.

"And without our family of girls, what are we?" Cat asked me.

I squirmed. She no longer expected an answer. She expected submission. And with a hopeless surge of self-loathing, I knew she would get it.

Joan stared, open-mouthed, unable to participate in this

one-sided conversation. Alice remained silent and invisible.

"Nobody," Cat said. I hated her at that moment, with a white-hot rage. I hated her almost as much as I hated myself. "Unwanted and unloved."

Misery swept through me, scouring away all resistance. I sank down onto the bed, a glacial emptiness yawning in my heart. She was right. Without the girls, without Cat, I was . . .

"Nothing."

FOUR DAYS LATER, A BLACK PAWN FROM ALICE'S CHESS SET LAY WRAPPED in the piece of lace in the wood-and-leather coffer. I tucked it beneath the papers and jewels of the duchess's shifting wealth. The key lay in Cat's smooth, open palm, a pale pink ribbon dangling from it.

"Oh, Cat!" Joan cried. "You got it!"

"Aren't you clever?" one of the other girls murmured.

"We'll have wine and dancing again!"

"And boys!"

News traveled quickly in Norfolk House. The maidens' chamber was full, in the middle of the day. It was a wonder the entire household didn't grind to a halt with no one to tend the duchess's fire or fetch her spiced wine.

Cat smiled. I waited for her to say it was me. I hadn't wanted to do it. I hadn't wanted any part of it. The least I could get was the credit.

She opened her mouth, and all around her quieted.

"Tonight," she said.

The cheer that arose rattled the shutters on the windows.

I couldn't breathe, stifled by Cat's treachery, and by Joan's willingness to accept it. Only Alice observed me through low-ered lashes, pity or contempt on her lips. My heart contracted with the realization that I probably deserved both.

The dancing and cheering stirred the dust and mites from the reeking rushes littering the floor, and nettled my eyes to tears.

I stumbled from the room. No one noticed. They were too busy congratulating Cat, who lapped it all up.

The top two stairs complained bitterly at the weight of the wretchedness I carried with me. I moved to the far left of the stairwell and crept unheard down the more secure runners near the wall. Cat had taught me that little trick when we were ten and raided the buttery at night.

I slipped through the oak gallery, which ran the full length of the house. Autumn sunlight fell heavily on the carved paneling, the duchess's allegiances spelled out in oak. I passed an ancient pomegranate carved in 1509 for King Henry's first queen, Catherine of Aragon. A Tudor rose carved for Henry himself. A falcon—abraded and indistinct—for Cat's cousin, Anne Boleyn, the king's ill-fated second wife. The third, Jane Seymour, hadn't lived long enough for the duchess to change any of the panels for her, having died quickly after giving birth to England's only prince.

The door at the end of the gallery squeaked a little when I opened it and I paused, breath held, before escaping into the garden.

Finally, my lungs functioned again. The sun angled over

the haphazardly shaped hedges. One may have been a griffin, another, a lion. The duchess wanted to keep up with social trends, but had no interest in paying a decent gardener, so the shrubbery grew wild and bizarre. Few people ventured outside, anyway. The duchess cultivated a very *indoor* household, so I often had the outdoors to myself. In the house, I was always surrounded by others, their noise and odors tangible. Outside, I could breathe.

I quickly passed through the garden and exited the grounds. The duchess forbade us to go out alone. She warned us of the murderers, scavengers, and vagrants who hid in the woods. Highwaymen waiting to prey on vulnerable young girls. The only things she didn't mention were harpies, trolls, and the descendants of Gog the giant.

I never went far—just through the narrow apple orchard on the southeastern edge of the duchess's garden, up a slight rise to the wooded area the duchess called the "park." Because Lambeth consisted primarily of marsh and mansions, the duchess coveted the little forest, owned by some long-feuding neighbor who was never willing to sell.

An arch between two oaks led into a clearing made by a huge fallen beech. The tree itself created a sort of bench, albeit one with arse-poking branches at regular intervals. It was the one, magical place where I could be alone. Not even Cat knew about it. My trips to the forest were my secret.

I hoisted myself onto the tree, gathering my skirts around me to avoid snagging. I held myself still, listening to the night-loving forest dwellers rising from their beds, and watching the

sky above me transfigure from white to gold. The trees exhaled the tired scent of autumn. All quieted, and my head sang with the silence.

My seething anger left me, replaced by a dull, familiar ache. Cat served herself well. It was remiss of me to expect anything different. Befriending me was one of the few selfless things she'd ever done. She'd found me, homesick and melancholy, saved me a place next to her at dinner, made room for me in her bed. Gave me my name. That first night, she'd wrapped an arm around me and said, "So, Kitty, would you like to come to court?" and the next day we entered the palace of her imagination, playing a game that never really ended.

Cat was still queen.

I sighed and lay back on the tree. It wasn't comfortable. Prickly. Awkward. But it allowed me full view of the crumbling leaves and the sky.

A squawk shattered the stillness. Three ravens, grumbling and croaking, bolted from the branches of a tree far to my right and flapped blackly across my view.

The sight of them felt like an omen. A chill crept over my skin like a million tiny feet, and I sat up. A noise froze me. Like an animal, large and clumsy. Or so big it didn't require stealth. It crashed through the underbrush, through the carpets of fallen leaves crusty from the lack of summer rains. Distant, but approaching quickly.

I pressed my hands against the rough bark of the fallen tree. My fingernails dug into it until flakes came off beneath them. I

couldn't decide if I should run or stay still. My limbs made the choice for me. I couldn't move. I hoped whatever it was would think me part of the forest itself.

I strained to look between the spindles and barrels of the bare tree trunks, feeling grievously exposed. A whip of white on the far side of a scramble of hawthorn caught my eye. A flash of gold.

The crashing stopped, cut off by a cry of anguish and replaced by a hungered grunting. It had caught whatever prey it chased.

And then something that sounded like laughter. Not the ravens. More like a man.

My skirt tore with a hoarse whisper as I slid from my bench. I ignored it and crept forward to the low, hedgelike hawthorn. The leaves were just beginning to fall, the berries blood-red against them. I hid, camouflaged in my moss-green gown and heavy brown sleeves, silently thanking Cat for making Wednesday green.

The leaves and branches obscured my vision. I saw one figure. Two. Movement. Leaves. Cobwebs. I used one hand to pry open an eyelet.

Not far away, a man fell to the ground in a patch of dappled late-day sun. He didn't live at Norfolk House, but obviously came from privilege, judging by the gold braid on his doublet. He was long and lean with blond hair, dark eyes, a straight nose, and a jutting jaw. His beauty was surprising, down near the forest duff.

He held himself up on his hands. His hose slipped down to reveal pale buttocks glowing in the fading light. Something swathed in dirty white writhed beneath him. A woman.

He crushed his face to hers, and a growl escaped him.

"I know you want this."

For one startling instant of intense clarity, I felt the woman's pain, the man's lust. My heart kicked me in the chest. Pummeled me. Screamed at me to flee. But my stomach sank right down to the roots beneath me and locked me where I knelt.

Two more men stood beyond, grimacing like the disembodied heads of traitors on London Bridge.

One looked down, his head bent at the angle of a suppliant. He watched the spectacle, one foot planted firmly on the woman's left wrist.

Her right hand dug spasmodically at the earth.

The other man was really a boy. Not much older than me. A swag of rich golden hair framed a round face and wide-set brown eyes. He stared out into the forest.

And found me.

He squinted. Bewilderment clouded his features. Then comprehension cleared them.

I recovered my feet and ran. Crashes and snaps echoed in my wake. Thin fingers of tree limbs yanked at my skirts and wrists. My legs leadened. My breath came in choking gasps. It was like fleeing pursuit in a nightmare, but knowing I couldn't wake.

I strained to hear a shout of alarm. A cry to give chase. I heard none. Just an exultant howl of satisfaction.

I reached the arch of the oak trees, crossed into the light of civilization. I ran back to the house with the visions I had seen streaming out behind me like a veil, twisting and unwrapping but never tearing completely free.

5

I CROUCHED IN THE HEDGES BEHIND THE BRICK MONSTROSITY THAT was Norfolk House and disgorged every morsel that had passed my lips that day. I shook like someone with the sweating sickness. If only I had the sweat, which left its victims delusional and babbling, dead within hours. I would prefer anything to the image engraved behind my eyelids, the image of that poor woman, contorted by pain and humiliation. The sound of the man's voice vibrated beneath my temples.

I sat back and wrapped my arms around my knees to stop the quaking. The moisture from the earth soaked through my skirts, and the night air cooled around me. I should have flown at the men in a rage, frightening them off like a harpy. I should have picked the woman up off the ground, tended her bruises. Offered her bread and wine in the duchess's kitchen. I should have stopped them.

I had done none of those things. I had done nothing. Fear had swaddled me in cowardice. Too weak, too pathetic to help, I was as much to blame as the man who held her down. As culpable as the boy who stood watch. Who saw me.

Why hadn't he called out? Why didn't they give chase and

hunt me down? Why was I not now weeping somewhere on the forest floor like that poor peasant?

I rolled forward onto my knees and retched again. Nothing but bile and self-loathing spilled from my mouth.

The man who had abused her looked prosperous, well fed, sure of himself. The richness of his clothes and the arrogance of his manner characterized someone who expected life to hand him everything he wanted, and if it didn't, he would take it.

I thought about what he had said. Had she, at some point, wanted him? She hadn't appeared to anymore, her face screwed up against his words, her arm pinned down by his crony. No one wanted that.

I hoisted myself off of the ground, brushed the soil from my hands and knees, and staggered back to the house. The duchess was right. It was wiser to stay closeted indoors.

I might never leave the house again.

The twilight filtered into the oak gallery, shadows like bars running the length of the paneling.

My skirt hissed along the floor, carried somehow by my trembling limbs. I reached the corridor to the back stairs, and a creak above me took my balance. I fell back, one foot caught on a stray bit of hem, my left hand grasping wildly for support. Anne Boleyn's falcon caught me.

"Kitty, if you grow any taller and more awkward, you'll need your own usher to keep you upright," Cat laughed, skipping down the last of the stairs and twirling me, stumbling, into the darkened gallery. "Still, as long as he's handsome . . ."

"Cat," I interrupted, and stopped the giddy dance, "I have to tell you something."

"Oh, but Kitty," she said coyly, "it can't be nearly as important as what I've got to tell you."

"No," I said. Meaning, no, don't tell me. No, don't speak over me. Don't tell me your news is more important than this.

"*Exactement,*" she started toward the north wing of the house. "Let's find Joan and Alice. They have to hear this, too."

She turned when I didn't follow and looked at me critically.

"You're filthy," she said. "You spend far too much time out in that garden. And you really shouldn't go out there alone."

"I've done something horrible," I blurted.

"So have I!" Cat cackled, pulling me through the back stairs corridor and into the servants' vestibule. I crawled after her, mind ablaze with agony.

"I've dumped the contents of every pot in the maidens' chamber into the one under the duchess's bed!"

When I didn't respond, Cat huffed in irritation, waiting in the doorway to the front vestibule.

"It's Mary Lascelles's job to empty it!" she cried. "She'll never get down the stairs without spilling, the silly cow. But she brought it on herself. Fools find their own misery."

She brought it on herself. She wanted it.

"And I rubbed rancid fat in her pallet while I was there," Cat whispered as we walked into the main withdrawing room, clustered with girls and women sewing. "Her bed will be full of maggots by week's end."

"Cat!" I gasped, one final desperate attempt to get her attention.

Cat's aunt, the Countess of Bridgewater, looked up. A pale woman, she wore pale clothes and engaged in pale activities. But she observed—and reported—everything.

"Hush!" Cat hissed. "Do you want everyone to know what I'm up to?"

She sauntered to the far corner of the room, swishing her skirts. I watched her go. She seemed so sure the world contained no greater wickedness than the perfidy of Mary Lascelles.

She was right about one thing. I shouldn't have been out in the forest alone. I should have stayed in the house, cloaked in the drama of stolen keys and sloshing chamber pots.

That night, after the party, Cat sent Francis from the bed early. She curled against me, breath sultry from kisses.

"Now, tell me," she whispered. "Tell me everything."

My throat closed with the enormity of it. Cat knew. As if my own thoughts were hers.

"You're upset," she said.

I nodded, still unable to speak.

"Over something that happened today."

I nodded again.

"Something you wished to tell me earlier."

A sigh escaped and I started to cry.

"It's the key, isn't it?" she said.

But I couldn't stop crying. I couldn't tell her she was wrong.

"I had to let them believe it was me," she whispered. "In case

someone blabs. I can't let you get thrown out, Kitty. You're like a sister. Better than my real sisters. You're a sister of my soul. What would I do without you?"

My head flooded with *ifs*. If she hadn't taken credit. If she had just stolen the key herself. If she had never opened the coffer to discover it. Terror and anger and blame welled up in me and I caught them in a gossamer bubble before it all escaped and ruined our friendship.

I couldn't spew it on Cat. Not the vitriol and spite. It wasn't her fault.

Fools find their own misery.

I certainly had.

6

In the days that followed, I stumbled through the house in a swamp of wretchedness. I did my chores, followed orders, smiled when it was expected. I couldn't enjoy the midnight parties anymore. The presence of men made me want to creep out of my very bones. Even when the men didn't come, I couldn't sleep, and when I did, nightmares bruised me. I thrashed so much, Cat threatened to move to another bed.

But time acted as a purge, and as the days grew cold and frost crept across the grass, I slowly came back to myself. Thinner, paler, bitter and inadequate, but extant.

As the winter drew on, the rains came. The walls of disused rooms ran with damp, and the rushes on the floors turned black within a week. The bed curtains hung limp and took on the vinegar smell of mold. The fire in the maidens' chamber wasn't lit, so at night we drew warmth from each other and sought out other rooms during the day.

When boredom overcame us, we went to what we called the tapestry room. The walls were lined with detailed hangings, bought at a discount from the estates of traitors, their coats of arms carefully picked out and covered with the Howard crest. The cold and colorless Countess of Bridgewater held court by the fireplace, but the bright designs and heavy fabrics gave the illusion of warmth, no matter where we sat.

Joan and Cat claimed a corner as far from the countess as possible. Joan sewed ribbons of silver tissue onto the duchess's blue velvet bodice. And Cat was repairing the hem of the duchess's widest farthingale—endless tiny stitches of eye-straining sameness.

"Damn the desperate canes on this thing," she muttered. I grinned. I had a reprieve from mending. The duchess had requisitioned another piece of lace from me, and I worked knots of white by the feeble light from the window.

"Shut up, Kitty Tylney," Cat muttered.

Alice slipped through the door and dipped a curtsey to the older ladies. None of them acknowledged her. Alice smiled.

"Alice," I said when she pulled a stool closer to us, "they didn't even see you."

"Exactly," Alice said. And smiled again.

Cat turned to me and raised an eyebrow. I knew what it meant. Cat would have thrown a fit if she'd walked into a room unnoticed. But Alice? Alice seemed pleased.

"What news do you have today, Alice?" Joan asked, sucking the end of a piece of silk to a point in order to thread her needle.

Alice leaned forward and we all leaned with her.

"The Lady of Cleves is on her way."

The Lady of Cleves was the king's wife-to-be. A German princess from an unknown duchy, she'd been chosen by Thomas Cromwell, the king's chief councilor. Not by the king himself, this time.

As one, we all sat back.

"Is she bringing her own household?" Cat asked, poking at the fabric with her needle, but not making any stitches.

"She travels with German ladies, but I believe the king wants to fill her apartments with English nobility."

We took a moment of silence to digest this.

"Imagine," Joan crooned. "All those gorgeous dresses. Velvets and brocades and delicious silks." She ran her hand down her thigh as though stroking a well-clad lover.

"Think of the parties," I said. "Masques and banquets and dancing." So much more than the midnight feasts in the maidens' chamber.

"Think of all the gossip," Alice said.

"Think of all the *men*." Cat's eyes shone. "There must be ten of them to every woman in the court. All with money. And power."

"Is that what you're looking for in a man?" I asked. "What about poor Francis?"

"He does possess many qualities I admire," Cat said. "High cheekbones. A chin dimple. An air of rakish danger."

"But no wealth or power."

"And to tell you the truth," Cat whispered, "his codpiece gives no indication of his actual anatomy. The sword is no match for the scabbard, if you catch my meaning."

"So you want to go to court to find a rich duke or earl with a big pizzle!" Joan laughed.

"And for the dresses and the gossip and the parties," Cat said. "I want it *all*."

"Do you think there's really a possibility we'll ever to get to court?" I asked. Our dream of going to court seemed just that—a dream. The only way to get a position was by petition from a patron or family member. A man. My father was unlikely to come through for me. But all our games couldn't have been practice for nothing.

"I have to. Or my life will be wasted." Cat echoed my own thoughts.

"If anyone gets there, you will, Cat," Joan sighed. "The rest of us have no connections."

Cat was a Howard. It was the appellation of the richest, most ambitious and pugnacious family in the kingdom. Unfortunately, it was all Cat got from her father, a negligent wastrel who had died virtually unmourned in March, leaving his third wife and ten children without a penny. Cat might have come from the gauche side of the family, but in our world, a name could be worth more than currency. The rest of us had nothing but our dreams.

"Speak for yourself, Joan," Alice said. "My husband has a position with Lord Maltravers."

I caught Joan's eye and then rolled my gaze to the ceiling. If Alice's husband didn't care that she existed, I doubted Lord Maltravers would. I also suspected that his opinion held little sway. Joan giggled.

"But there's more," Alice said, ignoring us. "The Duke of Norfolk is coming to visit."

The dowager duchess's stepson.

The most powerful and influential nobleman in the country.

"He's looking for girls to place in the new queen's household as maids of honor." Alice paused to let her words sink in. "He's looking for girls from here."

"So is he going to check our teeth and test our sure-footedness like hunting horses?" I asked as we hurried down the stairs for dinner with the duke. A masterful cleaning campaign by the duchess had brightened even the darkest corners of the stairwell.

"No, but he might give us all a good ride to break us in," Cat said, waggling her eyebrows and leering at me.

"Oh, Catherine, don't be disgusting," Alice sniffed. "He must be at least sixty."

"That doesn't stop him from dragging his mistress with him everywhere he goes," Cat said, slowing as we neared the great hall.

"I feel sorry for his wife," Joan said, slightly out of breath. "Out there in the country all alone."

"Sympathy," Cat scolded, "gets you nowhere. The English court is beautiful and cutthroat, and anyone going there has to be both. Or at least act as if she is."

"Well, I'll never get there, then," I said. Cutthroat I wasn't.

Cat stopped just outside the door of the hall and put an arm around me. Another Tuesday, and her pink gown made her skin glow. She hadn't let the rest of us choose our best gowns, not even on this occasion.

"Oh, Kitty," she said. "None of us is beautiful."

Alice snorted, and Joan looked aghast. I wanted to pinch Cat.

"We're not. We're decidedly average. It's what we do with it that counts. We have to be clever. Make yourself vital to someone's happiness, and suddenly you're the most beautiful creature in the world, and he will fall madly in love with you."

I didn't think I could ever make myself that vital to anyone. So far no boy had given me so much as a second glance. I suspected cleverness alone wouldn't merit a first glance, let alone a second, so Cat's falsely fortifying words fell hollow all around me.

We stepped gracefully and demurely into the great hall, into the shadows ever present there. No amount of candles could fill that cavernous space with light, and in the duchess's mind, even the duke's visit didn't merit additional illumination. The stone walls were covered in tapestries depicting tales of chivalry. Ladies, retainers, and ushers lurked in the shadows, the duchess's servants and dogs weaving in and out between them.

The girls craned their necks to seek out fresh faces in the duke's employ.

"That one," Alice said. She nodded ever so slightly toward a boy, almost a man, who stood at the back of the hall, near the linenfold paneling that hid the servants' entrance from view. He appeared to be a gentleman usher, lean, but not gangly, with a mop of sandy hair that fell over one eye. He shook his head to remove it and looked back at us.

The rustle of girls turning from his gaze attracted the attention of the duchess, who sat in an armchair on the low dais near the fireplace. She beckoned imperiously from the high table, and we approached cautiously.

Thomas Howard, Duke of Norfolk, sat next to her. He was four years older than his stepmother, our patroness. Yet where the duchess held her age aloft like a flag of truce, the Duke covered his with a veneer of athletic bellicosity. He had a hooked nose that dominated his small face and eyes that gave the impression of seeing into your very soul. And what he saw never pleased him.

I avoided his gaze, afraid to see the curl of his lip at my appearance and height.

"He's looking at you," Joan whispered. "No, amend that. He's *staring* at you."

All feeling left my face and my lips grew numb.

"The duke?" Could he really be considering *me*?

"No, he's watching Cat," Joan said blithely. "I meant the new boy. The good-looking one. He's watching you."

The blood rushed back to my cheeks and I met his eye. His

mouth turned up crookedly. On the verge of laughter. I looked away.

We curtseyed then waited on the duke and dowager duchess throughout the long, tedious dinner. The dowager duchess ordered variations of every kind of meat and fowl when the duke came to visit, as if to remind him of her importance to the Howard family. We carried platters, weaving in and out between benches and trestle tables at which most of the rest of the Howard clan sat, unwilling to miss an important gathering. Everyone wanted a place at court.

"The Lady of Cleves knows no English," the duke was saying as I brought forward a wide wooden platter of venison. "Nor any French nor Latin. She will need clever girls in her household."

"To help her adjust," the duchess agreed.

"To make her path smooth," the duke said.

I studiously avoided looking at the duke's new usher. It was a great honor to be a maid-in-waiting, or a lady-in-waiting, to the queen. Noblewomen climbed over and clawed each other to get a place. With the help of male relatives, of course. My only hope was the duke. And he certainly wouldn't help me if I were caught flirting over his shoulder at dinner.

"If we are not careful," the duke continued, spearing a piece of venison with his knife and beginning to gnaw upon it immediately, "the new men appointed to nobility by the king will

take over the court and run it like a brothel, salting the queen's apartments with the freshest and most desirable female flesh. We must take the opportunity to bring truly loyal blood to court."

"We have the Lady Rochford," the duchess said.

The misfortune-plagued Jane Boleyn. Once married to George Boleyn, brother to the king's second wife, Anne. Court gossip said that Jane was instrumental in getting Queen Anne beheaded by accusing her of adultery. And incest. George was executed, too.

I turned to take the platter to one of the lower tables, but the duke reached for my sleeve. I stopped, hardly daring to breathe.

"We need a girl," the duke said. "Virginity is temptation, and temptation will bring promotion to the house of Howard."

I felt sick. I didn't dare to look into his ferrety little eyes. The duke despised the idea of the queen's household being a "brothel," except when it was he who stocked it with whores of his own choosing.

Not bothering with a knife this time, he pulled a fatty piece of thigh meat from the bone with his thumb and forefinger and dismissed me without once looking at my face.

"That one," I heard him say, and I turned back to see him pointing with a lazy flick of his greasy finger. He indicated the girl with the pink cheeks and shining eyes, the glossy auburn curls and perfect curves. The girl who could make a man shud-

der with desire by throwing her hair carelessly over her shoulder. I left the platter on a side table and slipped invisibly back to my place amongst the unchosen.

"Catherine Howard," the dowager duchess called. "How would you like to go to court?"

"You could be a little bit happy for me," Cat said.

"I am happy for you," I said, stretching a smile across my face.

Knowing that I wouldn't be picked to go to court and actually not being picked were two different things. Before the duke chose Cat, at least I had hope, if only a thin sliver of it. And not until the candles guttered and the duke fell asleep in his chair had hope left me completely. He only needed one girl, and that girl was Cat.

"No, you're not," she said. "Not really. You're disappointed that you weren't picked, and that makes you feel guilty."

It could be unnerving, Cat's ability to read my thoughts. But often, it was like being wrapped in a heavy winter cloak to shut out a storm. Comforting to know I wasn't alone.

"Also, you're going to miss me." Cat crept over to put an arm around me. "We've never been apart. I don't know what I'll do without you. But don't worry, I shall find a way to get you to court, too."

"Now who's being silly?" I managed before my throat closed

again. Because she was right. It wasn't just jealousy that I felt. It was bereavement, as well.

"I will," she said. "I promise. Just you wait and see."

Her childish voice made her enthusiasm all the more appealing and lit again the hope that she was right. Because court was the only place either of us really wanted to be. If anyone could find a way to get me there, Cat Howard could.

I squeezed her back. "I'm very glad you will be there, ready to show me how it's done."

"Well, I will have no such mentor," she said. "So I have to get this right before I leave."

We were practicing her curtsey, just as we had every day since the duke's visit. Cat's skirts whispered against the rushes as she bent once more, her tiny frame curving over her knees, hair veiling her features.

"It looks perfect, Cat."

"No, Kitty," she said to her knees, and then stood up and repositioned herself near the door. "Watch this part. Pretend to be the king and tell me to rise when the time is right."

She walked with measured steps from the door to me, her head bent. No one looked the king in the eye until he spoke. No one turned away from him. All these things we had practiced into oblivion.

When Cat came within three feet of me, she fell again into a curtsey and remained there, the picture of humility. I considered making her wait, but figured she would only want to practice it again.

"You may rise, Mistress Howard." I affected a booming tenor.

Cat lifted her face first, a shy smile playing on her lips. She met my eyes briefly and then looked down again, her lashes brushing her cheeks. Subtly, she pulled her shoulders back, an action that caused her breasts to thrust forward, swelling just slightly out of her bodice.

"Jesus, Cat," I said. A little laugh escaped me.

"What?" she stumbled to stand straight and came to me. "Is it too much? Too little? What?"

"Isn't that a little obvious?"

"Obvious that I'm doing it on purpose?"

"No," I acquiesced. "Not so much. Maybe just to me."

"Well, it's not you I'm trying to impress," she said and turned away to recheck her box of clothes.

"Well, any gentleman you encounter will be. Impressed, that is."

"But will the king?" she cried, exasperated. "I want him to look at me and to see that I'm different! That I'm not just another maid-in-waiting."

"What do you want from him, Cat?" I asked. "He's already getting married."

"Whoever said I needed marriage?"

"Wait a minute. Are you trying to tell me that this whole act is so that you can be a mistress to the king? A fat, aging man with an ego the size of France and a temper the size of the Roman Empire?"

"I don't know!" she huffed. "Maybe I just want someone to notice me!"

"Well, *that* will certainly get you noticed," I gestured dismissively at her breasts.

"Don't you see, Kitty?" she said. "This is my chance. My ruin of a family has finally come through for me, and I don't want to bungle it. I could get *anything* if I have the king's attention. At court, that's all that matters. Getting into his favor. And staying there."

Getting noticed was one thing. But what about the consequences? Manipulating the king of England could open a whole Pandora's box of repercussions.

"Besides," Cat said with a wicked grin. "I'm just displaying my assets."

"No, Cat," I said, blinking my eyes bemusedly like Joan, "I think your ass is something else entirely."

Cat threw her head back and laughed. Crisis averted.

"At court, with the king's favor, I could get anyone," Cat declared. "A lord. A viscount."

"You could enamor an earl or bewitch a baron," I added, though a cold shiver ran to my stomach, a fear that when she became a famous lady, she would forget me.

"Bedevil a duke," she said. "Shame Charles Brandon's already taken."

"The Duke of Suffolk?" I asked. "But he's over fifty years old!"

"That didn't stop him from marrying Catherine Willoughby," Cat said.

"Hasn't he been married four times? And Catherine is younger than his children."

Cat smoothed the gowns at the top of her cedar chest. A bit ragged. Worn at the elbows. But presentable enough.

"Rumor has it he's great in bed," she said.

"He'd have to be."

"Imagine having a title of my own!" Cat crowed, slamming the lid of the chest. "I just want to *be* somebody."

"You will be."

"I don't want to marry some lame old fat man and die in secluded anonymity in the country. I've lived in the shadow of the Duke of Norfolk my entire life, just as my father did. Father was a nobody, and so am I, but when I go to court I could become a countess or at least a lady. Not plain Catherine Howard."

"You'd never be plain."

"Oh, Kitty, they shan't know what hit them. I will dance more than anyone and laugh more than anyone and eat the best foods and drink the best wines and make everyone laugh and love me. I will exhaust them."

"You certainly will," I said with a grin. I could picture it.

"I will be queen!" she cried.

My shock stifled any reply.

"Oh, Kitty," she said, whisking at me with her hand, "I mean the Queen of Misrule. I wouldn't *poison* her for pity's sake."

I looked over my shoulder to see if anyone was listening, but the maidens' chamber was empty. Everyone else was off performing the duchess's daily tasks—simpering, sewing, tending to imaginary aches and misgivings. Even speaking of poisoning royalty could lose Cat her head. And me mine, for hearing it. Keeping treason secret is treason itself.

"Cat," I warned. "You can't say things like that. Especially not at court."

"Then I shall have to come over every day and tell them to you. I shall have to tell you all about the horrible old lecherous men and the wonderful *young* lecherous men, and the bitchy girls who hate me because all the men lust after me."

I laughed. But her humor didn't dispel the creeping disquiet her other words had instilled in me.

"But Kitty," she said, her eyes widening with a sudden anxiety. "What will I do when we are at Hampton Court? Or Windsor? And too far away? Oh, Kitty, whom will I talk to then?"

Her eyes brimmed, and I wondered for a flash if the tears were real or conjured for my benefit. But I quelled the thought.

"You will just have to send me a letter."

Cat made a face and sat on the chest, arms crossed and pouting.

"Ugh," she said. "Writing is so tedious. Besides, if there's one thing I do know about court gossip, it's that you never, ever put anything on paper. At least nothing you don't want everyone else to know."

"You'll just have to save it all up, then." I sat beside her. "And tell me everything when you come back to visit." I reached out to stroke her hair. I knew she wouldn't come back. She knew I knew.

"Oh, Kitty," she cried. "Who will brush my hair?"

And in that sentence, she summed it all up. It's not everyone you let touch your hair. You can't trust just anyone to make you look your best when you have no mirror.

"You'll just have to wear a gable hood."

Cat mumbled a laugh and leaned into me. Just for a moment. Then she stood and walked quickly to the door.

"Come, Kitty," she said. "You must help me. Before anything else I have to do this one thing."

I followed her down the stairs, but paused before leaving the house. At sunset, the topiary animals cast leering shadows across the paths and the knot garden appeared to harbor wraiths and specters. Cat grabbed my hand and pulled me forward, marching like a nurse with a recalcitrant child.

A dark shape twisted from behind a tree. It moved swiftly, silently, and before I could scream, it reached for Cat. Wicked panic slashed through me, visions converging of men in black. I wrenched my hand from Cat's grip and she let out a little shriek. Then she scowled and twitched her shoulder from the grasp of Francis Dereham. I pressed my lower lip against my teeth with my knuckles, the pain sharper than the fear that burned my throat.

"Why didn't you tell me?" Francis asked, twisting his

empty hands together. I had never seen him so pitiful before. Cat liked her men confident and a little arrogant. Francis normally fit the bill perfectly, from his self-assurance in his anatomy to his swaggering air as a self-proclaimed pirate. But there in the garden he looked like a lost little boy, crying for his mother.

"Why do you think I'm wandering the gardens?" she admonished. "I asked you to meet me, remember?"

Francis looked at me. I shifted from one foot to the other. I had spent several nights in bed with the two of them, but this was by far more uncomfortable.

"Don't look at Kitty," Cat snapped. "She's no use in this matter."

Francis turned his eyes back to her. I wanted to sink into the mud.

"What about—?" Francis started to ask, but Cat cut him off.

"I'm going to court and there's an end to it."

She thrust out a hip and laid a hand upon it, the gesture of someone impatiently giving the appearance of waiting. She raised an eyebrow.

Francis glanced at me again, his misery contagious. He licked his lips.

"But you are my wife," he whispered.

A shock went through me, but before I could say anything, Cat slapped Francis with the quickness and ferocity of a striking snake. Francis flinched.

"Don't you dare say that to me again, Francis Dereham!"

Cat hissed. "I never want those words to pass your lips. Ever. To anyone. Do you understand me?"

Francis remained silent.

"We were not married in a church," Cat continued. "There were no witnesses. We never signed a contract. *We are not married.*"

"In my eyes we are," Francis said. "I love you. I have known you as a man knows his wife. If you leave me, I will go to sea to find my fortune, and when I come back, I will be able to grant you anything your heart desires."

"You can do what you like," Cat said. "But I am going to court. And I will not wait for you."

Shadows fell across Francis's face. I had always thought him a bit of a peacock, but he looked broken in the fading light. Cat could be hard and pitiless with her enemies, but I was shocked to see her treat someone she loved with such flinty disregard.

Francis reached for his belt and brought up a small velvet bag.

"Here," he said, handing it to Cat, "take this."

She peered inside, then back at him, her mouth open.

"There must be a hundred pounds in here," she whispered. "Where did you get this?"

"I've been saving it. For the day you and I might live together." His voice broke. "I give it to you for safe keeping."

"No, Francis," Cat said, her voice a warning.

"I will not ask for anything from you," he said. "I . . . I release you. If I do not return, the money is yours. If you are . . . taken when I come back, this money is all I will ask for."

It was perhaps the most honorable statement I'd ever heard him utter. Cat narrowed her eyes, obviously thinking the same thing and not trusting it.

"Fine," she said, and pocketed the velvet bag. It sounded a muffled clink.

"Will you leave me with a kiss?" Francis asked.

"No," Cat said, but held out her hand. He seized it with both of his, as if he would take it with him.

"Come, Kitty"—Cat drew away from his grasp—"or we will be late."

She walked back to the house, her head up and spine straight. She banged through the great oak door and disappeared into the gloom of the entrance hall. Only I looked back to see Francis watching her.

Cat started talking as soon as the door obscured the light behind me.

"That didn't happen," she said, her hand in her pocket jingling Francis's gold angels. The cold stone walls echoed the sound back to her, and she stopped.

"You're married?" I asked. "Without permission?" We weren't allowed to choose our own husbands. It was beyond imagining. Our families considered it contemptible. Despicable.

Cat placed a hand on either side of my jaw and pulled me

down until our noses touched. The fading light from the high, dirty windows barely illuminated her face, making her appear almost translucent against the dark.

"I am *not* married," she whispered, her words brushing against my lips like a kiss. "There was no ceremony. There was no priest. I am not his wife. And no one will hear any differently. Ever."

Even if they hadn't married in a church, an *agreement* could make any subsequent marriage invalid. If a rich and powerful husband found out about it, he could have the marriage annulled, and Cat would be out in the streets with no money, no man, and a tattered reputation. Not even her family would take her in after that, for fear of being tainted. A rich and powerful man could make life very uncomfortable for anyone who knew about her past and didn't mention it beforehand.

"I am untarnished," Cat continued. "Virginal. Innocent. I can make a good match at court. I can meet a man who will give me the kind of life my father wasted. A man who can throw a hundred pounds away on a single doublet, not present it to me like it's a fortune."

We stood there, suspended, locked by eyes and words and secrets. I could neither nod nor speak. Her gaze shifted from one of my eyes to the other. Searching. For hope. For acknowledgment.

"I need your help, Kitty. Please. Make sure no one from this household ever breathes a word of my life here. It's your duty.

To our friendship. To our sisterhood. The men of my past must vanish."

She let go and I swallowed.

"What men?" I whispered.

"Good girl."

1540

9

CAT LEFT FOR GREENWICH AND NEVER CAME TO VISIT. FRANCIS DISAPpeared, leaving behind the odor of thwarted love and a note to the duchess that rendered her silent with vexation. The midnight parties slowed and stagnated and then stopped altogether. And the rain and slush kept us indoors, cold and damp, compressed by the weather and our own lethargy.

When I couldn't stand the walls closing in on me anymore, I closed my eyes, counted to five, and stepped outside into the wide, wet world. I kept to the paths and remained in sight of the house, counting hedges between myself and safety.

I liked to watch the river flow, sluggish and churning when the tide came in, fast and raucous when it raced the tide to the sea. Even in fog, the air felt cleaner and sweeter than the air inside the house, where sides of beef charred on spits and men and dogs urinated in the corners of the great hall. I liked to look downriver to the great old palace of Westminster and imagine what life was like for Cat at court. Westminster—which the king avoided in preference for more modern palaces like Hampton Court—seemed to reflect my own state, abandoned and unloved.

In February, my father sent a message to the duchess that his scheming to get me married had so far come to naught. None of the men he'd contacted were interested. The duchess let me read the letter, addressed to her. It didn't include an inquiry after my health or a desire to be remembered to me. I meant as little to him as an aging carthorse or piece of bogland.

Joan found me sitting on the riverbank, staring into the water with my eyes open wide, trying not to let the tears fall.

"Bad news?" she asked, standing behind me.

"I'm going to rot here." Like the damp tapestries on the walls. Like the filthy rushes. Like the tattered cuffs and hems of my slowly decomposing gowns.

"Don't be such a melancholy Madge," Joan said, and nudged me in the back with her knee.

I turned my head to look at her.

"Why don't you sit down?" I asked.

"Because you're sitting on a mucky riverbank," Joan said reasonably. "You can get away with it in that sludge-colored kirtle. But I'm in blue. For Friday." She said the last with an emphasis that couldn't be denied.

"Oh," I said. Without Cat, I could wear whatever I wanted, whenever I wanted. No one said a word. I realized that only Joan kept up with the color roster.

"Do you think we'll ever go to court?" Joan asked, her eyes on Westminster.

Cat had promised. But I hadn't heard from her. And she hadn't promised Joan.

"I don't see how."

"Maybe we'll marry rich, important men, and we'll go to court with them?"

"Right now it's unlikely I'll marry *any* man," I said and turned back to face the empty palace. I neglected to mention that she was already married. And William Bulmer never went anywhere near court. Or Joan.

"Everyone who's anyone is at court," Joan mused. "All those banquets and parties and beautiful gowns."

"And not always being stuck in the same place," I agreed. "Dancing and masques and *movement*."

"Don't forget boredom and backbiting and intrigue," a voice behind us said.

My heart nearly throttled me.

We both looked around to see sandy brown hair flopping over grayish blue eyes and a freckled face lit up by a delightedly crooked grin. The duke's new usher. Staring at me again.

"How dare you spy on us like that!" I struggled not to return the smile and leapt to my feet to face him. Joan squeaked and wedged herself behind me.

"I hardly spied on you," he said. "I merely approached to ask directions."

"You sneaked up on us," I insisted. "We didn't hear you at all."

"Is it my fault I have a light step?" He failed to look remotely innocent.

"And what did you learn from listening to girls' gossip?" I asked. Joan remained mute.

"I learned that girls are as desperate to go to court as men are."

He wasn't even going to deny listening to our conversation.

"And who are you to be spreading gossip about the court?" I pursued. "You don't even know whom you're talking to."

"You could be anyone," he said, nodding sagely.

"Exactly."

Then I realized that the reverse was also true. I was standing in the garden speaking with an absolute stranger. He could be a molester or a spy, come to gather tidbits of scandal. A prickling flush crept up my neck.

"Allow me to take pity on you," he said, and bowed.

"No need to take pity on me," I bristled. "The onus is on you, entering the garden unannounced and interrupting a private conversation."

I looked him full in the face. We stood the same height. But that didn't seem to intimidate him. It was only when he looked in my eyes that he faltered and looked back down at the ground. I remembered Cat's criticism of me. *Your eyes are too knowing. You look at men and they want to slink away.*

"Forgive me, Mistress Tylney," he said quietly. "I forgot we had not been introduced."

He knew my name. Joan wrung my hand like a kerchief. I squeezed back once before I pulled away.

"After the banquet the duke attended, I made discreet inqui-

ries," he said. "I know you are Katherine but prefer Kitty. You are distantly related to the dowager duchess and have been here for longer than most of her servants can remember."

He bowed before me. "I am William Gibbon, gentleman usher and general dogsbody for the Duke of Norfolk."

William Gibbon. I pressed the name into my memory like a late summer bloom into the leaves of a book.

He had narrow shoulders for a man, or perhaps it was just the cut of his doublet, not the extra-wide shoulders preferred by the king and those who wished to be like him. But they balanced lean, muscular calves and thighs. My gaze traveled up his legs. He straightened and I blushed from the thoughts that flitted through my mind.

"You are well met, Master Gibbon." I made my voice sweet and cast my eyes down in an imitation of Cat's flirtation practice from so long before.

"I am entrusted with a message for the dowager duchess and regret that I must deliver it quickly."

"Regret?" I asked, risking a glance at his face. It showed relief. At what, I wondered, amazed at a retainer who had yet to learn the art of hiding all emotion.

"I would much rather stay out here with you two lovely ladies." His smile lit the garden more than the piddling winter sun. I nodded stupidly, the word *lovely* ringing brightly in my mind.

"We shall accompany you," Joan said, nudging me with her elbow. Joan, ever the matchmaker. I'd forgotten she existed.

"I'm glad you're no longer angry," William said. "It was never my intention to offend you."

The reason for his relief came clear. And he surprised me again because he spoke so honestly.

"How is the duke?" I asked in an attempt to make conversation as he fell into step with us.

"Bellicose. Impatient. Slippery."

"You certainly tell what you see," I said, taken aback. No one at court or in the Dowager duchess's household ever talked about anyone except in the most glowing terms. Or in secret.

"The Duke of Norfolk is my employer. I must tolerate his moods so that I don't lose my position, but he knows I am not a crouching lickspittle. He says he is grateful for my honesty and knows I will follow any order he gives me without question."

"What if it's something you don't want to do?" I asked.

"My loyalty is to the duke."

I stopped in the chilled and begrimed entrance to Norfolk House. "That doesn't answer my question."

"Do you have no one in your life that you feel loyalty to?"

I thought of Cat. My loyalty to her had turned me into a thief, a liar, and an enforcer of secrets.

"Your family?" William prompted.

"My family does not inspire loyalty," I said wryly.

"Perhaps one day your husband," William suggested.

"Not if he's someone my parents select," I retorted, my voice

higher and harsher than I had intended. It echoed peevishly off the dirty windows. We slowed as we neared the duchess's withdrawing room from which light and warmth crept over the stone floor.

"You prefer to make your own choices?" he asked. He turned to appraise me. My height. My hair. My eyes.

"Yes," I said without thinking at all. "I do."

"That's good," he said. "I like a woman who knows her own wants." I felt a spark begin to glow in my chest.

"Master Gibbon." The duchess's voice, like sand on paper, swept into the gallery. The heat and color of the room assailed us—fire and candlelight, tapestries, carpets, and the duchess herself decked in crimson and jewels. She saw me and Joan standing in the doorway and shooed us away. William strode to her place by the fire without a hint of good-bye.

"Charming," I said, my voice laced with sarcasm. But I loitered in the entranceway in the hopes of seeing him exit.

"Handsome," Joan added.

"I suppose."

"Oh, admit it, Kitty! He's handsome. He likes you."

I shrugged, but her words blew on the spark that kindled into something like happiness.

"And in service to the duke," Joan continued.

"Joan," I said. "I'm never going to get a chance to choose my own husband, so why should I even bother?"

I wondered, though, if my parents would accept a "contemptible" personal choice if only to get me off their hands.

If they couldn't find me a match, maybe I should find one for myself.

"You sound so bitter."

"I suppose I am," I said. "I mean, if a man marries someone who doesn't please him, he can find a mistress who will. He needn't stay at home with a woman he finds repulsive. He can go to court or to Ireland or go out to work. But the women have to stay home no matter what. Sewing and needlework and making clothes and seeing to the food and nothing else. Boring."

"But Kitty, men have to fight in wars, too. That's fearful."

"Yes," I said, grudgingly. But somehow the life surrounding war seemed much more interesting than sitting around and waiting for a man to return from it.

"And Kitty." Joan's thoughts dawned slowly across her face. "That's all we do here. Sewing and needlework and all the rest."

"Yes, Joan. That's how I know it's boring."

"You *do* sound like Cat sometimes, you know."

"I suppose someone has to talk sense when she's gone."

"Well," said Joan, putting an arm around my shoulder and whispering in my ear as if divulging a delightful secret. "If Cat were here now to talk sense to you, she would say that your marriage will happen one way or another, so why not indulge yourself now?"

Why not indeed?

I could do worse than a gentleman usher to a duke. And my father certainly hadn't done any better on my behalf. Could it really be possible? To make my own choice?

"A little flirtation never hurt anyone," Joan finished. "But desperation does. Don't let him find you waiting for him."

I didn't.

But I hoped the duke would need to communicate with the dowager duchess more often in the future.

10

But the duchess's next caller wasn't William Gibbon.

It was Francis Dereham.

He came trailing a cloak of mystery and bitterness. Creases fanned the corners of his eyes and he walked with a newly rolling gait, as if he had spent much of his time on a ship's deck, squinting into the wind. But he hadn't been gone long enough to get very far, which left me wondering where he had acquired his counterfeit swagger.

If we hadn't seen his arrival ourselves, we would have heard it shortly after, for the shrieks echoed from the duchess's withdrawing room and bowstrung the nerves of the entire household.

"You leave here without word or warning and expect to return to your old position? Do you wish to make a fool of me, sir?"

Joan and I dawdled at the stairs, dropping and refolding our embroidery. Alice was nowhere to be seen.

"Heartbroken!" the duchess cried in response to Francis's murmur. "Don't be daft! You may have been a favorite of mine, but this is unforgivable."

More murmurs. Sonorous. Sensuous. Persuasive.

We took a step nearer to the closed door.

"Eavesdropping wenches!" The steward's bark from the top of the stairs frightened Joan into dropping her embroidery again.

"Out!" He surged down the stairs and smacked her with the back of his hand when she bent to retrieve the fabric and thread. I sprang to help her, dodging blows, and began to giggle.

"We'll never compete with Alice," Joan panted as we raced through the Oak Gallery in a bid to escape. "She probably knows the whole story already."

"We'll just have to find Francis himself," I said. "Catch him before he leaves."

"You go right ahead, Kitty." Joan rubbed her backside. "I'll wait to hear from you."

I sneaked through the south door that led through the back courtyard to the kitchens, knowing I could pass through them to the vestibule and the chapel beyond. Another trick Cat had taught me as a child. We had stolen sugar from the cook on feast days and devoured it behind the duchess's screen by the altar. Later, Cat had made use of the same passageways and pew for stealing kisses.

I sat in the chapel with my head bowed, winter sun diagramming angels in the southern window.

"Kitty!"

Francis slid down the polished bench until his hip touched mine. A jolting reminder of when we used to share a bed.

"Returning to the scene of your crimes?" I asked.

"Love is never a crime, Kitty," he said sadly. "I had to come here, to where she first kissed me."

"I thought you might."

"Everything here reminds me of her."

I knew that well.

"She never loved me, Kitty," he said, his face fallen into crags formed by sunlight and shadow. "And now she treats me like a stranger."

"You saw her?" I asked. "You went to court?"

"I did," he said. Only Francis would walk unannounced into court to speak with his ex-lover.

"How is she?"

"Fat and happy," he said. "Exactly where she wants to be. She's surrounded by jewels and great ladies and has no need for the likes of me. She has found someone new."

His voice broke, and I looked for tears in his eyes but saw only jealousy.

"Really?" I asked. "Who?"

"A little weasel in the king's privy chamber. Handsome and cocksure and full of the king's good graces."

Power. At least one of Cat's criteria fulfilled. As she'd said, the king's favor meant everything.

"What's his name?"

"Culpepper. Thomas Culpepper."

Francis spat the name in the hush of the chapel and slammed himself to his feet.

"At least I got my hundred pounds." He grimaced.

"Where will you go? Back to sea?" I asked, hoping he would tell me where he'd really been.

"Hardly." He laughed. "Piracy doesn't suit me. And I doubt the duchess would tolerate my absence a second time."

"You got your position back?" *Even after all that shouting?* I added silently.

"The duchess is like putty in my hands."

"I'm surprised she played into them. I suppose I should say welcome home, then."

"Not exactly. She's none too pleased with me. Doesn't want to see my face. I'm leaving my goods and coffers here, but she's exiled me to the Horsham estate."

"Good luck." I reached out to shake his hand.

"Oh, I won't be there long, Kitty."

He took my hand and kissed it—a bit wetly—winked at me, and swept from the chapel with a flourish, a swashbuckler in his own mind if nowhere else.

I wondered about Francis's rival, Thomas Culpepper. He'd have to be pretty seductive to win Cat's attention over the barons and earls and dukes.

"She'd never have stuck with him anyway." A rasping voice startled me as I made to leave the chapel myself. Mary Lascelles, her mouth twisted in disapproval, blocked my way. Her blue eyes swam in the pale pool of her face.

"Oh?" I took a step back. Mary always stood too close.

"He's beneath her. He's beneath her *family*."

"Are those your words? Or your brother's?" I had a feeling he shared his opinions freely.

"My brother doesn't know any of this!" Mary cried. "If he did, he would take me away. He would punish me just for being here."

For a moment, I felt sorry for her. Until her next words erased all sympathy.

"Cat believes you're beneath her, too, you know."

"I don't see that it's your business," I replied sharply, brazening out the pain she inflicted.

"But *she's* the one not worth the Howard name. She may imagine she's royalty, but she acts just like a common slut."

"Oh, shut up, Mary," I said. "I don't want to hear your venom. She's not the one emptying chamber pots and sleeping on the floor."

"Even the highest will be brought low," Mary intoned.

I laughed. "Perhaps you ought to tell the king that."

"I just think," she said, "that if she continues as she has begun, she shall come to nothing."

"I don't care what you think," I said, and walked away.

"And if you depend on her," she said, her voice rising to reach me, "you will be nothing, too!"

Francis departed and the rain returned. Cat sent no word from court. I began to suspect that she couldn't wield the influence to get me there, and her promises were for naught. Doubt nibbled at the back of my mind that perhaps, to a certain extent, Mary Lascelles was right. I wondered if I was actually beneath Cat, or at least beneath her notice.

I turned sixteen in the middle of Lent. Joan wished me the best and Alice smirked and we had no meat or cheese and the day swirled away like effluent in the river.

I spent that afternoon outside, alone. I felt that the water of the Thames itself flowed in my veins, toilsome and murky. The colors of the river and the sky melded perfectly, running together on the far side and seeming to drip across Westminster like an unfinished painting. I stared at the palace, lost in imagining the riot of color and intrigue behind those dreary gray walls.

"Much more beautiful up close."

I startled, slipping on the slick clay of the riverbank, and fell headlong into the mud. My heart beat an erratic rhythm of fear until I looked up and it nearly stopped at the sight of William Gibbon.

"Let me help you," he said, extending a hand. Amusement lit the one blue eye that remained unhidden by his sandy hair.

"I can manage," I said, ignoring the hand. And the eye. And the freckles. And the enticingly crooked smile.

I hauled myself from the mire. "You know, you really must stop sneaking up on a person." I tried to give him a withering glare. Unfortunately, it didn't work. He looked at my dress and burst out laughing.

The entire front of my bodice and skirt had changed from blue to a saddle brown. The thick clay coated the fabric so thoroughly that the piping and embroidery didn't show.

"I don't see what's so funny," I said, my embarrassment making me pettish.

"My apologies," he said, his sincerity marred by a twitching at the corners of his mouth.

I wiped at the mud ineffectively. William coughed. If he started laughing again, I thought I might smack him.

"It's a lovely color on you, Kitty," he said.

Lovely color. It was a horrible color. Reminiscent of bodily functions. In spite of myself, laughter burbled in my chest.

"I look frightful," I admonished him. "Mud is a color flattering to no one." I caught a smile creeping across my own lips.

"Monks' habits are often that very brown."

"We don't see many monks around here, anymore," I

reminded him. Not since King Henry had shut down all the religious houses. "Besides, I don't think I'd be accepted into a monastery."

"Oh, really?" he asked with a grin. "Skeletons in your cupboard?"

"Wouldn't you like to know?"

"Actually," he said, "I find secrets get in the way." And suddenly his expression opened. Vulnerable. I could read everything he was thinking. He looked shy. And hopeful.

"That's good," I said. "Because I have none." None of my own, anyway. I looked away to hide the hope my own face reflected.

Westminster Palace stared back at me from its empty eye sockets. I remembered what William had said before I fell into the mud.

"Is it really more beautiful up close?" I asked. From Lambeth, it didn't look beautiful at all.

"I didn't mean Westminster," he said quietly. I felt his gaze on my face and couldn't move. Could hardly think. "I meant you."

I turned so quickly I nearly fell again, but William caught me with an arm around my waist, turning my insides liquid. His touch warmed my entire body and made me feel I could run the joust against the king himself. And yet I hesitated even to carry my own weight for fear he would let go.

"Watch your step," he breathed into me.

My thoughts spun like leaves on the wind, whisked high

and giddy with no direction or destination. I nodded, struggling not to laugh out loud at the joy of it. I looked up to see the laughter mirrored on his face. But he wasn't laughing *at* me. I bit my lip to stop myself from kissing him right there. The movement drew his eyes to my mouth. To the rest of me. I felt the flush return to my face when he looked me in the eyes again.

"Perhaps the monks will take me," he whispered.

"What?" I gasped. I took a step backward, onto the dry, rocky path. "One moment with me and you're ready to join a monastery?"

"I believe I already wear the color of their robes." He indicated a line of mud that ran up the length of his body. Were we really that close? I quavered at the thought. Deliciously.

"The duke will have my ear for this," he said with a laugh. As though he didn't really care.

"The duchess will have our hides if she sees us both and jumps to conclusions," I added. Because even she would be forced to ask about two bodies coated in mud.

"Then she shouldn't see us together."

My heart sank. He couldn't go yet.

But instead of leaving me and going to the house alone, he offered me his arm and led me in the opposite direction.

We walked past Lambeth Palace, the residence of Thomas Cranmer, Archbishop of Canterbury. Just ahead of us, the landscape opened and fell away, the path rising above it, almost like a bridge. The river stretched to our left, gray-green and rippled.

Lambeth marsh lay flooded to our right. I could see forever. No strangers lurking behind trees.

East, down the river, London town splayed on the horizon. It looked black and grimy, choked and swarming.

"Is the city very frightening?" I asked.

"My father used to take me when I was younger," William said. "We still have a little house there. Near Cheapside. I remember watching a tournament from the window."

"You *are* a gentleman, then," I said. Surely good enough for my parents.

"The tenants give us a little money," he said, the crooked grin growing sad. "But personally, I'd rather be here. Outside, with the sky and the river."

"And the mud."

"That, too."

"Not at court?" I asked.

"I suppose I prefer a quieter life." He made a face. "At court, there is so little time, so little room to move. Everything is dictated by someone else's desires, telling you what to do, what to think, what to want."

My elation flickered for a moment, caught like a fly against glass. Could I choose a man who wouldn't be at court—who would take me far away from everything I'd ever dreamt about? Away from Cat?

"I can see you're not convinced," he said with a wry smile.

There on the riverbank, the possibilities seemed so distant, the ultimate choice so remote. That I could go to court. That

I could choose a man I wanted. That William would even ask.

"Convince me." I smiled back. In the meantime, the least I could do was flirt a little. And put those years of practice with Cat to use.

"It may take time." He took a step closer. So close we nearly touched again. "And persuasion requires frequent contact."

"Oh?" my voice barely a whisper. "How frequent?"

"I will be returning often."

"Is there much news to share between the duke and the dowager duchess?"

"Apparently so," he said. "I'll show you spring as it comes. I'll show you why I'd prefer to be here. With you."

I smiled, my words lost on lips ready to kiss him.

"When the weather clears," he added, blushing as if he could read my mind. "And the mud dries."

We returned to Norfolk House, the narrow path necessitating close proximity. Our knuckles brushed once, sending a flash of sensation up my arm. William spoke of his family home in the country, his face animated with delight. And I listened, bewitched by the cadence of his voice.

When we arrived at the garden, he bowed and turned to the grand entrance at the front of the house. I watched for a moment and then ran around to the kitchen, startling the cooks and scullery maids and setting up a racket amongst the dogs. I literally tripped up the back stairs to the maidens' chamber, banging my shins and leaving gobbets of mud on

the risers, but I didn't care. I was too caught up in my own jubilance.

He wants to see me again. One thought pivoted, so I could see it from all sides. *He wants to see me again*.

Happy birthday.

And he did. Twice more in March and on the first of April, William arrived with messages and walked with me in the gardens. Even in the rain.

I couldn't sit with him inside because the duchess hectored him until he returned to court. But he wanted to be outdoors, anyway, so he could convince me of its merit, unaware that it was something I already knew. Something I feared. But over the course of his persuasions, I found myself, slowly, becoming comfortable with the world outside the walls.

He always caught me unawares. I never had time to dress up or even tidy my hair. And he liked me anyway. The more he came, the more I wanted to be with him. Not just walking. I yearned to hold his hand, to feel his skin against mine. To have him kiss me.

I remembered how his arms had felt wrapped around me.

I wished we still had the midnight parties, so I could invite him.

I wished more than ever for Cat to be with me. To offer advice and assurance.

Then, after Easter, as if conjured by my inclination, she returned.

On a day we all felt fractious and at odds, she blew into the house in Lambeth like Zephyrus, bringing summer and light. She wore an azure gown, the bodice studded with pearls and edged with satin rosettes. Her sleeves flowed about her arms like a sunset, orange silk slashed with yellow.

She spun once on her own, her skirts belling around her in a rustle of luxury, before we descended on her.

"How did you get here?" I threw my arms around her.

"Where did you get this?" Joan nearly bowled us over onto the hearth as she joined the embrace.

"Why didn't you tell us you were coming?" Alice sounded vexed that she didn't know in advance.

"I wanted it to be a surprise," Cat sang, causing the Countess of Bridgewater to grouse and shuffle. "I want all of April—all the rest of our lives!—to be one brilliant surprise after another."

She flung herself at me in a swirl of skirts that propelled us into the tapestry of Solomon and the Queen of Sheba.

"I can't tell you how happy I am to see you," she whispered.

I was about to tell her the same. Tell her I needed her advice. But she leapt from the wall as if pinched and pulled me with her.

"Come!" she said. "All of you."

She led us up through the gloomy entranceway and into the oak gallery where our voices and footsteps echoed.

"So what's it really like?" I asked. "Living at court?"

"It's actually hard work," Cat said. "I have to help the queen dress and plait her hair. Not to mention sewing for the poor and providing entertainment for the king."

"They have no servants?" I asked.

"Kitty, we *are* the servants." She navigated the stairs as if she'd never been gone. "The queen can't be attended by common peasants. The worst part is when the older ladies think they can order me around. Like my stepmother, even though all she did was marry my scattergoods of a father. She thinks she can play *ma mère* now that we live in the same household. I may just be a maid of honor, and she one of the 'great ladies,' but I'm there to serve the queen, by the Mass, not Margaret Jennings."

"She is a Howard now."

"Margaret Howard. *Lady* Howard. I don't care."

"Do you get along with the other girls our age?" I asked, waiting to hear I'd been replaced.

"Like who?" Cat paused at the top of the stairs. "Mary Fitzroy the Duchess of Richmond? She's actually a Howard, daughter of the Duke of Norfolk. Wouldn't she be a fine confidante, tattling every word I utter? Then there's Katherine Carey, Mary Boleyn's daughter, and possibly the king's, though he won't admit to it. I don't blame him: the whey-faced ninny thinks marrying Francis Knollys is the epitome of courtly delight."

Cat dropped names and dispensed sentences with such

worldly abandon that I began to feel hopelessly provincial.

"Is it true the king might be her father?" Alice asked.

"Aren't you always on the lookout for gossip?" Cat said.

"If she was, surely he would claim her, like he did the Duke of Richmond," Joan said.

"But she's a *girl*," Alice argued. "Only boys are worthy of a king's acknowledgment."

"There's no way of knowing for sure," Cat cut in. "Her mother was Mary Boleyn. I mean, the king of France called Mary his English mare when she served over there because he'd ridden her so many times!"

We dissolved into giggles that silenced when she pushed open the door to the maidens' chamber. The room had been completely transformed.

Swathes of fabric lay across several of the beds. Yellow damask. Green velvet. Silk an incredibly pale blue like the center of a snowdrift. Four different pinks, from a magenta brocade to a rose-colored satin. The layers of cloth carried the exotic odors of foreign lands and spices from the holds of ships.

"What's it all for?" Joan asked, her voice hoarse with awe. "New gowns?"

And even I heard the unasked question: *For us?*

"Isn't it gorgeous?" Cat said, stepping into the room and whirling in a dizzy spin. "Can you believe the dried-up old bat finally broke down and got me something nice?"

"It must have cost a fortune," Joan breathed, but disappointment washed her face.

"And it's all for me!" Cat grinned. "Not a hand-me-down. Not something cut from someone else's leftovers. Mine. Made especially to fit me."

I couldn't quench a spark of envy. Cat and I had always been the same. The same age. Both unwanted daughters. Both wearing castoff clothing. And suddenly she was away at court, meeting new people, wearing new gowns. I was beneath her, just like Mary Lascelles said. A sickly petulance overtook me.

"Jesus, Cat," I muttered. "How many times can you put *me* and *mine* into one breath?"

Joan squeaked. Cat fixed me with a glare like a rapier thrust. I felt it pierce me. My envy mingled with anger and shame. I wanted to take back what I had said. I wanted to say more.

She approached me with a swagger like a lioness ready to pounce.

"I am the face of Norfolk House at court. The duchess can't have anyone believe her house or her family is shabby. I represent the entire Howard family. I *need* new clothes. Do you deny me that?"

"Of course not," I said. "No one is happier than I am that you're finally getting all you deserve. Beautiful clothes. Jewelry. A man you love."

She stopped moving. Stopped breathing. Then snapped, "Get out," over her shoulder, and Joan and Alice disappeared as quickly as dandelion fluff on the wind.

"Who told you?" she asked, her voice more deadly than ever. "No one knows."

"Francis," I whispered, my voice a paroxysm of nerves.

"Francis *Dereham?*" she asked.

"Yes," I said. "He saw you at court. Then he came here to get his old job back. I spoke with him."

"*Francis?*" she repeated, and her eyes opened wide, radiating surprise, or possibly fear. "He's here?"

"No, the duchess sent him to Horsham," I said, confused and shaken. "He said you were in love. That you sent him away."

"I told *no one.*" Her voice rose to a shout. "What did he say about me?"

"He said you loved a man named Thomas Culpepper," I said.

Cat began to giggle. The giggles came in little puffs at first. Then in a surge, like bubbles from the bottom of a pond. And suddenly, she was giggling so high and so hard that she couldn't catch her breath and had to bend over, hands on her knees, eyes streaming.

This wasn't the Cat I knew. The Cat who whispered dreams in my ear at night. The Cat who sneaked around Norfolk House, kissing and canoodling with Francis in the chapel. This Cat jumped from one extreme to another. This Cat didn't like me. This Cat was frightening.

"Cul-Cul-Culpepper?" she gasped.

"That's what he said!"

"Silly Kitty." She took a stinging swipe at my cheek.

"Culpepper is in the past. Culpepper is no one. He was just a . . . nothing." Her eyes unfocused a little, "Though so *seductive*."

She shook her head as if to clear it.

"No, Kitty, I have a better catch now. I have everything I want right here."

She opened her tiny hand and showed me her empty palm. Then she snapped her fingers shut like a coffer.

"It's all I'll ever want, Kitty," she said. "It's all I'll ever need."

CAT STAYED, THE EPICENTER OF A WHIRLWIND OF FABRICS AND FIT-
tings, ribbons and pearls. She and I reached a truce that hinged
on us both keeping silent regarding Francis, Culpepper, and
her mysterious new man. And William. I wasn't ready to share
my unblemished feelings for him. And I wasn't sure she would
approve. We'd never had secrets from each other before, and it
felt odd and strained. The awkward tension made me mute on
all but the most mundane subjects.

Fortunately, the duchess embarked on a campaign of clean-
liness and enlisted the assistance of everyone in the house,
thus preventing the possibility of long, private conversations.
The stairs were swept and washed with lye. All the gold plate
gleamed in the buffet of the great hall. The dogs were banished
to the kitchens and courtyards. Even we were doused in cold
water—our hair scrubbed with lavender—and left out to dry in
our camisoles in the weak spring sunshine.

The steward began to lose his corpulence because he had no
time to eat. He had to be fitted for a new doublet, the duchess
muttering over the expense of velvet.

Cat sat in the tapestry room as if holding court, sewing

embellishments from twisted gold tissue to her new bodices. Occasionally, she begged the duchess to release us from drudgery in order to assist her. As we did, she would regale us with tales of court like a traveling minstrel, and we hung on every word.

The duchess tried to keep it a secret, but we all knew the reason for the uproar.

The king.

Sometimes, it was a good thing to have Alice around.

"But why would he be coming here?" Joan asked, hunched over tiny stitches of silver on silver in the drab light from the window.

"He has to visit the nobility," Alice said. "They expect it."

"It's the same reason he has a progress," Cat agreed. "He has to get out and engage with the lords and dukes. Be seen by the people. And see his country."

"But why is it a secret?" Joan pursued. "If he wanted to be seen by the people, wouldn't he be telling everybody? So the peasants know he's coming and can see him? And besides, we're right across the river from him. It's not like he's never seen Lambeth before."

"Well, this visit isn't exactly like a progress," Cat conceded, and frowned.

"But it is a great honor," I added.

"Of course!" Joan dropped her stitching. "Oh, I didn't mean anything else by it. I just don't know why he would want to come *here*."

"Are we that boring, Joan?" I asked.

"The duchess is a great noblewoman," Alice sniffed. "Of course he would want to come here."

"Right." Joan sounded unconvinced, and looked up to ask another question, but was interrupted by a commotion outside.

Horses and carts and men in livery filled the courtyard. Everyone seemed to be shouting orders, and no one seemed to be heeding them.

"The duke," Joan said.

I stood and brushed my skirts. Perhaps in the chaos I could at least catch a glimpse of William, if not a word with him.

"Where are you off to?" Cat asked.

"Nowhere," I said, feeling the word a betrayal to both Cat and William.

"Kitty's going to see the boy who works for the duke," Alice said. "The one who brings the messages. William Gibbon."

My cheeks flared.

"You have a boy, Kitty?" Cat asked, hurt in her voice. "You didn't tell me."

"He's handsome," Alice said.

"He likes her," Joan grinned.

"He stops by to say hello when he delivers a message sometimes," I said. "That's all."

It was the truth. So far. I just wished it were more.

"I think Kitty has a secret lover," Alice said. She stretched out the last word like a sticky sweet.

"He's not a lover," I said quickly, the heat on my neck refus-

ing to fade. He was the closest I'd ever had. The only one I'd ever wanted.

"Then you won't mind if *I* talk to him?" Alice said.

"Do what you like!" I cried, all bitter nonchalance. Confusion tied my tongue and baffled the truth.

"But, Alice, you're married," Joan protested. I could have hugged her.

"So are you," Alice said. "And that doesn't stop you from prancing about with Edward Waldegrave."

"But you can't take Kitty's boy," Joan said.

"Kitty says she doesn't care," Alice said.

My heart threatened to spill from my sleeve and all over the floor, I cared so much.

"Well, that's all right then," Cat interjected. "Because I have my eye on someone for you anyway, Kitty Tylney."

We all stopped and stared at her.

"Don't think I've forgotten my promise to get you to court," she said.

Joan gasped, a look of uncensored hope gilding her features.

"And when you get there, you'll have your pick of some of the most eligible men in the country," she continued.

Joan sighed, a mournful note of envy.

"But I don't . . ." I said. "I'm not . . ."

I didn't want anyone else.

"It's true, you're nobody," Cat said quickly. "But there are plenty to choose from even at your level. The king likes to keep young men around him. His privy councilors have become so

old, but some of his gentlemen pensioners and yeomen of the chamber are really quite luscious."

Like Thomas Culpepper, I thought, but carefully didn't mention it.

"One in particular," she said. "A yeoman. Looks like a lion, with this gorgeous golden hair. You would kill for it." She reached up and smoothed down a shock of my own hair that had escaped my plait. I felt it fly away again when she was done.

"He would be good for you," she said, quietly, in my ear only.

I nodded and smiled. But I didn't want Cat's choice. I wanted my own.

Perhaps I didn't want to go to court after all.

"The king's barge!" A cry went up from the garden.

The galleries filled with the sound of running slippers and pounding boots. I had never seen the elder members of the household move so quickly. Even the duchess exerted herself enough for pink to rise beneath the white lead on her cheeks.

We fell into line outside the great door of the house, a welcoming committee of flouncing skirts and adjusting doublets. The duke's men waited at the landing. I could see William's head amongst them.

The duke had insinuated himself and supplanted the dowager duchess as head of Norfolk House. He'd marched through the rooms and galleries, sniffing out the ugly and inconstant with his powerful nose. He tolerated no idling. And no flirting. I hadn't seen William for three days.

"There it is!" Alice whispered. We all craned our necks to look. The royal barge appeared, painted in scarlet and gold, with detailed filigree and intricate designs. The canopy of cloth of gold was embroidered with the initials of the king. H and R. *Henricus Rex.*

On the king's barge were select retainers. This was to be a

private party. An intimate meal with only the king's beloved friends. All two hundred of us.

The king faced us, his clothes and hair and beard a riot of red and gold. He looked like a giant standing there, one foot resting on a cushion as if he had just conquered it.

"He never ages," Joan whispered.

But even at a distance, I could see a slight stoop to his shoulders, the swell of his chest and belly. He was no longer the lean knight who had escorted Queen Anne Boleyn to London when we were children. He was something else now. Weighted.

"In line!" the duchess snapped as she strode past us, black and gold damask rustling, jewels winking on every surface. The Duke of Norfolk kept pace with her, his little bowlegs scissoring in his black hose.

The barge landed, and we all sank into deep bows and curtseys. We were supposed to stay that way, crouched on the muddy path, until the king exited the barge and waved us all up.

Cat had told us that the king suffered from an ulcer in his leg, brought on by an old jousting injury. He had trouble getting around, and sometimes his temper was incredibly short. The entire court would walk on eggshells, wondering who would be thrown out of the chamber for sitting or smiling or breathing. I knew what the duchess was like when she had one of her migraine headaches. I tried to imagine that kind of power and pain in a king.

Still, it took him forever to get out of that damn boat. My own knees began to ache from the stupid curtsey, and my thoughts ran to treason.

"Norfolk!" the king cried, his voice surprisingly high for someone so large. It made him more human.

We took our cue to stand, and I was able to look at the king from beneath my lowered brow. Dressed all in crimson and fur, he blocked out the sun, which created a halo behind him. I wondered briefly how many animals had to die to construct his ermine cape. He towered over the duke. And he was *wide*. It couldn't all be fat, because he wasn't round, just prodigious. And intimidating. He stood with his feet planted far apart and his hands on his hips, like Colossus straddling the entrance to Rhodes.

He finished listening to the flattery of the duke and dowager duchess and strode toward the house. We all sank to the ground again. I curtseyed gratefully, not wanting him to see or notice me. He was too big, too beautiful, with his gold-trimmed clothing and neatly cut beard and fingers burdened by heavy rings.

But he stopped in front of me. I trembled, unable even to look at his shoes.

"Mistress Howard," he said. Of course it wasn't me. It was Cat. "I believe I have seen you at court."

"Yes, Your Majesty," Cat said, and rose. "I wait on Her Majesty the Queen."

"And how do you like it?" he asked.

"I like it well, Your Majesty. She is a good mistress, and you are a good master."

"Loyalty is a virtue," the king said.

"Your will is mine, Your Majesty."

"I like that in a woman," the king murmured.

Cat's skirts rustled, and out of the corner of my eye, I saw her sink back into a curtsey.

"Come, Mistress Howard," the king said, his voice quick and hearty. "You shall sit by me this evening."

I couldn't help but smile, wondering what the duchess's face looked like. Little Miss Nobody usurping her place at the high table. Cat rose and I remained in my curtsey, watching her satin slippers practically skipping down the path.

The duchess laid on a banquet of epic proportions for the king, even though in theory, he was "just stopping in for a bite to eat." Venison, spit-roasted pig, a boar's head, pike, sturgeon, rabbit, and lamb. Peacock, pheasant, duck. The very best wine, not the vinegary, watery stuff she usually served.

Because we weren't important, Joan, Alice, and I served the far end of the room, not even able to sit down. Others enjoyed the privilege of serving the king, and then the dishes were passed down the tables. We got the worst cuts of meat, and little of the sweets and marzipan, but it was still like Christmas and Easter all at once.

Cleaning and decorating had rendered the hall almost

unrecognizable. The scratched benches, ancient wooden tren-
chers, and dogs were all gone. The floor gleamed from repeated
scrubbings, as did the tables. The king sat in a brand new chair,
on a velvet cushion, the back carved in elaborate designs of
stags and Tudor roses.

"Just look at the fabrics he's wearing," Joan sighed.

"Look at all the gold," Alice said.

From a distance, the king's eyes appeared to recede into the
fat of his face, giving him a mean and piggy look. Cat looked
like a doll beside him.

"What do you think of his men?" I asked, glancing about
the room at the few courtiers he had brought with him. None
of them looked to be Cat's type. They didn't appear dashing
or dangerous. They didn't have sexy smiles or chin dimples or
shapely calves. But they must have had influence, to accompany the king for such a private party. Power and riches. But
could she give up looks?

"The two men behind him are passable," Joan said, dragging
her eyes from the king's furs.

I had to squint a little to see them properly. One had stringy
black hair but broad shoulders. He stood in a good imitation
of the king's stance. The other man was older and indifferently
handsome.

"Well, they're not too bad, I suppose," I said. Perhaps it was
the second man Cat was interested in, but she paid no attention to either of them.

She seemed perfectly content to wait on the king, to smile at

his comments, to speak rarely. For the king didn't really seem to want to converse as much as impress. I couldn't hear what he said, but he did most of the talking. How could Cat bear it? She hated being around people who talked about themselves more than about her.

But then again, he *was* the king.

"I wonder what he's saying," I said.

"Whatever it is, it must be riveting," Alice said. "Look at Cat's face."

Cat watched the king talk as if it were the most fascinating thing in the world. She looked . . . *avid.*

"She has to look that way," I said. "If she looked bored, he would cut off her head."

Alice puckered, and Joan gagged on her wine.

"I didn't mean it," I whispered hastily. "It was a joke. It just slipped out."

"Jokes like that could lose you *your* head, Kitty," Alice muttered. "You must watch your tongue."

I nodded, voiceless.

Joan sighed, leaning back against the wall. "Cat has all the luck."

"She certainly does," Alice said. "She has the family connections, the looks, and now the clothes, too. Is it any wonder the king noticed her today? Her duckies are practically bursting out of that bodice."

"Now who's making inappropriate remarks?" I asked.

Alice made a face, and Joan giggled into her hand.

"I desire a dance!" the king cried, and clapped his hands. "Mistress Howard tells me that she and her friends here in Lambeth love to dance."

The duchess called for more musicians, and the servants scurried to remove the trestle tables and benches. The king had brought no ladies with him at all, so even the lowliest among us had a chance for a partner. Trust Cat to open every window of opportunity for us all.

One of the king's retainers took Cat's hand and she accepted impassively. Joan giggled at the invitation of Edward Waldegrave. Alice partnered the other courtier, but I kept my eyes on Cat. The man opposite her was tall. A little old perhaps. Blandly good-looking, with a narrow face that stretched into a pointy wedge-shaped beard. Cat smiled at him once but paid him little notice.

"I don't see what you find so interesting about Anthony Denny."

I turned to see that William Gibbon stood before me. I blushed.

"I didn't see you."

"It appears your attention was elsewhere." He held out his hand and we began the galliard.

"I was just . . ." I couldn't finish without giving away Cat's secret, so I stuttered into silence.

"I've been out on business for the duke," he said, rescuing me. "And have returned just in time."

I smiled. The galliard was athletic and inhibited conversa-

tion. But when the music stopped, William led me aside into the shadows so we could watch—and whisper—unimpeded. He held my hand lightly, his touch like summer—like the shape and feel and scent of a plum—intoxicating.

"You dance well," he said.

"Practice." I laughed. Thinking of late nights in the maidens' chamber made me feel warm. "Late night dances with Alice. Though I usually play the boy's part."

"Really?" he asked. "Why?"

I looked at him to see if I could detect a trace of guile, but saw none.

"It's impossible for someone like Alice to lift me," I said simply, and indicated my height. "I'd probably crush her."

"Funny," he said, slipping an arm around my waist. "I had no problem at all."

"You are a bit taller than she is," I said, but my voice caught slightly. "I'm huge compared to her."

"I think you're just right," he whispered.

I sensed every place his body touched mine. One hand on my hip. His arm along my back. Chest just touching my side. His right knee lost in my skirts.

"Kitty," William said, his mouth so close to my ear I could have kissed him with a turn of my head. "Kitty, I think I . . ."

He paused and I turned. So close. He raised his other hand to stroke a wisp of hair from my forehead. I felt lost in the lightness of his touch.

Then the musicians fell silent, breaking the spell, and we

looked back to the room. The king had risen and made his way slowly to the empty floor.

"A pavane!" he called. A slow, stately dance, one that wouldn't trouble his leg.

He turned and held his hand out to Cat. She curtseyed, and when she rose, a triumphant smile lit her face. She didn't like slow dances. But her countenance reflected no boredom or irritation. Far from it. She looked . . . radiant.

She no longer looked detached. No, she watched the king with every step she made. In the light, in the dance, beneath her gaze, his features lost twenty years.

The king and Cat only had eyes for each other.

I felt as if I had been struck by lightning. I stared, prostrate with the knowledge of who had replaced Culpepper in Cat's affections.

15

"I, CATHERINE, TAKE THEE, HENRY, TO BE MY WEDDED HUSBAND," CAT said solemnly.

The king told everyone he had been unable to consummate his marriage to Anne of Cleves. Her body repulsed him. His conscience pricked him.

"To have and to hold from this day forward . . ."

Anne had been engaged before. To the Duke of Lorraine. The ambassadors from the Duchy of Cleves were unable to produce the proper paperwork proving the contract was null and void.

"For richer, for poorer . . ."

A betrothal was as good as a marriage, legally binding. King Henry balked at bigamy. When it suited him. Queen Anne could be lost in translation and become the King's beloved "sister," no harm done.

"In sickness and in health . . ."

I saw the appeal of losing status rather than losing your head, but who would willingly accept being superseded by a little girl? Seeing one of your *maids* crowned queen while you sat by and smiled and pretended not to understand?

"To be bonny and buxom in bed and at board, till death do us part *are you listening to me?*"

The sharpness of the words startled me away from the open window in the maidens' chamber. The sun was out, carrying waves of the scent of the fresh June leaves in the apple orchard.

"Of course I am, Cat," I lied. I'd heard the words so many times already I could have said them myself.

"This is my *wedding*," Cat snapped. "I have to get it right. It has to be perfect."

"It will be," I assured her. Not that any of us would be there to see it. We weren't invited. We didn't even know what day it would be.

"What does it mean?" asked Joan, who lolled on her bed, rummaging through Cat's new cast-offs. Every day brought a new gown, a new jewel, a new bauble. Cat, festooned with attention, dripping with royal favor, passed on the least of her wardrobe to the rest of us. The poor.

"Bonny and buxom?" Joan grinned and hefted her own breasts to illustrate.

"No!" Cat said. "Bonny means cheerful. And buxom, obedient."

Henry wouldn't say that part. No man was expected to owe cheer and obedience to his wife. So it might as well have been breasts.

"What will happen to Queen Anne?" I asked.

"He's giving her Richmond Palace," Cat said. "And bucketloads of money. And don't call her that. She'll be the Lady Anne soon."

She'd be able to live on her own. Without having to answer to anyone. But she'd be alone. I wondered if the trade-off would be worth it.

"It's her own fault, really," Cat added. "She rejected him."

"No, she didn't, she married him. He's rejecting her."

"No, I mean before she married him. She was in Rochester and he disguised himself as a traveler. Rode hard from Greenwich to meet her. I mean, how romantic can you get? He couldn't wait to see her, to kiss her for the first time. But when he got there, she pushed him away."

"But if he was disguised, how did she know it was him?"

"Well, everyone else did."

"But she'd never seen him before," I said. It seemed unjust that she was vilified for a natural reaction. A strange old man comes up and tries to kiss you, who wouldn't push him away?

"That didn't matter to him. You see, he still thinks of himself as the handsomest man in Christendom. The golden hero. The statuesque godlike figure of classical art and mythology. The man she rejected was a dilapidated, fat, smelly old man. After that, whenever he was with her, that's how he felt."

"But I make him feel like the Greek god," she finished. "And as long as he sees himself that way through my eyes, he'll be happy. And once I get that crown on my head, I will give him no reason to feel any differently."

"I hope you're right," I said.

"Of course I'm right," she replied, laughing. "I'm always right. I was right about us going to court, wasn't I? When I'm

queen, I shall bring you to be my favored guest. You shall supplant the greatest ladies of the kingdom in status and in my affection."

When she's queen. Cat Howard.

"Cat," I whispered. "You're going to be queen."

"I know," she said, her eyes alight, an edge of awe creeping into her confidence.

"You're going to be the Queen of England!"

I threw my arms around her and danced her up and down the room, our laughter echoing up the long gallery. Joan sat still on the bed, smiling, rubbing the raised velvet brocade on her new skirt.

"And you'll really take me with you?" I asked when we caught our breath.

"I promised, didn't I?" she said. "When I left, didn't I tell you I'd find a way to get you to court? For us to be there, just like we always dreamed?"

"Well, you certainly found it," I said.

She grinned.

"And we'll do just what we always said. We'll eat too much and dance all night and flirt with *all* the boys," she paused. "At least you will."

"I'll flirt," I said to soothe, though I didn't mean with all the boys. Just one. "But we'll both dance."

16

At the end of June, Anne of Cleves moved to Richmond with her furs and her head intact. Cat moved back to court. Throughout the spring, Norfolk House had been in a continual furor. If we weren't planning a dinner for the king, we were cleaning up from one—usually both at once. Now, the absence of Cat and the king was like the space of a missing tooth. I kept probing it to see if it was real.

Even more painful was the fact that William returned only infrequently. And I waited as impatiently as the duchess for news from her stepson at court. He came once, mid-July, on what felt like the hottest day of that hot, dry summer. The duke and dowager duchess sequestered themselves in the cool cave of the downstairs withdrawing room. And William coaxed me outside, where the sun had bleached the topiary and cast a diamond reflection off the river.

"Why don't we venture outside the walls?" William said. "I spotted a little grove of trees on a rise just south of here . . ."

He trailed off, watching me. In my mind, I knew those men no longer lurked in the shadows beyond the apple orchard. But in my heart I felt them waiting outside the gates.

"You don't like the park?" he asked.

I hadn't set foot in the woods since that evil afternoon the autumn before.

"Actually, it's one of my favorite places," I blurted. The quiet. The birdsong. The ever-changing, myriad shades of green.

"But?"

I couldn't tell him. Because I'd done nothing. Nothing to help. Nothing to hinder. I'd run. I'd saved myself. And still I didn't feel safe. I never felt safe.

Except with William. I managed a smile and moved toward the gates.

"Don't." He laid a hand on my shoulder. "Don't do something just to make me happy. This isn't only about me. It's about both of us."

Freckles dusted his knuckles like they did his nose. His nails were short and even a little grubby. William didn't spend all his time indoors drinking wine and flirting. He worked. I liked that.

He took his hand back, ducked his head, his hair concealing his embarrassment. I loved that his face told me at least as much as his words, and sometimes more.

"When I was little," I told him, "I used to pretend that the arch in the oak trees was a gateway to the fairy world. I could walk through there and be in the forest where the leaves changed the color of the light and the bluebells formed a carpet more luxurious than anything produced by man. I always felt it was there that I truly belonged because no

one expected anything of me. No one told me what to do or what I wanted or who I was. No one told me I wasn't good enough."

I took his hand from where he held it behind his back and smiled.

"A magical gateway." He sounded dubious.

I nodded. It was my turn to feel embarrassed.

"That is something I must experience for myself." He began to run up through the orchard, pulling me with him. Elation and terror mixed within me. The sun illuminated the arch like a golden door, and when we reached it, William swept me up into his arms to carry me through.

The light patterned through the leaves like stained glass. William set me down but didn't take his hands from my waist. The fairies must surely have lived there, for I forgot, in an instant, all that had happened in that forest.

"This will be our special place," he said, his gaze so keen I lost sight of the sun itself. "No one here will tell you that you aren't good enough." The dappled sunlight played across his features, chasing the emotions that sped from elation to confusion to determination. He leaned forward and pressed his lips against mine.

For one startled moment, I stared directly into both of his gray-blue eyes, then I closed my own and kissed him back. A kiss that dissolved with spice and sweetness on the tongue.

My arms ached to wrap around him, but I didn't know how.

His waist? His neck? Could I run my fingers through his hair? In the end, I stood still, arms straight at my sides and fingers splayed.

William stepped back and looked at me, blinking surprise.

"I'm sorry," he said.

"I'm not." Something about him drew the truth out of me.

"I have no prospects. I'm nobody. I have nothing to offer you."

"Neither have I. I have no family connections. I will bring no dowry. We're equals." The word ignited something in me. We were the same. The wonder of it made me smile.

But William didn't. Deep in the shadows of that shrouded wood, the expression that crossed his face combined anxiety with a half dose of despair. But his eyes still held hope. Just a shred of it.

"I am dependent upon the duke," he said. "My loyalty to him is based solely on need. The need to make the right connections."

I nodded. The sunlit warmth had fled from my body, and I shivered. I was not the right connection.

"He knows this," William continued. "And doesn't let me forget it. That my choices are not entirely my own. But you're related to the dowager duchess?"

"Distantly," I said. "Very, very distantly."

"He couldn't say no," William said quietly.

To what? I wanted to ask, but held my tongue. I didn't trust myself to speak.

"When I first saw you, at that banquet, I couldn't take my eyes off you," he said.

I remembered. With a blush.

"You were so different from the others."

So much taller. So much more awkward.

"So much more real." William took my hands in his. "You didn't preen or simper or bat your eyes. You didn't wear cream to make your skin pale or paint your cheeks. You wore a plain gown."

I had to.

"You didn't flirt with the duke when you served him."

Ew.

"In fact, it appeared you couldn't get away from him quickly enough. Despite the fact that he could get you to court."

Maybe that's why the duke didn't pick me.

"I liked you before I even knew you, Kitty," he said, and stepped closer still. "But getting to know you has made me like you even more."

When he kissed me again, my arms went around his neck of their own accord. My hand reached for his hair and buried itself in the thick, textured luxury of it. My tongue found his, and I lost myself in the brilliantly faceted sunlight and shadow of his touch.

17

I SLIPPED IN THROUGH THE FRONT DOOR OF THE HOUSE, ONE HAND TO lips that felt green and renascent, like spring itself. The entrance hall dozed, languid, in the afternoon heat, buzzing with the hum of a single fly.

And voices. From the duchess's little withdrawing room.

I tried to slip past, but was caught by the sound of my name.

"Katherine?" the duchess said. "You try telling that snip of a girl what to do. I've tried for years now, and she still does whatever pleases her."

A shot of fear passed through me that someone had seen me with William. That the duchess disapproved not of my choice but of me making it.

"Perhaps that is why she is so headstrong," came the duke's voice. "She has never been punished for it."

"Are you trying to tell me how to run my own household, sir?" the duchess cried.

"I would never do such a thing, my lady. Though others might wish to if they discover the laxity of your control. Especially in the past."

"No one will ever learn Katherine's secrets."

Secrets? I had none. At least none the duchess knew. Or so I thought.

"Which is exactly why we must fill her chambers with those allegiant to the house of Howard. And one in particular who will be willing to tell us everything. What is said and by whom. Who is in favor and who is out. When they consummate the marriage. How often and how vigorously."

I realized which Catherine they discussed. And why.

"We will need to know every detail of her monthly courses," the duchess agreed.

"God forbid that she have them," the duke interrupted. "For what we really need is a Howard heir in the royal cradle."

The duchess murmured her agreement. I started to creep away, having no desire to be privy to the rest of their conversation. But the duke's next words stopped me.

"We will need help. Someone close to her. Someone we can trust, but whom she must trust as well. A sister?"

The duchess let out a condescending laugh.

"She hates her sisters," she said. "No, it will have to be someone closer than that."

"Someone loyal," the duke reminded her.

"I know just the person," the duchess said. "Loyal to the grave."

It was what the duchess had called me, many months before. *Loyal to the grave.* Closer than a sister. When Cat fulfilled her promise to bring me to court, would I be expected to tell all her secrets to the duke?

On July 28, Thomas Cromwell, who had engineered the marriage to Anne of Cleves, lost his head for his singular lack of judgment.

Cat married King Henry the same day.

Cat followed instructions and appointed great ladies to her household. She kept Jane Boleyn, the Lady Rochford, widowed sister-in-law to the first Queen Anne. And she selected several candidates from amongst her family members. Cat's half-sister Lady Isabel Baynton, thirty years older and infinitely more tiresome, and Cat's stepmother, Lady Howard, retained the positions they'd had in Anne of Cleves's household. Cat's aunt, the pale Countess of Bridgewater, and Lady Arundel, another half-sister, rounded out the Howard retinue.

And then Cat appointed the dowager duchess herself.

Cat finally had them all where she wanted them. She wielded more power than her stepmother. More influence than her aunt. More status than her grandmother. Cat had won. Finally.

But she didn't have us. As the long, hot summer stretched on, we received no word. The duchess packed up her house. Dismissed her servants.

Wrote letters to the parents of the girls in her care.

We waited as the summer scorched the earth. Into the dry autumn when the leaves dropped from sheer exhaustion. The wheat withered in the fields before it could be harvested. Cows and sheep and men and women battled starvation.

Joan started to cry.

"Don't worry, Joan," I said, barely able to console myself. "She promised, remember?"

"No, Kitty!" Joan cried. "She promised *you*."

I froze, one hand on her shoulder. Had Cat only promised me? And how much was that promise worth?

"I was there, remember? In the maidens' chamber. The day she was practicing her vows. She said she would make *you* her greatest lady. Her greatest friend. She didn't promise me anything. She didn't even look at me."

"Of course she meant all of us," I said helplessly.

"You can't really think that," Alice said. Quiet as ever.

"We've always been together," I said.

"It's always just been the two of you," Alice said. "Kitty and Cat. And me and Joan on the side. You were always the important one."

Not important enough.

"But I might have certain benefactors working in my favor," Alice announced.

"In *your* favor?" Joan said, petulance generating a shrill falsetto.

"Well, yes," Alice said. "My husband does work for Lord Maltravers."

I looked at Joan and mouthed *Lord Maltravers* with simpering, pinched lips. She smiled weakly.

"I even wrote a letter to Cat," Joan sighed. "I reminded her of our friendship. Of our history together."

A sudden fear clenched me.

History. Joan knew all Cat's history.

"And you put this down on paper?" I asked, barely able to form the question. A piece of paper could take on a life of its own. In the right hands, it could bring down a queen.

"It was pretty sickly," Joan admitted. "*Remember the love my heart has always borne towards you.* That sort of thing."

"And that's all?" I asked.

"Of course." She nodded, her face blank and guileless.

The other girls dispersed to the bosoms of their unloving families. Mary Lascelles cried piteously over the punishment of having to return to her brother's keeping. But whatever Joan had written must have jarred Cat's memory, because the summons came. For all three of us.

I had my chance to go to court. To be someone different. Someone important. Someone desired. Someone beloved of the queen.

19

WINDSOR CASTLE APPEARED ABOVE THE GOLDENING RED ASH OF THE surrounding forest, the gray stone glowing white against the painfully blue October sky. This was a true castle, not a modern approximation of one. Not like the duchess's house of brick and spit-shine. This was a castle built for defense with thick slit-windowed towers and crenellated walls.

"There it is!" Joan yelped. We had already traveled many long, boring hours and now she leaned over her horse's neck, as if hoping it would get her there sooner.

I found myself leaning forward, too. My horse danced sideways slightly, caught up in my excitement. The castle on the hill looked so far away.

"Let's race," I said.

"Most unladylike," Alice muttered. She rode primly in her dark brown riding habit, eyes straight ahead, completely unaware of the smudge of dirt across the side of her nose.

"Last one there tends the duchess's bunions!" I shouted, an old joke from when we were children.

My horse leapt forward when I dug in my heels. She seemed as keen as I was to enter the magical realm of chivalry presented by such an enchanted scene.

"Katherine Tylney!" Alice cried.

"We're not ladies!" I shouted back to her. "We're chamberers!"

Joan's laughter undulated over the warm-cold ripples of sunlight and shadow and I knew that she followed. Alice couldn't be far behind.

Our horses kicked up dust on the dry road and over the cracked-earth gardens and pigpens. We slowed as the road narrowed between rows of tall, half-timbered buildings—the kind occupied by merchants and town leaders, sellers of fabrics and slippers and lace to the court, all eager and bustling because the king was in town.

Suddenly the right side of the road opened out and up the hill to a great stone gate, looming above the rest of the houses. Protection. Defense.

We stopped. Almost as one.

"Here we are," I said quietly.

"We made it," Joan agreed.

Alice only nodded, all confidence drained from her face.

The guards at the gate recognized our escort and allowed us through. The air cooled considerably as we passed beneath the arch, heavy and dark. Then we came blinking into a wide, gaping courtyard, studded with knots of gem-colored courtiers.

We dismounted, and stable boys scurried to lead our horses away. I felt bereft at the loss of my palfrey's bulk and warmth. I pressed the anxiety beneath my stomacher.

To our left rose a perfectly rounded hill, topped by an ancient tower, thick and heavyset like an old man's chest. To our right,

the castle wall enclosed the quadrangle and all the activity that spun within it. And directly ahead, a looming gray residence studded with towers squinted at us through narrow windows.

The entrance yawned wide, ready to swallow us whole.

"This way," our escort said with a noise halfway between a laugh and a cough.

I realized we had stopped again, the three of us open mouthed and gawping. My skin burned with embarrassment. We giggled nervously and started forward again.

"*This* way," the guard repeated, and indicated the western wing of the building, the door hidden behind the tennis court—the servants' entrance, illustrating the fact that indeed, we were not ladies, or anything remotely akin. We were chamberers, and therefore not entitled to the same privileges. No matter what Cat had promised.

The courtiers looked up and ogled as we passed. One, a yeoman in scarlet Tudor livery, faced the others, and I admired his broad back, clipped narrow at the waist by a shiny black belt. He had gorgeous golden hair that I would have given my left hand for. The thought tugged a memory. *Hair you'd kill for.* Was this the man Cat had in mind for me?

He turned as we walked through the narrow space between the building and the tennis court, and I stumbled over the cobbles. His brown eyes widened, round face slack with surprise. And recognition. He'd seen me before.

In the forest.

20

Joan muttered a curse when I tripped over her in a scramble to escape. She looked up and saw the man staring.

"He's delicious," she breathed, looking at my red face. "And he's staring right at you!"

"We can't stop," I hissed, and urged her toward the building.

We slipped in through the narrow doors. Not the kitchen entrance, but certainly not the state entrance. After a stuffy vestibule, the building opened up to a giant room with a massive staircase.

This was obviously the place to be and to be seen. And it was crowded, so therefore also a good place to hide. Women clustered together like peacocks at a spill of grain. They were dressed in bodices of rich damask, with matching overskirts and complementary colors in their kirtles. Their sleeves were puffed and slashed to reveal vivid silks beneath, looking a bit like bread ballooning from the heat of the oven. Gowns of velvet trimmed with gold braid. Hoods decked in pearls. And all sorts of dazzling adornments—chokers and collars and pendants of gold, brooches the size of my hand, studded with gems, rings like jeweled knuckles.

I risked a glance at my own clothes. My Wednesday green dress was smudged with mud from the road. The tear in the skirt was coming open, like a secret dying to be let out. My face was likely splotchy, my eyes probably wild, my hands trembling.

I looked behind me, afraid of being followed.

"Watch where you're stepping!"

I turned to see that I had almost trod upon the bejeweled slipper of a small, compact woman. Her sleek chestnut hair peeked out from beneath a French hood the color of the sky just before nightfall. Her gown was of the same color velvet, simple, without the dazzling chaos of brocade, the sleeves a lighter blue shot with silver. She had wide-set eyes the color of wheat, like a cat's, and they looked up at me critically. I was yet again reminded of my great height and ungainliness.

"Excuse me," I said, and curtseyed. I assumed, from her dress, that her status would be higher than mine. I assumed everyone's would be. Surely the presence of this woman would offer some protection.

"Nicely done," she said, and smiled. It changed her appearance dramatically. Her pale face brightened and her pointed chin smoothed. From seeming somber and somewhat world-weary, she became a coy beauty. I couldn't help but smile back. Her gaze did not stray to my unsuitable attire.

"I am Jane Boleyn, Lady Rochford," she said. Her eyes never left mine, gauging my reaction. And I could imagine the many she got when she introduced herself. People likely recoiled in horror at her intimacy with the infamous Anne Boleyn. People

would pity her widowhood. Her dependence on the Duke of Norfolk. Not something I would wish on anyone.

I didn't look away, and smiled more broadly, determined to judge her on her own merits and not the gossip surrounding her. Determined I wouldn't mention Anne Boleyn or the painful past.

"I am Katherine Tylney," I said quietly, and curtseyed again.

"New chamberer to the queen," she said.

"And these are Joan Bulmer and Alice Restwold." Joan stared openly. Alice's mouth sliced into a smile.

"I believe you are called Kitty," Jane said to me. "You may call me Jane when we are in private company, but Lady Rochford when you speak to or of me in the public of the court."

"Of course," I said, a little nonplussed. No lady, especially not one so great as a viscountess, had ever asked me to call her by her first name. It seemed misplaced. Odd.

"The queen awaits you," Jane said, slipping her arm through mine, "but I must take you first to St. George's Hall to meet the king."

I risked a glance over my shoulder. The man with the blond mane was nowhere to be seen. Jane's arm pulled mine slightly.

"I believe you have met the king already?" she asked, probably assuming I felt nervous entering the royal presence. "I was under the impression that you lived at Norfolk House in Lambeth, and he visited there."

She tactfully did not refer to the fact that Cat was not queen

then. That, in fact, there had been another queen altogether at the time.

"I have never spoken to the king," I said.

"Well, it will be unusual if you get a chance to speak with him today," Jane said. "We will enter, you will be introduced, and we will leave. The king is a busy man and rarely takes any particular interest in the queen's household."

"Oh," I said, unable to think of anything else. I figured it would be churlish to say *good*.

She drew us up the broad staircase, whispers and a few snickers following us as we traveled. And then we stepped into a riot of color and sound. Great, painted wooden beams curved across the vaulted ceiling high above us. Embroidered tapestries cloaked the walls, sewn of pure gold and silk, embellished with pearls and sparkling stones. Courtiers milled about, bedecked in diamonds and bound in gold braid. A man could spend a year's wages on a single item of clothing. Each of them glittered. Each of them wore a dagger *and* a rapier. Beautiful and deadly.

Everything smelled of sweat and dust, breath and lavender.

"Sir Anthony Denny"—Jane pointed to a man in a pale green doublet trimmed with yellow velvet—"the king's Chief Gentleman of the Privy Chamber." I remembered him from the first banquet the duchess gave for the king.

"Thomas Wriothesley," she said, pronouncing it Riz-ley. Jane's lively face took on a fixed smile as she nodded to the man next to Denny. He was dressed in black, the slashes in his

sleeves revealing chevrons the color of blood. "Stay away from him if you can. He's like a ferret. Small, hungry, and with very sharp teeth. Most likely, you'll never come in contact."

Wriothesley caught me staring, scanned my face, my clothes, and my companions. I could *see* his mind ticking off items and columns as he did so.

A man who looked like a younger Duke of Norfolk, resplendent in orange and brown, stood to one side of the room. He was engaged in conversation with a bigger, broad-shouldered man who sported a mighty beard and scanned the room with keen eyes that lit only on the women.

"The Earl of Surrey, Henry Howard," Jane said, following my gaze. "And Charles Brandon, Duke of Suffolk."

"Is the Duke of Norfolk here?" I asked, a squeak in my voice. I scanned the room for the possibility of William.

"He's at his estate in Kenninghall," Jane said.

But not before a figure caught my eye. A figure and face I knew. A gasp became trammeled in my throat, ensnared by panic.

"Lady Rochford?" I said, trying to keep from choking on my own breath. "Who is that?"

Jane craned her neck to see around the broad shoulders of the Duke of Suffolk, and then smiled.

"The new girls always spot him right away," she said.

He was tall and lithe. The blue of his doublet matched the silk that winked from his slashed yellow sleeves. He had chiseled cheekbones and a straight, jutting jaw. His dark eyes

danced, assessing those around him. Handsome. But repulsive. I knew him well, because he haunted my nightmares.

This was the rapist from the woods.

I struggled to remain composed, my muscles poised for flight, my heart pounding to escape.

"That, my dear, is the king's usher, Thomas Culpepper. A bit of a gallant, if you ask me, playing fast and loose with the affections of a dozen girls at once."

Thomas Culpepper. He had once been the object of Cat's affections. He was still at court, free and whole and unscarred.

"And never far from his company is Edmund Standebanke," she added. "One of the yeomen of the chamber."

A lion's mane of hair inclined as its bearer whispered into Culpepper's ear.

"Kitty!" A girlish cry nearly dropped me to my knees. "Joan! Alice! I'm so glad you're here!"

We turned to see Cat scampering the length of the great hall, dukes, duchesses, and courtiers scattering, bowing, and curtseying in her wake. Everyone watched her progress to see whom she considered important enough to greet with such ecstasy. The sleeves of her crimson gown billowed, tucked in at the wrists by gold-embroidered cuffs. A series of pearl-and-ruby ropes hung around her neck, anchored by a gold pendant enameled with a brilliant crowned rose.

Jane pinched my sleeve and I followed her into a curtsey of my own. It felt so strange making obeisance to my best friend.

"Oh, stand up for pity's sake," she cried, and threw her arms around me.

"Kitty," she said, and then whispered in my ear, "finally, someone I can talk to!"

She hugged Joan and Alice in turn. Around us, the murmur of whispers sounded like the hiss of disturbed geese.

"Joan, thank you for the kind note you sent," Cat said, a slim, cold edge to her voice.

"Your Majesty," Joan said, a blush turning the entire top half of her body pink.

"And Alice, always a pleasure." Cat gave a tight smile. "How fares my uncle?"

"I do not know, Your Majesty," Alice said, her eyes darting in confusion. "Lady Rochford says he is in Kenninghall."

"I swear you've grown," Cat said, ignoring her and turning back to me. "Soon you'll be too tall for any man save the king, and I'm afraid he's already taken."

The women around us tittered behind their hands, and I smiled weakly, accepting the butt end of the joke. I kept my eyes on her. I had the protection of the queen. No one could harm me. Cat would be my shield. From the laughter. From Culpepper.

"Come meet my husband." Cat giggled. She dragged me by the hand to the dais at the front of the room. The king sat in a velvet-laden chair beneath a cloth-of-gold canopy. Cat ran up the shallow steps to him, and he shifted his weight gracelessly to look at us.

"Who are your acquaintances, my love?" he asked. He must have seen us a hundred times at Norfolk House, and yet he hadn't noticed us once. Now, with Cat's introduction, I felt overly conspicuous and uncomfortable.

Not to mention the fact that he had his arm around her, his huge, meaty hand resting precariously close to her breast.

"Your Majesty," Cat replied. "This is no mere acquaintance, but my best friend, Mistress Katherine Tylney. We are more like sisters than my own sisters, for we grew up together."

"Ahh, Mistress Tylney," the king said. "A pleasure to meet you."

Since he had spoken to me, I was allowed to rise, but found that I couldn't.

"Thank you, Your Majesty," I said, curtseying to the floor again, my voice barely a whisper. Cat laughed.

"This is Kitty's first royal audience," she said. "I think you intimidate her."

"Ah, no," the king said, and I looked up to see him smiling in mock horror. "Surely I inspire awe and not fear?"

"No, Your Majesty," I said. He looked shocked and I realized my mistake. "I mean, yes, Your Majesty."

Cat laughed, and the king chuckled. He moved his arm around her waist and stroked her hip, a smile flickering across his face. He looked besotted. Smitten. Lustful. I gagged on my embarrassment.

"I shall go to my apartments," Cat told him, gently extricating herself from his grasp.

"Much to catch up on with your friends," the king said, and smiled again. Like an indulgent grandfather. Cat flashed him a grin and slipped through the hall, pulling me behind her, beckoning Alice and Joan to follow.

"Your Majesty." A short, stocky woman with a rather masculine face approached Cat and curtseyed.

"I don't need you, Lady Howard," Cat said, airily. So this was Cat's stepmother.

"As you wish," the woman said, seeing that Cat held fast to my hand. Her face twisted out of a grimace that I could read clearly. A Howard, passed over in favor of the prosaic, the homely, the minion?

Cat turned to the other women who had hastened to her side. The dowager duchess, resplendent and ravenesque in silver and black. The Countess of Bridgewater, drab as a sparrow, bland brown eyes receding into the shadow of her bland brown hair. And Lady Baynton, Cat's half-sister Isabel, pinched features and disapproving lips making a mockery of her swanlike neck and graceful bearing.

"I don't need any of you."

A look of venomous jealousy crossed the face of Lady Baynton. The others were shocked rigid by the dismissal. No one had pretended interest in Cat when she lived in Lambeth but everyone seemed keen on her company at court. The ladies quickly smoothed their faces to compliant smiles for the queen. But Lady Howard couldn't rid

herself of the expression that suggested she smelled something repugnant when she looked at the rest of us.

"Ignore the Coven," Cat whispered to me and proceeded out the door. "They bark, but they don't bite."

I turned. The ladies clustered, hissing whispers and angling their necks. The men stood in their knots of color, making negotiations and preparations and telling secrets. And Thomas Culpepper dazzled in his inky wickedness like a beacon. Watching.

21

THAT NIGHT, CAT DISMISSED ALL OF HER LADIES—ALL OF THE DUCH-
esses and marchionesses, the daughters and wives of nobility.
She even excused Joan and Alice. She abandoned her giant
feather tester bed and crept onto my little straw pallet with me,
her shoulder pressing against mine.

"Just like old times, Kitty."

"But now we're living the dream."

"I'm glad you came," Cat said. "I need you here."

"Where else would I go?" I asked with a laugh, the double
meaning hanging in the air. I'd go where Cat asked. No one else
wanted me.

"I need loyal friends, Kitty. It's a nest of vipers out there."

"The Coven doesn't seem very friendly," I agreed.

"They're all right," she said. "They're Howards. Just looking for advancement. But the rest. The Seymours and the
Wriothesleys and the Cromwells. All looking for a crack into
which they can wedge a fingernail. To chip off the gilt."

I shivered.

"Cat," I said. "Even the Howards aren't trustworthy."

I told her of the conversation I'd overheard between the duke
and dowager duchess.

"You should just forget you ever heard it," Cat said.

"But how?" I asked. I had fretted over it for weeks, wondering who would betray her. Who would nestle into the duke's pocket and whisper in his ear.

"I already have the king. That's all they care about. When I came to court, they hoped I would look pretty and spread my legs in return for family advancement."

"Cat, that's so vulgar."

"Vulgar, but the truth. But I've gone beyond their wildest dreams. I don't just have the king's interest—I have his *heart*. No one can touch me."

But I couldn't shake the anxiety I felt at the duke's involvement. He frightened me with his sheer feline scheming, his false front of inflated aristocracy hiding a heart of pure unprincipled deviousness.

"They didn't reckon on me charming the king so much he'd want to leave his wife for me," Cat continued. "Not just a mistress. More like my cousin Anne Boleyn than her sister Mary."

"That's dangerous talk, Cat." It seemed a jinx.

"All talk is dangerous. Every word you speak can be turned around and turned against you. You can express your love for the king and someone else will say you've imagined his death, a hanging offense."

"Aren't you afraid?" I asked, thinking of the secrets, the lies, the gossip.

"Afraid?" she echoed. "Afraid of the king? Why, Kitty Tylney, how dare you doubt my husband?"

Cat proved her statement that all words could be turned to

mean something else. Something that implied wrongdoing by the speaker.

"Afraid of the court," I said, speaking generally but thinking of Thomas Culpepper. Knowing now that the face had a name.

"I am queen," she said, turning onto her side. "The court should be afraid of me."

I smiled and turned too, our backs stretched the length of each other like conjoined twins. Cat would protect me.

"You always wanted to be queen," I murmured.

"The Queen of Misrule," she replied, her voice almost lost in the luxurious darkness of the room.

22

We quickly fell into the routine of Cat's household. Alice, Joan and I were "chamberers," a few steps below the ladies, but a step above the common servants. It was our job to check the huge feather tester bed for knives and poison. We made sure the fires kept burning and the rush mats stayed fresh. We slept in Cat's bedchamber each night on our straw pallets on the floor.

Within the citylike structure that was Windsor Palace, Cat had her own little warren of apartments. An audience chamber, profoundly more grand than the duchess's, where she held public interviews and where her privy council asked her opinion on state matters, much to her amusement. A withdrawing room, bedizened with gilt and tapestries, where she sewed quietly with the Coven and listened to music. And her bedchamber, with its bulky four-poster bed festooned with heavy curtains.

She even had a garderobe for her own private use—no more chamber pots for Cat. She got to sit on a velvet cushioned bench in a tiny chamber closed off by its own little door. It was quite possibly the only privacy she ever got.

The king had his own suite of rooms above the north wharf overlooking the river. His Groom of the Stool (the man who accompanied the king to his own garderobe, therefore ensuring the king never had any privacy at all), Sir Thomas Heneage, came to Cat's rooms with news every evening at six. The king himself visited frequently. I found another place to sleep on those evenings.

Culpepper stayed in the king's rooms, a royal favorite. He was always surrounded by a gang of young men, Edmund Standebanke among them. Fortunately, the queen's ladies remained apart, in her apartments. A completely separate household. Most of the time.

When I could stand it no more, I found a quiet moment to ask Cat. Obliquely.

"What of the king's favorite, Thomas Culpepper?" I asked.

She looked at me sharply. Not forgetting that I had once connected his name to hers. The Coven shifted by the fire.

"What about him?" she asked, focusing again on her sewing.

"He seems . . . dangerous," I said lamely.

"Oh, Kitty," she said, her voice pitched low, "he is dangerous."

"What do you mean?" I asked, my limbs tensed as if ready for flight.

"He is as handsome as the day is long and cunning as a fox."

"I was wondering"—I licked my lips, my mouth suddenly dry—"why he remains in the king's chambers. If he's . . . dangerous."

"Oh, he's only dangerous to innocent girls," Cat said with a grin. "He would eat you for breakfast."

Isabel Baynton tittered.

"Diverting as that may sound," Cat continued, "I couldn't let it happen."

"Oh," I said, horrified. "I'm not interested."

"Good," she said, with a snap of the shirt she sewed for the king. "Because I have my eye on someone else for you, Kitty."

I recalled her saying this before.

"Who is it?" I had hoped she would give up her matchmaking. "It's not some lame, old, fat man, I hope."

As one, the Coven sucked in a breath, drawing all the air from the room.

Cat stared at me, dumbstruck. She hesitated for a fraction of a moment and recovered herself, a blush barely touching her cheeks. Mine flamed in response. The old joke struck too close to home.

"No, Kitty," she said. "Nothing like that."

"I'm sorry—" I began.

"No need for apologies."

But I saw there was a need. Cat went back to her tiny stitches. Her forehead puckered and she bent closer to the fine fabric. The bitterness of anger radiated from her.

"The king told me how much he misses her attention to detail," she said. "The first Queen Catherine. She made all his shirts. Even after he tried to divorce her."

I didn't have time to respond, because Alice and Joan dashed into the room together, setting the Coven to clucking.

"Cat, you'll never guess what," Joan said, flouncing to the floor at Cat's feet.

"A ghost from your past." Alice spoke over her, rushing to get the news out first, and tripped over her own skirts, almost landing in my lap.

Joan giggled. But Cat threw her sewing to the floor and stood, eyes sparking dangerously.

"Do you not make obeisance to your queen?" she asked.

"Of course." Alice curtseyed and Joan leapt to do the same. Cat let them stay down longer than absolutely necessary before she sat again and motioned for them to rise.

"And don't call me Cat. The king thinks it sounds too harsh and feral. He prefers *Catherine*. Or better yet, Your Majesty."

"Yes, Your Majesty," they said in unison, curtseying again.

"Much better. Now what is your news? You mention a ghost, but there is nothing in my past that could possibly haunt me."

Her voice remained calm, but the pointedness of the words drove them home.

Joan bit her lip and glanced at Alice.

"It's nothing, really," Alice said, the wind of her gossip removed from her sails.

"It's obviously not nothing, Alice," Cat retorted.

"It's Mary Lascelles."

Cat's hands stilled in her lap. "Mary Lascelles?"

"Yes, she was once chamberer to the duchess," Alice said.

"And now she has petitioned to be a member of your household here," Joan added, still slightly aglow with the news. "She was sent by her brother."

"A horrible man," Alice said. "Apparently she gets her holier-

than-thou attitude from him. He considers it his duty to infect all society with saintliness."

"Well, we shall have none of that." Cat managed a weak air of mischief. "Make sure she is sent away promptly."

I released a breath I hadn't known I held. Cat's temper had lit like straw but extinguished quickly. And it would be easy enough to rid herself of the tattling Mary Lascelles.

"And empty handed," I added.

"No," Cat said, stopping Alice before she carried the message. "Send her home to her brother with a chamber pot. For old times' sake."

Fools find their own misery.

23

In December, the court moved en masse to Hampton Court Palace. Built by Cardinal Wolsey, sacrificed to the king, it sprawled along the banks of the Thames, blocked out in lines and angles, squared against the semicircular curve of the river. The turrets and gates, the buildings and towers glowed in the winter sun, embellished with red and white and gold. I had lived half my life across the river from a royal palace, and spent two months in another, but had never seen anything so majestic.

It seemed the entire country came with us, preparing for the Christmas season. Parties and banquets were never-ending and the rooms and halls and galleries perpetually rang with music and laughter, the pounding of feet, the whispers of expensive fabric and the rattle of gold and pearls.

Cat's true raison d'être as queen was to fill the court with as much pleasure as possible, planning a seemingly endless succession of feasting and dancing. Former queens had helped the poor, changed the king's views on religion, or begged for mercy for rebellious commoners. Cat enabled him, in his decrepit old age, to enjoy life again.

She dressed in a new gown every day, discarding them just

as she had said she would. She pushed her ladies to do the same, bringing some to the brink of bankruptcy. Queen Jane had insisted every lady dress modestly, her control reaching all the way to the number of pearls on a bodice. Queen Catherine Howard insisted that they dress for a party every day. That every lady at court wear a French hood, eradicating the ugly gable. And that everyone make merry. Or at least give the impression of it.

Christmas hit us like a snowstorm, and Cat was deluged by a blizzard of gifts, including a brilliant brooch, glittering with diamonds and rubies, edged with pearls. Cat counted them all.

"Thirty-three diamonds," she declared. "And sixty rubies."

And a sable muffler edged with rubies and pearls. And a square gold brooch containing twenty-seven table diamonds. And hoods of velvet and cuffs of fur and goblets and plates of gold. Enough to make the faint-hearted edgy and unnerved, but Cat accepted it all and asked for more.

On Twelfth Night, she received a collar fashioned from links of gold and enameled Tudor roses, flashing at the throat with diamonds arranged to form the letter *C*.

"You finally got your name in jewels," I said, lifting it to help her put it on. Remembering her threat to steal the duchess's *A* long before.

Cat pulled the collar from my hands and studied it.

"Do you know what the ancients believed?" she asked. "That diamonds are supposed to shine brightly before the innocent

and darken in the face of guilt. I wonder if the king is testing me."

"That's a myth, Cat," I said, reaching again to fix the jewels around her neck. "Diamonds symbolize constancy. Fidelity. Commitment. It's a beautiful gift. And one you deserve."

"It's not enough. He doesn't give me what I really want."

"What do you want?" What more could she possibly ask for?

"I want him to have me crowned!"

"He will."

"He never crowned her," she said. "Anne of Cleves."

"You told me he knew from the beginning he would get rid of her."

"That's what I mean!" She turned on me, speaking urgently. "If only he had me crowned, I would feel secure. I would never need or want another thing."

"He loves you, Cat," I said. More than that. He thought the sun shone out of her. "Why are you so concerned about this?"

"Because my entire family is breathing down my neck about it!" she cried. "Every twenty seconds the duchess mentions it or my stepmother makes a pointed comment or the duke is whispering in my ear about it."

"The duke is here?" I asked. I hadn't seen him, so rushed was I with Cat's preparations. But if the duke was in attendance, William might be, too. I hadn't seen him for three months.

"Of course he is," Cat snapped. "The whole world is here."

I hurried to finish getting her ready, suddenly desperate to get away. My fingers faltered and I held my breath, hoping

she wouldn't mock my desire to see William. Or, God forbid, remember her pledge to find me someone else.

"All they ever want is more, more, more," she said, oblivious. "As if I haven't given them enough already. Every wretched member of the family has a position at court. Everyone I know wants a piece of me. A piece of what I have. What a bunch of leeches."

"I suppose it's because court is the place to be," I said quietly.

"Oh, Kitty!" Cat threw her new jeweled brooch with its thirty-three diamonds and sixty rubies onto the bed and grabbed both of my hands. "I didn't mean you! You and I will always be Cat and Kitty."

She threw her arms around me in a hug like someone drowning. "No matter what, don't ever leave me. Promise me that."

My thoughts ran briefly to William. To a place in the country. To quiet and forest and open spaces.

"I need you, Kitty," Cat whispered.

"I know, Cat," I said. "I promise."

As a chamberer, I was not invited to the festivities, much to the delight of the Coven. They swept past me in the gallery that separated Cat's apartments from the king's, clucking and warbling, with barely a glance in my direction.

The gallery, empty of people, filled with shadows cast by the swiftly setting sun and the lowering fire that barely warmed the queen's audience chamber. Instead of following the gallery to the king's processional route, past the chapel and down to the great hall, I took the back galleries, through the rapidly emptying rooms, down to the clock court.

I craned my neck to look up at the carvings inside the gateway, brilliant yellow, white and red even in the dim light. Tudor roses proclaimed their dominance. More subtly, the paint beginning to age, the letters H and A entwined. HA HA. Painted for Anne Boleyn. Ha, ha, indeed. I slipped out from under those ill-omened designs to view the windows of the great hall.

I felt rather than heard the rumble of six hundred voices. Imagined the riot of color of everyone's finery. The aching beauty of the tapestries on the walls and the gilded ceiling. The smell of sweat and smoke and roasted flesh, the cacophony of overindulgence and exaggerated laughter.

"Wishing you were inside?"

I turned to see William striding across the courtyard. The sight of him stilled me and set my heart to racing all at once. He broke into a run and caught me before I could move to meet him. His arms around me felt like a blanket made of daylight—bright and solid and safe.

"Hmmm," I said, my cheek pressed against his shoulder. "A crowded hall where everyone ignores me or some time alone with you? Difficult decision."

"I'll wait while you make it," he said. He stepped away from me, hands behind his back as if at attention, waiting for orders.

"Perhaps I'll just see what they're serving." I turned as if to go, laughing.

"You can't get away that easily." He pulled me back and kissed me lightly. I closed my eyes and felt his lips on mine, his breath a sigh within me, his touch dancing between imagination and reality. The entire length of him fit with me perfectly.

"I'd never try," I murmured against his lips.

With unspoken agreement, we turned and walked beneath the king's great clock that tolled the hour and described the minutes, seconds, and phases of the moon. It displayed the astrological constellations and even predicted the running of the tides. Gold and blue, larger than the windows, it gleamed like a beacon of the enlightened prince who ran the country.

William held my hand, his thumb tracing circles around my knuckles as we walked without the need for words through the base court, beneath the empty eyes of the royal apartments and the rooms of the courtiers housed there, through the final gate and out into the garden and down to the Thames, flowing cold beneath the first glittering star of the evening. And I finally felt, for the first time in my life, that I belonged.

William stopped above the riverbank and drew his cloak around us both. Motionless, we watched the darkness fall.

"The duke is to be sent to Scotland," William said after a sudden breath. He wouldn't meet my eye. The Scottish borders were the very edge of civilization. The Scots were constantly encroaching, pillaging in violent disputes over land and authority. The Borders were dangerous. And very far away.

"Do you have to go with him?" I tried to keep my voice light, almost a tease. But the pain leaked through.

"I depend on him," William said quietly. "Not just for my livelihood but for my reputation. I may not agree with him. But I have to do as he asks."

"And what I want doesn't matter?" The words were out before I could stop them.

His body went rigid and he pulled away. He ran his fingers down my arms and clasped my hands in his, but when he looked at me, his face was cast in shadow.

"What do you want, Kitty?"

It was on the tip of my tongue to say one word. *You.* But I denied myself even that simple truth. I had made Cat a promise.

"I want the possibility of seeing you. No matter how busy we are. I want you here. At court."

"But even you don't want to be at court. Not really."

I balked. I had told him the truth—or part of it—and he denied me my own thoughts in the matter.

"We've been dreaming about it since we were little girls," I said. "It's all I ever wanted."

"Is it?" he asked. "Or is it what Cat wanted? Because I think you need to know the difference."

"Are you telling me I don't know my own mind?"

"I'm telling you that Cat's desires seem to eclipse your own. Her need for clothes and jewels and furs and fashion. That's all she cares about. Getting the crown and not thinking of what goes along with it."

"That is not all she cares about," I argued. "She cares about friends and family and . . ." I couldn't think of anything else. Truth be told, I didn't actually believe she cared about her family. But I had to defend her. I would be no one if it weren't for Catherine Howard. I would be hiding in corners and swishing out chamber pots like Mary Lascelles.

"No, Kitty," William said. "*You* care about those things. And more. You are not like her. She wants you to be her shadow. You can only truly be yourself if you cut her off."

"Cat cares about me!" I cried.

"No, she doesn't. Cat cares about Cat."

"How dare you?" I said, suddenly breathless with anger. "You don't even *know* her!"

"I know many like her," William said. His hands remained stiff at his sides, his profile turned to me. "She's just like her uncle. Ambitious and court-blind, seeing only the surface and not what lies beneath."

"And yet you stay with the duke. No matter where he goes."

"I have no choice."

The breach between our bodies was no more than a hand's breadth, but I couldn't find the words to bridge it.

"Neither have I."

"Yes, you do," he said urgently. "You need to get away. You don't belong here. You don't want to be like her—mercenary and artificial."

Before I knew what I was doing, I slapped him. The resonant sting in my hand surprised me and I clutched it back to my chest, nursing the hurt in my heart.

"You can leave court if you wish," I snapped. "But I won't go with you." Not that he'd asked.

I bit down on my tongue, relished the metallic taste on it. The punishment for lying was to cut the tongue, was it not? But the lie had to be brazened out, so I straightened my spine, and my gaze didn't waver from his.

He broke down first. His head sagged and he stepped aside, a weak gesture telling me I had clear passage.

"You shouldn't be with people who tell you what you want." William's sadness imbued his words. "What to think or feel or do. Like Cat does."

"Don't you see?" I croaked, my voice barely a whisper. "That's exactly what you're doing."

I couldn't feel my feet as I walked away, and my knees didn't bend properly. I felt like a wooden toy, inflexible and heartless. I left my own heart, crushed, on the riverbank at William's feet.

The duke left for Scotland at the end of January.

William didn't come to see me before he left. And I didn't say good-bye.

1541

25

"That's good," Cat said absently when I told her what had happened. We were making endless circumambulations of the upstairs gallery, cloistered by the rain, dogged by the Coven, who kept a meager distance.

I had suffered days of solitary anguish before I mentioned it. I waited until I couldn't bear it by myself any longer. And in the end, I didn't tell her everything. Not what William said about her. Not what I felt about him. I only told her that we'd argued and that I probably wouldn't see him again, the rupture in my heart growing with each word.

"Good?" I managed to reply. "The only boy who has ever noticed me?" And I'd lost him. Not just lost—discarded.

"Oh, no, Kitty," Cat stopped, causing the tide of ladies behind her to eddy and retreat. "Not the only boy. There is another."

I blinked at her, stunned.

"He is one of the king's yeomen of the chamber," she said. "A tall young stud. Mounds of golden hair. Looks a bit like a lion."

"Standebanke," I said, the word jagged in my throat.

"You've noticed him, then." Cat smirked.

"No, Cat," I pleaded, saw-toothed memories from the forest flashing behind my eyes, "He's not . . ."

"You think you can do better?" She finally looked at me, her blue eyes flinty. "You think you can get a Knyvet or a Neville or a Percy?" She thought I wanted nobility.

"It's not that."

"Is it still that Gibbon boy?" she asked. "Ha. I say good riddance to him. Or did you fancy yourself in love?"

"I don't know," I said. Cat's tone was so contemptuous. So bitter.

"Well, I'm here to tell you, Mistress Tylney, that there is no such thing. Not in this court, not in this life. But if you must continue your infatuation, just get him back and have both. It never hurt a girl to have two men at once."

"I can't, Cat." A shudder ran through me.

"Then don't. Give up Gibbon for all I care."

She didn't. I could see that. Didn't care that my heart was breaking over something I'd ruined. Or that she was pushing me into a relationship with a rapist's sidekick.

"It's not William," I said. I needed Cat to understand.

"Good. Because Standebanke is yours. He's *asked* about you. I shall set up a clandestine meeting for you personally." Cat positively glowed with mischief. Cat the matchmaker. The Queen of Misrule.

"Your Majesty."

We turned to find that Jane Boleyn had broken free of the pool of ladies behind us.

"What is it?" Cat snapped, her light mood changed in an instant. "Can't you see I'm speaking with Mistress Tylney?"

"Yes, Your Majesty." Jane lowered her eyes. "That is exactly the subject I wish to broach."

"Have you been eavesdropping on my private conversations?" Cat asked, her eyes aslant with suspicion.

"No, Your Majesty," Jane said and glanced once over her shoulder. Jane never spoke unless she knew who was listening. The Coven gaggled a few yards away. The other ladies and maids whispered at the far end of the gallery, hesitating by the door of the chapel as if unprepared for holiness.

Jane lowered her voice and spoke with her head bowed. We had to lean close to hear her. "I come to give fair warning to prevent ill feeling in the future. It is my job to keep your path smooth and your life comfortable, and I do my best to fulfill my function."

Cat snorted with derision and turned back down the gallery.

"And what do you wish to warn me about?" she said.

"There are ladies who feel supplanted in the queen's favor. Ladies who feel they deserve to be in the queen's company more than a mere chamberer. They think affection should be dictated by status. That you, Kitty, are good for nothing but stoking the fires, changing the rushes, and fetching wine."

"You mean," I said, "as a servant."

They thought I should be treated no better than Mary Lascelles back in Lambeth. I tasted the sour tang of inferiority.

"That's exactly what she means," Cat said. "That because

159

you're not blood-related, you're not worthy. Because you're not the daughter of an earl or the wife of a knight or the widow of a duke."

"Do you think this, Jane?" I asked.

"No!" Jane said, "I see that the queen is naturally attracted to others who share similar interests. You enjoy entertainments. Music. Excitement."

Her own eyes lit up at the words. I felt a rush of pity for a grown woman who craved the company and pastimes of girls. A thirty-five-year-old who wished to be a teenager again. But she understood the way the court operated. She had served five queens. She was a survivor, and wanted us to be, too.

"Well, then, it's no wonder the others are resentful," Cat replied. "They've lived for so long in stuffy decorum that they can't imagine a court full of sunshine and gaiety. They want life to be boring."

The worst epithet Cat could attach to someone. *Boring.* More damning than *badly dressed.*

"They may be boring," Jane said. "But they are also powerful. Enough that they could make life very uncomfortable for you. They would find ways to purge your household of people they found undesirable."

"What do you suggest, Jane?" I asked.

"Perhaps the queen might spend more time in the company of other ladies."

Cat let out an exasperated sigh.

"And if she fell pregnant . . ." Jane let the sentence hang. But

I knew what she meant. If Cat were to have a boy, she would be invincible. She could have everything she wished, and no one would think to question it.

"It is so difficult for a monarch to depend on a single child to succeed him," Jane finished.

King Henry especially. His father had ended the bloody years of civil war, establishing the Tudor reign. Both father and son had ensured their throne by executing any other possible claimants. Henry VIII would not want his lineage to expire.

Cat twisted her rings as if trying to wrench her fingers off, and her mouth settled into a rigid seam of ill humor. I recognized the signs of a major tantrum building.

"He has two daughters," I said, trying to sound like that could be the end of it. "Two healthy, intelligent daughters."

Jane laughed. "I think we all know how well women are regarded in this court. Would these men *ever* accept a queen to rule over them?"

I had to shake my head. The idea was ludicrous. The dukes would undermine the pious, earnest Lady Mary. The earls and marquesses would tear the beautiful little Elizabeth apart.

"Listen!" Cat exploded. "There's not much I can do about a pregnancy! I just wish everyone would shut up about it. No matter how many times he can't get it up, it will be all my fault if we don't have children. I *know*."

Jane glanced about as if the four horsemen were upon her, dragging the Apocalypse.

"You cannot speak so, Your Majesty," she whispered hur-

riedly. Everyone knew that George Boleyn hadn't been beheaded for incest with his sister, no matter what the official record said. His execution traced its origin back to a public statement about the king's impotence.

Cat glared at Jane.

"Thank you for airing your concerns, Lady Rochford," she said. "But I believe I shall return to my rooms, for I am feeling rather fatigued. Your presence is no longer required. I feel the need for the company of more *distinguished* ladies."

Jane curtseyed without comment, the Coven clucking as they passed her. I watched the other women amass behind Cat's skirts, struggling to keep up with the haste that carried her back to her rooms.

"Words will be her undoing," Jane said quietly when she stood again, her face white.

I shuddered at the foreboding in her voice.

"She will not be undone," I said, more to convince myself than her.

"That will be our commission," Jane said. "To prevent it. To ensure that the rumor mill doesn't grind her for grain. To *guarantee* she bears a son."

26

BUT THERE WOULD BE NO GUARANTEES.

In February, the king's ulcer closed over, and infection spread a fever throughout his great frame. He couldn't walk, couldn't stand, couldn't govern. He refused to see Cat. Refused her presence in his apartments. So we remained sequestered in her rooms, bound by the murmurs of the Coven.

Gossip was their life's blood. Especially when it came to the king and his health. Under normal circumstances, every cough, every limp, every bowel movement was scrutinized by the entire court. This illness had them all buzzing like flies around a corpse.

It was treason to mention it. Treason even to think it. But the king's death would change everything. And the Howards hoped it would mean a Howard regency until the toddler Prince Edward came of age.

The king feared his death with a palpable madness caused by a loathing of limitation. He brought to mind a furious, demonic bear, pent up and confined within his own flesh like the caged animals of the Tower menagerie. We could hear his raging all the way down the long gallery from his apartments.

Could gauge the power of his anger by the force of the explosion of courtiers from his room. Every man moved tentatively about the palace, afraid one false step would bring wrath like a fireball upon him.

The women just stayed away.

With each day, Cat grew more irritable, more jumpy. She couldn't eat and retired early, sparking rumors that she was pregnant. That she had miscarried. That the king planned to take back Anne of Cleves.

Cat tolerated only my presence, ignoring all others or else snapping at them. The entire populace of the court seemed poised for flight—ready to flee the royal circle out of sheer, desperate self-preservation.

But the outside world remained oblivious to the seismic disruptions at Hampton Court and pursued, unheeding, its own agenda.

And suddenly, my parents found me a husband. Apparently, being the best friend of the Queen of England had perks that some people just could not deny.

Lord Graves lived close by my parents in the far end of nowhere. Through marriage, his land would be ensured to Tylney heirs. I shuddered at the thought of producing them.

My fate was written and sealed with wax. Sold like a parcel of land or a breeding mare.

The physical person of my intended appeared in late February, entertained by the dowager duchess herself in her private rooms. My parents still considered the duchess my

guardian and had appealed to her to secure the match.

She did so with pleasure.

I was bestowed with the dubious honor of waiting upon them both. I wore a "new" gown, pieced together from Cat's discards, the rust-colored skirts skimming the tops of my slippers with no train and the bodice gaping obscenely if I didn't keep my shoulders thrown back like a soldier.

"My lord," I said, curtseying deeply and keeping my head bowed. Not out of respect, but because I didn't think I could look on his wrinkling, pox-marked face without crying. I couldn't even repeat his given name for fear it would make the whole thing real.

"Young Katherine," he said, and I heard an edge of lechery in his voice. He was practically drooling. "Rise and look on me."

I stood and looked.

And I saw my future unravel before me. The pits the smallpox had left glowed pink and shiny against his pale, papery skin. His jowls sagged as he gazed at me unsmiling. If anything, he looked bored.

"Turn," he said.

I turned.

This was how it was going to be. His orders. My obedience. The rest of my life, a vast expanse of mirthlessness and drudgery.

He reached for me. My skin tried to creep away, and I forced myself very still in order not to flinch.

"We shall marry in the summer," he said, gazing expectantly

at my flat chest and thin hips. As if he thought they might ripen in the sun in time for our wedding night.

"I expect the queen will be sad to see you go," the duchess said. I detected a trace of a smile in her voice.

"I had rather hoped Katherine's influence would find me a place at court myself."

"Kitty is a chamberer," the duchess rebuked him.

He wasn't fazed. "But beloved of the queen." He licked his lips.

I couldn't decide which was worse, leaving Cat to live on the Graves estate or having to see him every day at court. At least my position necessitated that we wouldn't share a bed.

"That will do."

Dismissed.

I hurried from the room, fighting down the bitter acid that rose in my mouth. I couldn't imagine being touched by him. Being kissed by him. I allowed one tear to escape. For myself. For my future. For what I could have had with William, if things had been different.

I ran straight to the queen's apartments. Looking for protection.

"Cat," I said, sitting down beside her on the bench beneath the window in her withdrawing room. "I need your help."

The Coven—sans duchess—erupted in a twittering dither in the corner.

"How many times do I have to tell you?" Cat seethed. "You have to call me Your Majesty!"

"Yes, Your Majesty," I said quickly, impatient to enlist her aid.

"And where have you been?"

"The dowager duchess called for me."

"So you, too, are prepared to spread rumors about me?" she hissed. "Groveling to the great ladies who secretly loathe you?"

The attack caught me off-guard and I shrank back.

"I don't know what you're talking about."

"You left me alone!" she retorted, causing another flutter amongst the Coven. Cat lowered her voice, "Abandoned in my time of need."

What about my time of need? I wanted to ask. I met her eye. The words formed at the back of my throat. She looked back at me, unflinching. But somewhere, in the back of her gaze, I saw fear.

"What is the matter, Your Majesty?" I whispered.

I heard the Coven creak and twist to hear what she said next, but her words fit only into my ear.

"I can't do it," she said. "I can't. I can't be brave in the face of his illness. I can't stand up to their pushing and gossip. I can't be the generous queen, giving alms to the poor. The poor make me cringe. I can't be noble. We weren't taught how to be queens, Kitty! We were taught how to be . . . property."

"We were taught how to be wives," I said.

"Same thing," she muttered. "Oh, Kitty, if I am so high, why do I feel so low? I am nothing more than the youngest daughter of an insignificant branch of the Howard family tree."

"That's what you *were*, Cat," I said. "But look at you now. You're Queen of England. You can do anything."

"Nothing queenly."

"So do something queenly."

"But I hate the poor. I don't care about religion. Politics bore me stiff."

"What about prisoners? You could save people's lives."

Like mine.

A spark flashed in her eyes, like a candle lighting right behind them.

"Thomas Wyatt is in the Tower again," she said. "You're right. What better thing to be known for than rescuing Anne Boleyn's former lover?"

I could think of many, but again held my tongue.

"What did he do?" I asked.

"What does it matter?" Cat said. "It will be a coup. He was one of Cromwell's men. That faction will love me. I'll get a reputation for a soft heart. For being a romantic. It's perfect.

"Oh, Kitty," she hugged me. "You are the best friend a queen could ever have."

The Coven shifted again in the corner. Gathering like pikemen prepared for conflict. Their attention flustered me, but I knew it was the right moment. To ask for help while Cat was in a generous mood.

But before I could open my mouth, she leapt to her feet.

"I must prepare my defense of Wyatt so I can present it to the king at exactly the right moment. I must look absolutely perfect."

She leaned in to whisper to me.

"I'll make the Coven happy, too." She turned to the room. "Lady Howard, Lady Baynton, Countess, I need to choose a very special gown. Attend me."

"You can help me practice later." Cat winked and left me, dumbstruck, by the window. Just as she was about to pass through the door in a cloud of women and silk, she paused and turned back.

"Kitty." My name itself an afterthought. "There was something you wanted to tell me."

The Coven waited, poised. Listening. Lady Howard narrowed her eyes.

"I'm to be married," I said weakly.

Cat smiled, her mouth pulled up on both sides like a marionette, her eyes untouched.

"Congratulations."

THE KING RECOVERED TO A COLLECTIVE SIGH—RELIEF FOR SOME, REGRET for others—from the court. The question of my marriage got lost in the scramble to return the court to normal. And the renewed requests from the king for Cat's company.

"Mistress Tylney, you will accompany me to the king's chambers," Cat said one evening in early March. She had been bathed and dressed, her hair bejeweled and her cleavage perfumed, and there was nothing else to be done. "I shall have supper there."

"Of course, Your Majesty," I said. At her suggestion, I wore a deep blue hand-me-down of Cat's, lengthened with a piece of silk the color of the winter moon.

"You look lovely," she whispered to me with a quirk of a smile.

A group of us moved through the palace in step with each other, walking when Cat walked, stopping when Cat stopped. Like a flock of birds, taking cues from a single source, whirling and diving in perfect harmony.

We made our way through the queen's apartments and out to the gallery. Courtiers and ladies, servants and messengers bowed to her as she passed, her smile widening with every step. She paused to speak with a viscount here, an earl there, just briefly, never engaging in a real conversation. But the number of people flocking the gallery made the short journey excruciatingly long.

We stopped at the door of the king's apartments and one of the ladies knocked. An usher opened the door, sweeping aside with a low bow.

"Your Majesty," he said.

"Master Culpepper," Cat answered, emotionless.

He stood and grinned at Cat as if she was a delicious sweetmeat, and she arched an eyebrow at him. The blood from my feet swirled in my ears. I wobbled. I reached out blindly and grasped an arm, a sleeve, to steady myself. The arm of the queen.

"Mistress Tylney, you do forget yourself," Cat snapped. She shook my hand off and glared at me. "You are excused."

Murmurs vibrated through the cluster of ladies behind us and one of the Coven sniggered.

"I beg your pardon, Your Majesty," I said, growing hot under their stares and whispers.

Cat leaned close to me, "Edmund Standebanke is off duty tonight. He waits for you in the clock court. You didn't think I'd forget, did you?"

She winked at me from beneath her lowered brow and gave me a push.

"Happy birthday."

Even I had taken no notice of the day. Trust Cat to remember. And to find a suitably Cat-like gift, dubious as it was.

I turned away from the ladies and the light of the king's apartments. Away from the gaze of the court. I couldn't flee. Cat would expect a full report. My feet took me back along the dim galleries, down the stairs and through Anne Boleyn's gateway. And there, under the timepiece, a man stood waiting. For me.

The other girls had all noticed Standebanke and commented on his golden good looks. Like a classical hero, he excelled at sports and games and physical tasks. He wore the king's livery well, tight in all the right places, sleeves flowing, chest and shoulders broad. The red hose, cut with the black lining, emphasized what were surely muscled thighs. Joan called him "swoony."

But all I could see was the monster from the forest.

I quickly scanned the courtyard. Dozens of courtiers, clustered in groups. He couldn't hurt me. He wouldn't dare. I was a favorite of the queen.

"Good evening," he said, and nodded a tiny bow. He was taller than I—though the extra inch or two could have been his hair.

"Good evening," I echoed, and dipped slightly.

"Mistress Tylney?" he asked.

I nodded, too afraid to speak.

"Would you care to walk in the garden?" he asked, holding out an arm.

"It's getting dark," I said, refusing the walk. Refusing the arm.

"And you are afraid of the dark?" he asked. He sounded sympathetic, understanding. I would have laughed had I not been so petrified.

"Yes," I said, surprised I told the truth.

"No need to be afraid with me," he said and patted the sword that hung at his side. "I am one of the king's own guard. I can handle the rats and owls that inhabit the gardens at night." Again he held out his arm.

"It is not the rats and owls I am afraid of," I said, and took up the courage to look him in the eyes. My arms remained firmly at my sides, and I struggled to release the fists I clenched.

He lowered his arm and leaned closer to me. I held tightly to my bones, which felt ready to fly apart.

"I knew it was you," he said quietly, his deep voice a rumbling purr. "I wanted to meet you. I wanted to tell you . . . the truth."

I looked upward. Watched the slow spinning of the clock. Waited.

"It wasn't me."

I snapped my head around to look at him.

"It was you," I said quietly, my fear coming out as vehemence. "I saw you. Standing there. Doing nothing."

"That's right!" his voice cracked. "Doing *nothing*. Kitty, James Millard was there, standing on her arm. He thought it was

173

sport. He laughed at me. Spited me. We fought and he's been thrown from court and I say good riddance to him. But . . ."

His words had come out in a rush like the Thames below London Bridge, spilling and dangerous. But now he slowed and looked at me, his eyes full of sentiment, making him look too young to be a king's guard.

"But what?" I asked. I studied his face for traces of deception. The high cheekbones, the strong chin just showing a beard, the full mouth. His eyes begged me to believe him.

"Culpepper. No one can refuse him. He's brash and daring and ever so brilliant." Edmund sounded almost fawning, then hardened. "But manipulative. And cruel.

"You've seen his cruelty, Kitty." He looked me full in the face. "Imagine it turned on you."

I had. In my dreams. Every night.

"But you watched," I said. "You did nothing to stop him."

"So did you," he replied.

I felt the words like a slap. The kind that wakes you from a faint. Because of course he was right.

"I was afraid," I admitted.

"So was I."

"How can you be his friend?" I asked.

"How can I not be?" Edmund said. "Surely, you of all people understand. A friend with that kind of power."

"Don't you compare him to Cat," I spat at him. "She's nothing like him." But felt a vibration of truth. I stilled it.

"Of course not," he agreed.

I swallowed. I remembered that night. I remembered that no one gave chase when I ran. When he saw me.

"You didn't tell him," I said. "That I was there."

He smiled then.

"I couldn't do that."

I took his arm. I understood.

28

Cᴀᴛ ʀᴇᴛᴜʀɴᴇᴅ, ꜰʟᴜꜱʜᴇᴅ ᴀɴᴅ ɪʀʀɪᴛᴀʙʟᴇ, ꜱᴏᴍᴇᴛɪᴍᴇ ᴀꜰᴛᴇʀ ᴍɪᴅɴɪɢʜᴛ. She snarled and squawked until we roused ourselves to attend her needs and do her bidding. Then she dismissed everyone else. Alice and Joan settled onto their pallets and the Coven bickered their way out the door.

"I've been sent away," she moaned. "Fetch me cloths and a warm stone."

Her courses. Cat suffered terribly from her monthly battle with womanhood. She used to retreat beneath the covers of our bed for a full day, sometimes two, groaning and twisting the blankets like a winding cloth. The duchess once offered to have her bled, but Cat had barked, "I'm bleeding quite enough already, thank you very much!" and that ended the discussion.

"Join me, Kitty."

The thick tester mattress of the best goose down was covered by fine-spun linen, beaten to skinlike softness. Real feather pillows cushioned our heads, and mounds of velvets and furs cocooned us with warmth. Cat curled up on herself, rigid with pain. Tentatively, I reached out to stroke her hair, as I used to in Lambeth. Her muscles unwound and she heaved a sigh the size of the king himself.

"So did you have a good time with the delectable Edmund?" Cat asked, the question laced with petulance.

"I suppose."

"Well? What did you do?"

"We . . . talked."

"You talked. You have a young, gorgeous, virile man at your disposal and what do you do? You *talk*."

Cat raised herself up onto an elbow, rested her head upon her hand and peered at me.

"But don't you think he's divine? All that gorgeous hair. I know you want to run your hands through it."

I considered running my hands through Edmund's hair. But my fingers remembered William's. Besides, I didn't know how much I trusted Edmund.

"Should you really be saying these things?" I asked.

"It's only you, Kitty," Cat said. "If I can't say them to you, who can I say them to? Everyone else in this viper's den will go running to the king if I so much as fart in their direction."

I stifled my chuckle, but Cat giggled out loud. Joan, fast asleep, tittered and muttered something about marzipan, which made us laugh even harder.

"But you have the king," I said.

"I have a husband who thinks a quick peck on the cheek is foreplay. I have to coo with pleasure when I'm really gritting my

teeth and wishing for it all to end. I'm trapped. I've made my own snare and I'm stuck fast in it."

There was no comfort I could give her and no option out. Except one.

"What about Francis?" I asked.

"Francis?" she said, surprise and condescension mixing with equal parts. "He wasn't really that much better. Just quicker."

"No, Cat," I said. "What if you were precontracted to him? He said you were married. What if he were to come back and claim you as his wife? Then your marriage to the king would be invalid and you could get an annulment. Francis would take you back. I'm sure of it." Even if the rest of the world shunned her.

"The king wouldn't let it be that easy," Cat said, her voice as small as the hope she harbored.

"He did it with Anne of Cleves."

"He's too involved with me. You've seen. He paws me all the time. He says I make him feel like he's young again. He wasn't able to . . . you know, with Anne at all. That's how they got the annulment. But we've consummated the marriage. I can never be free."

We lapsed back into silence. I watched the fire flicker light across the ceiling. It was decorated in bas-relief, gilded lovers' knots curling around Cat's emblem of a crowned rose. The petals of one had already begun to crack, painted before it had dried sufficiently.

"Kitty," she said, suddenly urgent, "you can't tell anyone

that I've said this. That I'm unhappy. That I want other men. Not the king, not my uncle, not even Alice or Joan."

"I would never betray you, Cat, you know that."

"Swear." She clutched my arm tightly. "Swear you will never speak out against me. No matter what."

"There's nothing to speak of," I said, uncomfortable. It wasn't a question or even a request. It was a command.

Sweat shimmered on her upper lip. "Swear it."

"I swear," I said. "I will never betray you. None of us will. We're a coterie. A circle that can't be broken. We'll make it through."

"An unbroken circle," she echoed.

She turned to me, her face flushed with emotion and the heat of the stones pressed to her lower back.

"But you're the only one," she said. "The only one who loves me, aren't you, Kitty? Truly. My sister of the soul." She grimaced and shifted position.

"Everyone loves you," I argued. "You're queen."

"But do they love me enough to believe in me?" she asked.

"What is there to believe?"

"That I am faithful. That I am untarnished. That the king is the one and only man in my life. That I deserve the crown."

"No one will question you," I assured her. "No one will believe any ridiculous tittle-tattle from your past."

"The queen a promiscuous little slut when she lived with her grandmother?" Cat asked in mock horror. "Preposterous!"

"Impossible!" I joined in.

"Unthinkable!"

"Absurd!"

We clutched each other, giggling, our breath growing more hysterical as we perched precariously between guilt and rumor.

"I'll just have to live vicariously through you," Cat said finally, a smile on her face, but none in her voice.

"I'll do my best to make it pleasant for us both," I said. But when I thought about making it pleasant, the face that manifested before me had a crooked grin and sandy hair.

"Then move a little faster with Standebanke," Cat said. She kissed my cheek and rolled over, falling quickly into sleep. Safe in the knowledge that her bidding would be done.

It was very late in the night—or very early in the morning—when I realized why Cat's words kept me awake. Until she married the king, we had all lived vicariously through her. Any girl would think we still were—her gorgeous gowns and furs and jewels, the luscious dishes and divine entertainments. And yet, Cat had given up any hope of love. Or even lust. She was already bound to the life we all knew would claim us eventually. The dullness of the marriage bed. Compensating with accessories.

29

CAT MADE HER INAUGURAL TRIP THROUGH LONDON WITH THE KING AT her side. Other queens had journeyed alone, to be admired on their own behalf. But the king insisted they travel together.

Their barge shot the roaring waters beneath London Bridge to the accompaniment of gunfire from the Tower. The north wind whipped us downriver, past Lambeth and Norfolk House, and the sound of the cannons followed us all the way to Greenwich.

Cat chose this as the perfect moment to exercise her influence as queen and plead for clemency. After careful consideration, the king granted Thomas Wyatt his freedom. The condition was that Wyatt leave his mistress and return to his wife, whom he'd left twenty years prior. He almost refused.

Greenwich Palace crouched on a riverbank between the Thames and the deer park. The king's gardens created an illusion of space and openness, while the rooms within the palace felt cramped and crowded. The lesser nobles had to find accommodation outside the grounds. But my position as chamberer allowed me to stay within Cat's rooms. Protected.

I took comfort in the knowledge that my fiancé's pleas for

placement were ignored. The king's illness had prevented him from attending to business. And Cat focused all of her energies on more parties. But I knew I lived on borrowed time.

To celebrate the end of winter and Lent, Cat planned the most personal entertainment of her royal career.

"It's going to be the best masque ever presented before the king," she declared.

She was determined that we would all participate. Cat took the lead role, but the younger ladies would dance, the chamberers provide background, and the Coven play elaborately costumed goddesses. Everyone was made happy.

Cat wanted the entire production to be a surprise for the king, so she dismissed the deviser of court revels and planned it all herself. She designed the costumes and sets. She cribbed the music from other sources and dispensed with all but the most basic script. We spent hours sewing filmy shawls from seemingly inexhaustible supplies of multicolored silks. We decorated hanging set pieces with badges embroidered with gold thread. Perhaps it wouldn't be the most elaborately staged masque in court history, but it would be hers.

Cat made us practice again and again and again. Two days before show time, we were all thoroughly sick of the whole thing.

She was insatiable. Manic. As if her life depended on pleasing the king with this one ostentatious evening.

Not that she needed to. He still caressed and fondled her

at every opportunity. He sat her next to him at every banquet. Gave in to her every whim and desire. She didn't insist on piety, like Catherine of Aragon. She didn't argue about religion or get insanely jealous like Anne Boleyn. Her presence didn't destroy his vanity, as Anne of Cleves's did. All Cat wanted was pretty things. All the time.

She got them. And she made sure we had them, too.

"I have a surprise for all of you," she said, dragging me, Joan, and Alice into her robing chamber the night of the masque.

"Your Majesty!" the Countess of Bridgewater honked. "Your ladies are ready to help you prepare for the banquet."

"My *ladies* will have to wait!" Cat called as she kicked the door closed on the surprised faces of the Coven.

Joan giggled and bounced on her toes. She only needed to clap her hands to look like an expectant five-year-old.

"What is it?" Joan said, and then she did clap.

Cat glided to a cedar chest and opened it carefully. It exuded a scent of resin and lavender so pungent it made my eyes water. Cat reached in, pulled something out and shook it loose. An underskirt of rich blue velvet. Joan let out a little moan.

"This is for you, Joan," Cat said, and smiled. She looked younger. Almost shy.

We all knew it was one of Cat's cast-offs. But the quality of the fabric should have designated it for one of the great ladies of the court. Cat swiftly reached into the chest again and pulled

out an overskirt of light watchet blue shot with gold thread and handed it to Joan as well.

"And this," she said, and continued with a velvet bodice of the same color, and sleeves with fur cuffs, and flowing oversleeves trimmed with the same fur. Joan sank to the floor in ecstasy, surrounded by fabrics and gold embroidery, and the sound that came from her was something between a hum and a sob. When she looked back up at Cat, a single tear had run down her cheek and into the corner of her mouth. She poked at it with the tip of her tongue.

"Thank you," she whimpered.

"It's nothing," Cat said with a shrug, and went back to the chest to remove similar clothing for Alice, only in the russets and browns that made her look healthy and cheerful. Alice stood dumbly and nodded.

My wardrobe was all in green. The kirtle was the color of sea foam, the overskirt and bodice brocade the color of pine.

"Green makes your eyes magical," Cat whispered. "Just remember to keep them in check."

We dressed quickly. The Coven would have clucked themselves to death, because Cat tightened our stays and tied on our sleeves. She helped Joan and Alice tie their hair into French hoods of velvet trimmed in pearls, and plaited my hair elaborately. She flounced our skirts and smoothed the creases from our sleeves, then stepped back to inspect her work.

"And now for the gilding."

She strung a gold chain around Joan's neck, weighted with

a gold pendant enameled in blue. A square brooch decorated with pearls and a single ruby was attached to Alice's bodice. And for me, a delicate collar of little green-and-white enameled daisies.

"These are for loan only," she advised us. "But the gowns are yours to keep."

"Thank you, Your Majesty," Alice murmured, and we all followed her into curtseys.

"Oh, get up," Cat said brusquely, but a delighted smile lit her face. She looked at us critically for a moment. "Just one more detail."

She opened a small silver coffer and removed precious unguents and pastes.

"Alice is pale enough," she said, smearing a little white on my face. "But you spend too much time outside."

"I like it outside."

Cat hmphed and moved on to Joan. She applied a little crimson to Alice's cheeks and cleavage and closed the coffer with a snap.

"Done," she said with a smile. "More beautiful than my jewels."

Joan giggled, and Alice's blush competed with her makeup.

"Go forth and conquer," Cat pronounced. "Dazzle every male in Hampton Court."

We dressed Cat in a gown of crimson and gold so fine it almost hurt the eyes. Joan brought a hood trimmed with pearls and rubies, but Cat shook her head.

"Tonight, I want to be different," she said.

She pulled out an elegant caul fashioned of gold gauze and studded with diamonds where the networked bands intersected. We parted her hair in the middle, and Joan carefully gathered the auburn curls into a loose knot and bound them in the net of the caul. Alice secured it all with a series of clasps fashioned of gold and rubies that ran from Cat's forehead to the nape of her neck and I attached similar, smaller ornaments to the coils of hair just above her ears. She bowed her head for me to fasten the gold and diamond collar the king had given her for Twelfth Night around her neck.

The Coven hissed to each other when we finally made our way out of the chamber, but dropped into placid curtseys and murmured plaintive flattery as we neared. Cat swept past them out the door, and they struggled into their queue of precedence and preferment, the dowager duchess taking the lead. Alice, Joan, and I took our place at the back of the throng, safe in the knowledge that we were the queen's true favorites.

For the banquet, Cat had ordered the cooks to outdo themselves: a peacock stuffed with game hens, roasted, then the feathers all reattached so it looked like a living bird; venison and boar, caught by the king and his men in the woods nearby; fish of every color, size and description; sculptures of sugar paste, glittering in the candlelight; wine imported from Gascony.

The great hall buzzed like a giant, polychromatic beehive.

Everyone was decked in their best, hoping to be seen, hoping to be noticed. Waiting for that one glance from the king that could launch a brilliant career. Cat and the king took their place on the dais at the far end of the hall, the gold canopy of estate over their heads. The highest-ranking courtiers sat near them. The rest of the hall milled with earls and lords, cardinals and ambassadors, fawning and filling themselves.

And despite Cat's pronouncement in her bedroom, attention remained fixed firmly on her. She drank it in like the watered wine in the golden goblet in front of her. I searched my heart for the green bile of jealousy but couldn't find it. I didn't want to be in her position.

But I didn't want to be in my position, either. The eyes of three men found me in that crowded hall, amongst the bejeweled women, the platters of delicacies, and the gossip that vied for their attention.

William Gibbon stood in attendance on the Duke of Norfolk.

"The duke is back?" I asked Alice.

"Yes, of course," she said as if this were common knowledge. "He was at Westminster. Didn't you know?"

I shook my head, unable to draw my gaze from the face I'd pictured a thousand times since Christmas.

William took in my new gown. The enameled daisy-chain collar. My hair carefully smoothed and pinned. My face whitened and powdered. I felt overdressed and naked all at once.

His eyes met mine, and pain froze the crooked smile before he looked away.

Edmund Standebanke stood behind the king, jesting with the other men. He wasn't in the king's livery but wore a doublet in a burnt orange color called lion-tawny and sleeves of bright yellow. He practically glowed. His eyes lifted. Searched the room. Lit up when he saw me. And stayed.

Thomas Culpepper, standing next to him, followed his gaze. Briefly, his attention twitched from my face to my hair to my clothes. He turned, whispered something to Edmund, and walked away. Edmund's smile faltered briefly. Almost imperceptibly. He shrugged and returned to the shadows at the back of the dais on which the king sat.

I found some shadows myself, remembering William's words about how he liked me plain and unadorned as I was in Lambeth. Wondering what he thought of me dressed in finery, the very image of all he held in contempt. Wondering what Thomas Culpepper could possibly have said to Edmund. Wondering what I was doing there at all.

When the feasting was done and the tables moved away, Cat had some servants drop the fabric set pieces from the minstrel's gallery. An awed murmur threaded the room, and then hushed as the music started.

The masque was based on the story of Persephone. Cat entered from behind the set pieces, her hair still bound in gold, but now with a cloth-of-gold tunic wrapped over her gown. The diamond *C* glittered and flashed at her throat.

Jane Boleyn, dressed in pale blue and green, acted the part of her mother, Demeter. They danced together between several ladies dressed all in white who held aloft bright yellow scarves to symbolize sunshine. The Coven watched from a high platform meant to be Olympus, frozen smiles on faces stiff with white paste.

But then Persephone was stolen by the dark lord Hades and pulled down to the underworld. Alice and I and some of the less pretty maids, covered in black scarves, plucked at Cat's sleeves as she shied away. We moved about, sylphlike, portraying the restive dead.

Persephone's cries, comforted by no one, rang out in the haunting sounds of a vielle, the musician drawing the bow across the strings in long, wailing notes. Men dressed in black patrolled the hall, extinguishing torches to achieve a more sepulchral gloom.

The masked man playing the lord of the dead hovered over her, touching her hair and her dress, and she grew more and more despondent and more and more lethargic as he sucked the life from her. It was almost as if she could change the hue of her gown, and it grew dull and lifeless, too.

"Enough!"

The shout startled all of us and we dropped our hands. Joan let out a little shriek. The musicians stopped playing the dirge of the underworld, and we all spun to look at the king.

He stood on the dais, his pendulous jowls purple with rage.

"You dare to compare my court to hell?" he bellowed, "My lady, you dare to compare me to Hades?"

Cat trembled, but stood up straight. She lowered her eyes.

"No, my lord," she said, barely audible.

"That is exactly what you do!" he shouted. The entire assembly muttered and shook.

"No, my lord," she repeated, and then looked him straight in the eye. "My lord, if you allow me to continue, you will understand my true motives for choosing this fable as the story of my masque."

She smiled then, a hauntingly provocative smile. One that promised a certain amount of wickedness.

"I have changed the story somewhat, my lord." She spoke as though it were only the two of them in the room, though a thousand eyes observed them. "Hoping to reflect how I felt when I came to live with you."

I heard the king's labored breathing from across the room. The surrounding silence magnified it until it seemed to be the breath of God himself.

"Go on," he muttered. He winced as he sat, and his face tumbled into crevasses of old age and overindulgence.

Cat nodded to the man playing the lord of the underworld and I just glimpsed something in her face, in her eyes. I had seen it before. It was the look she got when she saw something she liked, something she wanted. Like a crimson gown or a fur muff or a hood trimmed with gold and pearls. But more than that, it was the look she got when she knew she could get a man

to fall in love with her. To want her as he had never wanted anyone else. The look that led to ruin.

It disappeared a sliver of a moment after it began, and I wondered if I had actually seen it at all. And I realized that I had no idea who the man disguised as Hades actually was. He had never come to our rehearsals but had practiced separately with Cat while we were otherwise engaged—embroidering costumes or practicing songs and music.

An unusually full mask obscured his face, showing only his eyes, not his nose and lips like the traditional half-mask. His black cloak and shiny black boots hid the rest of him completely, and he faded directly into the darkness.

But his eyes sprung a memory somewhere, one that trembled fearfully before falling back down into the impenetrable depths of my mind.

"Kitty!"

Joan pushed me forward. I stumbled over my long black cloak and almost fell. Cat shot me an icy look.

I continued the performance without looking at her or the man who played Hades. I knew that he handed her a pomegranate, and that she lifted it to her lips to eat.

But here, Cat changed the classical story. In the myth, Persephone eats six pomegranate seeds, thus condemning herself to six months of the year in the underworld. Her mother, Demeter, goddess of the seasons and the harvest, mourns for her for these six months, creating winter.

But in Cat's version, Persephone refused even a single pome-

granate seed. She was halted in her attempt to take a bite by a beautiful vision: Edmund Standebanke dressed all in gold, a false red beard on his chin and a crown upon his head. All he needed was a placard reading *Henricus Rex*.

The king laughed and clapped his hands like a child at the sight of his double, and some of us breathed a sigh of relief. He could have erupted at the sight of a mere yeoman portraying him. Better, however, than a nobleman with pretentions to the crown.

Edmund reached out and plucked the pomegranate from Cat's hand. He lifted her up, her tunic and sleeves radiant again as she stepped out of the shadows and unveiled her natural incandescence.

The man playing Hades shook his fist at them and then sank to his knees, defeated.

Cat turned to the pretend king and he bowed deeply to her. The light of the candles created a halo of sparkles over her head, and she spoke.

"And so it is always summer with my lord, even when the days are short and the rain ever-present," she said.

The king rose again, applauding, immediately followed by all of the courtiers. All of us players bowed or curtseyed deeply to the king, except Cat, who stood and glowed with the adulation.

"Music!" the king shouted as he stepped from the dais and the players struck up a stately pavane.

And the king danced with his wife, firmly assured that it would always be summer and he would always be young and handsome, as long as he was with her.

A very clever piece of propaganda.

But when the pavane was finished, the king strode back to the dais, the merest of limps betraying his infirmity.

And the queen stayed on to dance the galliard with Hades, still dressed in black, but now without his mask.

Thomas Culpepper.

The king cheered and applauded and drank copious amounts of wine. He laughed with the Duke of Norfolk and remained completely oblivious to his wife and his usher making eyes at each other under the guise of dancing for His Majesty's pleasure.

I had to be wrong. I watched them dance, their bodies moving as if anticipating the other's actions even before they were made. I closed my thoughts to the possibility that Cat would consider adultery. Treason. I watched them until the dance ended and Cat practically sat in the king's lap, laughter on her face, delighted with herself.

I wished for something to hold onto. Something solid. I remembered another dance, holding William's hand, whispering, his mouth so close to mine. I looked to where he had stood behind the duke, but he was no longer there. I scanned the room and saw his sandy hair shining over the greasy, grizzled heads of the older courtiers. Headed my way.

My fingers grew numb. My lips as well. I couldn't think what I would say to him. How to apologize.

A dozen steps away, he slowed. Hesitated. Looked at me. No smile. He took two more steps, broke eye contact, and bowed.

To Alice Restwold.

He guided her to the middle of the Great Hall with one hand firmly on the small of her back. She turned and smiled up at him, chin tilted, eyes reflecting the bravura of the painted ceiling.

I crawled into the deepest shadow I could find and watched alone. I watched them dance, their bodies mirroring each other. I watched them move together as the music changed for the next dance. I watched him kiss her hand.

"We can't have the queen's favorite hiding in the corner, now, can we?"

The voice was smooth and rich like burnished mahogany. But the face set me back like an onslaught. Handsome. Angular. Rapacious.

"Master Culpepper."

"You know me."

I edged closer to the crush of courtiers making negotiations and assignations in the candlelight.

"You are hard to miss."

Culpepper's smile was at once charming and disarming. It erased any hint of debauchery from his features. And yet, I knew what he was.

"That makes two of us," he said. "You look ravishing this evening, Mistress Tylney. Shall we dance?"

"No." I didn't want to be near him, much less dance with him.

He staggered backward, dramatically clasping his doublet where his heart should have been. Several nearby ladies tittered, and he winked at them conspiratorially.

"You wound me, Mistress Tylney," he said. "Perhaps you are too proud for the likes of me, a lowly gentleman usher to the king."

"I am no such thing!"

"Then dance with me."

"No." I wished he would go away. Disappear. Prey upon someone else.

"One dance. I promise." He sidled closer, slipped an arm behind my back. Fear rent every shred of breath from me so I couldn't even scream.

"I'm afraid this dance is mine, Thomas."

Culpepper turned his charming smile to Edmund, and I felt faint at my deliverance.

"Edmund, you always get the most *delicious* girls," Culpepper said, the word overripe in his mouth.

"No, Thomas," Edmund said. "You've tasted the very best, I'm sure."

Culpepper trailed his gaze along my body once more, his tongue just visible beneath his upper lip, sucking on his teeth.

Then he turned without another word and walked away.

"You look a little nervous," Edmund whispered, and took my hand.

"He terrifies me," I admitted, willing to ignore his implication that I wasn't one of the very best.

"You want protection," he said, and pulled me deeper into the shadows instead of onto the dance floor.

I did want to be protected. From Culpepper. From Cat. From the future. From heartache.

Edmund wrapped his arms around me, the press of his muscles tight against me. He lowered his head and breathed in, as if drinking the scent of my neck, my hair.

I rested my face on his chest, the fur of velvet and scratch of gold embroidery, the sure, steady, unadulterated beat of his heart.

"You're right," I whispered. "I want you to protect me."

He ran his hands up the back of my bodice, fingers catching on the laces, pressing into my ribs, up to my throat. He pulled away, my face cupped in his hands, held me with his eyes.

"The only person I can't protect you from is me, kitten," he said.

He didn't exactly make me feel safe. Not protected, really. But *wanted*, definitely. That thought urged me forward and I pressed myself into him. He breathed again, a smothered moan, but didn't kiss me.

"Not here," he said. "Not now."

He pulled away from me. I was dumbstruck, not sure of what

to think. I watched him weave through the crowd. Few noticed his passing, despite his bulk and good looks. A yeoman of the chamber didn't merit interest amongst nobility.

He returned to his position behind the king's dais.

Where William stood in attendance upon the Duke of Norfolk. Watching me, pain and betrayal scrawled across his features.

30

IGNORANCE IS BLISS.

Or so they say. But I didn't find it so.

I ignored the presence of the duke and his entourage. The pain that threatened to smother me when I thought of William. The way I felt when I imagined Edmund's breath buried in my hair.

I ignored Culpepper and the memory of Cat's smile. I ignored the biting fear that arose in me whenever I thought back to that evening in the autumn woods. I couldn't eradicate the vibrant nightmares that hunted me in the dark, but I could ignore them in the light of day.

Turning one's back on knowledge is not the same as the lack of it, so bliss eluded me.

So did sleep. And comfort.

Because the court began to move. From Greenwich to Rochester, Rochester to Sittingbourne, and back to Greenwich. King and court were like a restless beast, unable to settle down, pacing back and forth behind bars. The mood caught everyone. Waiting.

Summer approached rapidly, the threatening cliff-fall of my marriage with it. But then, without my asking, Cat blocked Lord Graves's request to come to court. Had him held at bay.

"My reasons are entirely selfish," she said when I tried to thank her.

"What, you want me all to yourself?" I asked.

"But of course," she said, and waggled her eyebrows.

She was carefully composing a note at her little writing desk. Dipping the quill in the ink before scratching a word or two. Slowly. Painfully.

"What is the status between you and Edmund Standebanke?" she asked.

"I'm not sure," I said. I hadn't seen Edmund in several days, except in passing.

"Perhaps he thinks you're not interested," Cat said.

"Maybe *he's* not interested."

"Of course he's interested," Cat said. "You're young. You're beautiful."

I snorted. We both knew I wasn't beautiful. I wished she wouldn't keep reminding me.

"You're a favorite of the queen."

"That's probably the pinnacle of my desirability," I said. It was easier to put myself down than build up hope only to have it crushed. "Besides, I'm betrothed to another."

"All the more reason for something to happen with Edmund

now," Cat said. "Have a little fun before you succumb to Lord Poxy."

Cat's pet name for Lord Graves. Trust Cat to focus on the positive.

"Is it that William person?" Cat asked. "Are you still pining away for the gentleman usher of a mere duke?"

"William is no longer fond of me," I said, the truth pressed like a thumb to a bruise.

"Well, then, something has to change," she said. "You can't have two men lose interest unless you're doing something horrendous. Speaking out of turn or expressing too many opinions. You could make a little more of an effort with your dress, as well."

I glanced down. The midnight-blue gown she had given me earlier in the year had begun to wear at the hem and cuffs, and there was a stain on the bodice that couldn't be removed by water or rubbing. Cat didn't seem to understand that I actually had to work for her and couldn't wear my best gowns at all times for fear of ruining them.

"Perhaps you don't take enough baths." She wrinkled her nose.

"I don't smell!" I cried.

"Then you hold too tight to your favors," she said. "You have to give men a taste to keep them around. Sniffing about like dogs when the smell of fresh meat is on the snout of their leader."

"I am not fresh meat." I shrank from her comparison.

"Well, the loss of Gibbon might not be your fault, you know," she added sincerely, giving me a look of pure pity. "It could be Alice. She's managed to hook her claws into him somehow."

I thought of the two of them dancing after the masque. Alice's claws twisted in my own heart.

"Do you think he likes her?" I asked, barely a whisper.

Cat sighed and folded her note.

"Go to Edmund," she said. "Go and ride him for all he's worth. I know you want to."

I wasn't sure what I wanted. I had to admit to myself the possibility Cat was right. But I didn't know if I wanted to admit it to her.

"Such a suggestion coming from the divine mouth."

"Only the king is God's representative on earth," she corrected me.

"So you must be the devil's," I teased.

"If the devil spurs you to make Edmund Standebanke feel like he's never felt in his life, then yes, I am."

She reached into her pocket and pulled out a little gold ring.

"Take these to Jane Boleyn," she said, pressing ring and note into my hand.

Jane, because she was one of the "Great Ladies" of the household, had her own rooms in the palace. And her own servants.

I studied the piece of jewelry. A simple, gold cramp-ring.

"Is Jane unwell?" I asked.

"Lady Rochford is fine," Cat replied. "I'm just returning it to her."

I turned to go.

"Oh, and Kitty?" Cat called. "Would you ask her when I shall have the thing she promised me?"

"What thing?" I wondered what Jane and Cat could possibly be trading back and forth. Cat despaired of Jane's fashion sense.

"She'll know."

31

THE WARREN OF ROOMS AT GREENWICH WAS STILL UNFAMILIAR TO ME, and I made several wrong turns, cursing a court that couldn't stay put. Hampton Court I understood, blocked out as it was in great squares. Windsor was a distant memory. And the other places we'd visited, I couldn't keep straight.

I found Jane in an ill-lit room with north-facing windows, the smudge of fogged daylight barely penetrating the gloom. I stepped in quietly, caught her staring at the distant trees. She held a chain of pearls that seemed illuminated internally. From them hung a gold pendant.

"Jane?" I asked. I wondered if this was the thing Cat wanted.

Her hands moved, deft as hawk's wings, to cover and conceal the necklace in her sleeve. Then she looked up and saw me watching.

"Kitty," she said, and the pearls slid like water from her fingers, tumbling to the floor.

"Here," I picked it up. Smooth and heavy. The pendant a letter *A*, a single teardrop pearl suspended from the center bar. Like the one in the duchess's coffer back in Lambeth. A for Agnes Tylney. I frowned.

"It is mine," Jane said, sounding defensive. "It was given to me."

"By the duchess?" I asked.

"No," she said quietly. "By Anne. Anne Boleyn."

"Oh." No wonder she kept it hidden. No wonder the duchess never wore her copy of it.

"People say I hated her," Jane said. "That I was jealous. But she was my friend. For a while. And the Boleyns?" Her face twisted into an uncomfortable smile. "They always stuck together. Except for one."

"Like the Howards," I replied.

"Oh, no," she said as she gently put the necklace into the pocket that hung from her waist. "The Howards will cut you off as soon as look at you. Every last one of them."

I shivered at the coldness in her voice, her eyes as dead as river stones. I felt suddenly desperate to get away.

"The queen asked me to deliver these," I said, and handed over the note and the ring. "And asked about something you promised her?"

"I didn't promise it," Jane said quickly. "But tell her it will be delivered. Eventually."

I knew Cat would not be happy with that answer. Immediate gratification usually wasn't soon enough for her. And I would bear the brunt of her irritation.

I pushed my way back through the darkening rooms, trying to figure out a way to reorder Jane's words to the best outcome. Not looking where I was going, I tripped over a stool and cursed.

"Language, kitten."

Edmund's words triggered a rush of memory of my conversation with Cat about him. And his presence, warm and masculine, one hand on my arm in support, liquefied me.

"Are you all right?" he asked.

I realized I was trembling. Just a little.

"I'm fine," I said, trying to recover some semblance of courtly poise. I stepped back. The raised carvings of the wood paneling pressed into my shoulder blades. Tudor roses. Falcons.

Edmund moved with me. Hard oak behind me. Velvet, muscle, and bone to the fore.

"I think you're more than fine," he said quietly, his voice resonating through my body.

"What gives you that idea?" I asked.

"Your eyes," he said, and tucked a strand of hair back into my hood. "They say more than your words." His finger traced the line of my jaw to my lower lip and tugged lightly.

"Oh? What are they telling you?" But I knew. I just wasn't sure I agreed with them entirely.

"That you want to be kissed."

I pressed my lips into a line, and he laughed.

"I see your mouth doesn't agree."

I lowered my eyes. They said too much. Just as Cat had told me.

He drew his finger beneath my chin, forcing me to look at him again, and put his mouth on mine. I had expected the kiss to be like William's, soft and bright, like a smile made for

two. But Edmund's kiss tasted of smoke and felt like a mad rush, like shooting the waters of the Thames beneath London Bridge. Thrilling and dangerous. Part of me wanted to run. A small part.

He pulled away, his lips just inches from mine, a devilish smile playing on them.

"Now I see your mouth and your eyes want the same thing."

"And what is that?" My attempt at playful flirtation wavered at the expression on his face. He looked intently into my eyes for half a breath, then focused covetously on my lips.

"More."

I couldn't disagree. His kiss made me giddy, disoriented, out of control. I moved to close the gap between our mouths. His smile widened.

The sound of footsteps stopped me just before the point of contact, and we stood motionless, Edmund's breath cooling my lips.

"Forgive us!" Alice's voice echoed down the gallery and then she strolled into my field of vision. Followed by William Gibbon. "We appear to have waylaid a private *tête à tête*."

William said nothing, just stared straight ahead. Edmund stepped back and pulled at the bottom of his doublet. The action caught my eye and when I looked up at him, he grinned. He thought I was looking at his codpiece. I frowned at him, which only made him grin more broadly. Until he saw me glance at William again. Then his eyes narrowed.

"Or perhaps it was a *bouche à bouche*." Alice continued. She

grabbed William's arm proprietarily. "Please don't let us disturb you." She wore the dress Cat had given her, the russet bodice making her eyes sparkle and her cheeks glow. And at that moment, I was more jealous of Alice Restwold than I had ever been of Catherine Howard. The state of my stained and frayed gown suddenly sat heavy upon me.

"It is no disturbance," I said, unable to look at William at all. "I must return to the queen's apartments."

I hurried off, uncaring if they had heard my mumbled words or even noticed my consternation. Let William have Alice if he so chose. If he wanted a girl like her, he was more stupid than I had thought. Alice liked nothing better than a tight ass and association with the duke. All she wanted was to lord her knowledge and conquest over everyone else. Let her. I pushed past them, my eyes on the floor, hoping to hide my face, ravaged by stifled tears and embarrassment. I heard Alice titter again, and their footsteps as they ambled in the opposite direction.

I looked back.

Edmund stood where I had left him, watching. He smiled, turned on his heel, and walked away. As if he had been waiting for me to look.

As if he had known I would.

32

News came of unrest in the north. Once again. Years before, during the time of Queen Jane, some of the northern bishops and lords had committed treason by instigating the Pilgrimage of Grace. It was a backlash against the king's religious policies when he made himself the head of the church, breaking with the Pope in Rome and dissolving the monasteries.

The pilgrimage accomplished nothing, except the mass execution of the rebels. And a general, nagging distrust.

So now, the king decided to put an end to all of it. To make his presence—*his* Grace—known to everyone. He, and the entire court, would travel north. To York, the city of his grandfather, Edward IV. A great progress. Proof of power.

The court flew into a whirlwind of activity. The progress would begin in summer, and it seemed the king planned to move most of the palace as well as courtiers, guards, bearers, archers, and horsemen. Armor, arms, pikes, and cannon. It was like an invasion, albeit one dressed up as ceremony.

Cat ordered dozens of new clothes, all to be packed away and carried hundreds of miles so she could be beautiful and resplendent every day of the journey. Gowns made of cloth of silver that shone like a pond in the summer sun. Bodices of crimson velvet trimmed with gold. Silk sleeves every color of the rainbow. The king called for the same, his doublets and caps fashioned from cloth of gold. We packed their furs, jewels, hoods, trims, and bindings—everything that made the king and queen things of beauty.

Their wardrobes would awe the ignorant common people of the country we passed through. How could the uneducated peasants not believe that the king and queen were God's very representatives on earth?

An army of servants packed the king's most beautiful tapestries, stripping the walls of Hampton Court, Greenwich, Whitehall, and Westminster. All manner of gold and silver utensils, plates, jugs, and accoutrements were carefully laid in cedar boxes to be used throughout the journey.

Saddles, litters, and carts were requisitioned, decorated, or made from scratch to transport all the people and materials the court would be carrying. The king commandeered five thousand horses, carts carried two hundred tents to house us all, and we were to be accompanied by a thousand armed soldiers to keep us safe.

But the more days I lived, the less safe I felt.

In May, the duchess came grinning with a note from Lord Poxy, claiming what was rightfully his.

I took it to Cat immediately.

She read it carefully, one word at a time, and handed it back to me.

"What can I do?" I asked.

"I suppose it's your duty to marry him."

"But . . ." I scrambled to contradict her. "But what about the progress? What about you?"

"You mean, what about Edmund, don't you?"

"No," I countered. Though it was true I preferred him to Lord Poxy.

"You've kissed him, right?" she asked. "Anything else?"

"No, Cat."

"Why not?"

"I don't think I love him."

"I've told you before that love doesn't matter."

"Cat," I said. "I am not going to have sex with that man." Maybe.

"And defy a direct order from your queen?"

"I don't want to get pregnant."

"There are ways to meddle with a man and not get pregnant," Cat replied. "You *need* Edmund Standebanke's attention."

"Why?"

"Because he travels with a pack."

"Like a dog," I said, unable to shake myself of the image she had conjured weeks before—the men of the court sniffing about like animals.

"Exactly. It's easier to conceal something in a pack. It's difficult to keep secrets when you run rogue."

I got a sinking feeling. I thought of the pack in which Edmund Standebanke ran. I thought of the bellwether of

that group—the alpha male whom all the rest followed. *Culpepper.*

"Conceal what?" I asked.

"Never you mind," she said, then added, "Help me out of my bodice and sleeves. I'm ready for bed."

"I think you should be careful," I whispered.

"Oh, you do, do you?" she asked. "You, who have never felt the pleasure of a man, think I should be careful? I'm not surprised."

I bristled at her condemnation of me. But I couldn't let her get away with it. I couldn't let her destroy herself.

"Cat," I began. "It's dangerous—"

"Oh, God's blood, Kitty, I'm only flirting. Everybody does it. Queens and kings and courtiers. It's *expected*."

"Then you don't need me to cover for you."

"Why, in the French court, apparently, they have open affairs all the time!" It was as if I hadn't even spoken.

"The *men* do, Cat," I said. "Not the queen."

"Shut up, Kitty," she said. "Just shut up about it. I hate being queen. All the stupid responsibilities. I'm having a little fun for once. And because I'm queen no one can do a thing about it."

"But Cat," I pleaded.

"Listen," she turned to me. "It comes down to this. You can marry Lord Poxy. Go off and live on the Poxy estate and have twelve Poxy children. Or you can stay at court. Entertain Standebanke. And maybe have a little fun. You choose. And I will ensure your choice comes to fruition."

"It's hardly a choice, Cat."

"Good," she smiled. "Then I'll make it for you. I know which one you really want. We don't have room in the entourage for one more. And I need my dearest friend to come with me. Lord Poxy will just have to wait to get his hands on you."

33

THE KING ELIMINATED POTENTIAL TROUBLEMAKERS BEFORE OUR DEPAR-
ture. Prisoners long held in the Tower. Anyone who carried a
drop of non-Tudor royal blood posed a threat, as a standard
around which rebels could rally.

Margaret Pole, the Countess of Salisbury, was charged with
treason. She was daughter to Richard III's brother, sixty-seven
years old and frail. She refused to plead guilty or lay her head
on the block. It took the inept executioner ten or more strokes
of the ax to dispatch her.

On that sorry note, it began to rain. The roads quickly
clogged with mud and became impassable and we were forced
to remain immobile in Greenwich, looking dejectedly north-
ward, for three entire weeks.

There was no flirting. No lover's meetings. No men. Just
dreary boredom.

The Duke of Norfolk took his trusted servants and braved
the rain and muck, securing great houses and deer parks for
the king's use. Rumor was he would meet back up with the
court in Lincoln. I watched Alice for signs of distress, but she

dared not show them to me. I didn't know how, but the pain of William's absence was greater than that of his presence. Even though he'd chosen Alice over me.

We listlessly played music or repeated old gossip or embroidered tapestries or tried on each other's clothes, leaving kirtles and sleeves and bodices strewn about the chambers, too lethargic to pick them up again.

"Why don't we just call it a day?" Joan moaned, staring out the window at the waterlogged hills and swollen Thames.

"We can't call it a day, it's been a month," I said.

"The king has to go," Alice said importantly. "He has to get to York."

"But why?" Joan said. "I'm so sick of the rain and the mud already and we haven't even left yet!"

"And your comfort is so important to the king," I snapped.

"It's not just me!" Joan said. "Everyone's complaining."

"You're just complaining the loudest."

"No," Joan said, sticking out her tongue. "You are."

"Me?"

"Yes, you're complaining about me complaining!"

We stared at each other for a moment and then burst into laughter.

"Oh, really," Alice sniffed. "It wasn't that funny."

But the laughter bubbled up unbidden. Joan and I clung to each other and giggled helplessly, our hair coming unbound and our faces red and splotchy.

"There's really nothing to laugh about," Alice said.

I considered the rain, the prospect of the long uncomfortable, muddy journey ahead of us, and the executions that had so recently taken place. Alice's perfidy.

"No," I concluded, "I suppose you're right."

"At least it's stopped raining," Joan said to the window.

"For now," I grumbled.

"What sour faces my maids have!" Cat swept into the room, the hem of her rose-petal pink skirts skimming the floor. We all sank into curtseys and she laughed.

"Why so glum?" she asked.

"The rain."

"The mud."

"The boredom."

"Need we say more?" I asked.

"Well, I have thought of something we can do to alleviate the last item," Cat said, hugging herself and bouncing on her toes.

"What is it?" we asked in unison and she giggled.

"Hide-and-seek."

We stared at her in silence.

"We can play in the castle galleries," she said. "There must be loads of secret hiding places in the vacated rooms and courtyards."

Hide-and-seek wasn't my favorite game. My discomfort in enclosed spaces gave me an animalistic fear of being found. As

a child, I would hold my breath for so long I saw spots before my eyes. And when I wasn't near fainting, I was bored out of my mind.

"We do need something to cheer us up," Joan said hesitantly.

"Of course we do," Cat said. "And here's the best part. We'll get the king's men to do the seeking.

"Come," Cat commanded, and ran down the gallery toward the king's apartments, her skirts belling behind her.

"Send him away," came a voice from behind the door when I knocked. "No more suits. We must get to Lincoln. We must get to York." The king trailed into grumbles.

"I do not look for favor," Cat called from the doorway. Just inside the room, Culpepper watched her with hooded eyes.

"My lord," Cat said, skipping to the king to hug him from behind. He faced the fire, so we could not see his reaction, but he lifted his hand to touch her face. She removed it and kissed his knuckles perfunctorily.

In the closeness of the room, I smelled the wet clothes of the men, their unwashed bodies, and the crisp fir resin of the fire.

"I wondered if we could borrow some of your gentlemen," Cat said, and sneaked a glance at me. "And perhaps one of your yeomen of the chamber as well."

"What sort of mischief are you planning today?"

"Well," Cat said. "My ladies grow bored and restless, closed in all the time."

"Don't we all?"

"And I thought a game of hide-and-seek would dispel some of it."

"A children's game?" he asked.

"Yes," Cat said. "I thought perhaps the ladies could hide, pursued by the men. One man each."

"Don't you think the men already do enough pursuing?" the king asked with a hint of a smile in his voice.

"Ah, but my maids are too chaste to allow themselves to be caught," Cat said. "In a children's game, the seeker may finally achieve his goal."

"If only they should be so lucky as I," the king said softly, stroking her again.

"I shall sit here with you," Cat said. "And wait for the couples to come back. We will have wine and sweetmeats after they're caught."

"The rest of us can wager on who will be the last girl found," the king said, and looked up at Cat. "So you must hide as well, because you have a cunning about you that I cannot see any of my men matching."

"I shall do my best to win you a fortune," she said.

We established the rules that each man would hunt only his partner, but if he found someone else's partner, he could disclose her location to her hunter.

"However," Cat said. "If another man finds you, you may move. Find another hiding spot. But only if you have been discovered."

"I told you she was cunning," the king said.

We paired up, the men choosing their quarry. Edmund Standebanke chose me.

"I relish the hunt," he said. I enjoyed the warmth of his whisper on my face.

"And what do you do when your quarry eludes you?" I asked, looking at him directly, knowing my eyes would give me away. That they anticipated the plunge of another of his kisses.

"Oh," he said, his lips brushing my temple. "I never give up. Surrender is the only option."

"You're very confident of your success," I managed. His words, his breath, his very nearness were making me excruciatingly aware of my own body.

"Sometimes, the quarry *wants* to be caught," he said.

His words wrapped briery and cold around my spine, so closely did they echo those I'd heard in the forest.

"Not all," I said quietly.

"Are all of you prepared?" the king asked, breaking the spell.

I pushed away the illogical fear caused by Edmund's meaningless banter and smiled up at him.

"Are you?" I asked.

But my eye was drawn to the other side of the room. Cat twitched a filmy kerchief enticingly from the grasp of Thomas Culpepper. He cringed in mock despair. Cat kissed the kerchief and laid it gently in his hand. Culpepper raised it to his own face, almost to his lips, his eyes never wavering from hers.

"Have you a favor for me?" Edmund asked.

I turned to look at him, tilted my chin. A delicious thought came to me.

"Perhaps a kiss," I said with a smile.

"Perhaps more," he replied, his eyes fervent. "I will not let you be until I've had you. Remember, surrender is the only option."

The heat his words generated in me threatened combustion. But it was tempered by a heady dose of trepidation. The word surrender implied forced submission.

"Ready!" the king cried before I could speak. He grimaced as he stretched his leg out in front of him. "Begin!"

Edmund nudged me, his palm on my lower back, his fingers sliding lower.

I ran.

"Count to one hundred!" I heard the king call to the men. "In Latin!"

My height put me at a disadvantage. I couldn't hide in a cupboard or beneath a chair, not without pain. But I didn't want to be found, not for a good long time. I needed some time to think.

I slipped through the great hall. Knots of older men ignored me, busy discussing matters of state. I darted across a courtyard and headed for the kitchen. The boys who turned the spits giggled at me, and the cooks gave me dirty looks. As I stepped into the alley behind it, I breathed deeply, and then regretted it, as the mud and slops from the kitchen mixed below my feet, despite the king's declaration that all parts of the palace must

be kept scrupulously clean. I found a recess in the wall, half hidden behind a trio of spits hanging with the tattered remains of the previous night's meal.

I waited, straining to hear the sound of boots on the cobblestones or the giggling of another girl being found. And I thought about Edmund Standebanke.

I thought about his sultry smile and the way his kiss flashed through me like a cataract. And how he walked away afterward, as if he knew he was being watched. How he looked when he laughed with Thomas Culpepper. And how his words echoed Culpepper's demand for submission from the woman in the forest.

I thought about how my body reacted to him. Like a craving. How I could imagine his hands on me. But not his arms around me.

And with a pain like acute infection, my mind turned to William Gibbon, off in the wilds of the north. I wondered if he missed Alice, and I wished that he missed me. I wished it were he who would discover me in the kitchen alley.

I stood, alone, my toes growing numb in my thin slippers on the wet ground. Edmund couldn't have been looking for me very hard, no matter what he said. I wondered if the others had been found. If Cat had been found.

And I suddenly felt knocked down by a gush of insight.

The king was right. Cat's cunning surpassed all others. She was hidden. For once, she was by herself—something completely

unheard of at court. About to be found by Thomas Culpepper. *In a children's game, the seeker may finally achieve his goal.*

I needed to stop her. Before she ruined herself. Before she ruined her marriage. Before she ruined us all.

I slipped from my hiding place to search for Cat and ran straight into Edmund Standebanke.

"Wanted to be found that badly, did you?" he asked.

"No," I said, unable to shake the feeling of dread from my stomach. I couldn't think clearly, and the sight of Edmund, his lips turned up in a teasing grin, didn't help at all.

"I would never have seen you there," he said. "Why else would you jump straight into my arms unless you wanted to be found?"

"I have to go," I said.

"I believe you promised to bestow a favor."

He gripped my arms and kissed me. Urgently. As if his life depended on it. I was almost able to forget Cat. Forget the possibilities. Except for those that his kiss implied.

"We must claim our reward from the king," he said, pulling away, wiping his mouth on his sleeve. "The only girl not yet found is the queen. And he placed a wager on her, so she was sure to be the last one caught."

"The queen has not been found?" I asked. "How do you know she'll be last?"

"You've been at court long enough to realize we allow the king to win at everything that matters," Edmund said. "She

and Culpepper are probably hiding somewhere near the king's chambers, waiting for all of us to return."

The dread came back and doused me with a chill.

"We have to find them."

"I told you," he said, "they're hiding. Come with me to drink the king's health."

"We need to go to the queen's rooms first."

"No we don't, kitten," Edmund said, his voice a yard of tease and an inch of threat. "We need to go to the king's apartments and collect our prize."

"You go," I said. "I need to find Cat."

"I can't go alone, you silly girl," Edmund said, his grip and tone now equally steely.

I was a silly girl. I had walked right into a trap. My vigilance was down. The constant observance of the court was distracted. It was the perfect moment for Cat to find some privacy.

And I was too late to do anything about it.

I FOLLOWED EDMUND INTO THE KING'S CHAMBERS. THE OTHERS WERE already eating an extravagant indoor picnic of meat pies and good wine and cheeses. The king looked up when we burst into the room.

"Ah!" he said. "Mistress Tylney! You must have hidden well to have given Master Standebanke such a merry chase."

"Yes, Your Majesty," I said, and curtseyed. The bodies of others pressed in too closely. The fire burned too high. The greasy smell of the cheese mingled with those of sweat and wet shoes, conspiring to make me feel ill.

"But my wife is cleverest of all," the king said. "She has not yet been found. I doubt young Culpepper will ever find her. For when my wife sets her mind to something, she makes sure she does it properly."

"Yes, Your Majesty," I said, the words like dust in my mouth because he spoke the unknowing truth.

"Here is your reward, Mistress Tylney," the king said, and gestured to a servant to bring something forward to me. It was a small box, inlaid with shell and silver.

"Thank you, Your Majesty," I said, curtseying again. I didn't want the box. It was like payment for keeping quiet.

"No, no, Kitty!" the king said. "What is within the box is what counts!"

His use of my pet name startled me. I looked up at him, his eyes merry behind fat cheeks flushed with pleasure. He looked like a child, eager for praise.

The servant thrust the box into my hands and I opened it slowly. Lying on a scrap of blue velvet was a chain of gold from which hung a single pendant of startling emerald.

I nearly dropped the box, and the king laughed at my clumsy juggling.

"Thank you, Your Majesty," I said when I held it tight in my hand, and again I curtseyed. It seemed I spent all my days in obeisance.

"Stand up, Kitty," the king said, irritably. "Let young Standebanke here put it around your pretty neck."

I blushed at the king's use of the word *pretty*. Of course, it was only my neck about which he spoke.

Edmund reached around me for the necklace, his forearm just grazing my breast. He gently lifted the fabric of my snood to clasp the chain. His breath raised the hairs of the nape of my neck.

"There," he whispered in my ear, and allowed my snood to fall back, warming the gooseflesh.

"It's beautiful," I said, looking down.

"Come here, Kitty," the king said, and I knelt before him.

"I saved it for you," he whispered, and I looked up at him in shock. "Because your eyes are the same color green. I would have given it to you no matter if you were the first or the last girl found.

"You are my wife's closest friend," the king continued. "She told me this when you arrived at court. I have never forgotten."

"Thank you, Your Majesty," I breathed.

"Remain a friend to her, Kitty," the king finished. "She has many enemies at court."

He no longer looked delighted, just old. Haggard.

"I will, Your Majesty," I said. Knowing, as I said it, it would mean betraying him.

I bowed once more and caught a whiff of an odor, like meat gone bad. Like the rot at the bottom of the Thames. My nose wrinkled involuntarily.

The king moved his legs with effort, a grimace. He scowled at me.

His ulcers. Despite the bandages soaked in lavender, the king knew I smelled them. A tide of remorse swept through me, and an agony of sympathy for the man who had everything, but truly held nothing. Not the honesty of his court. Not the fidelity of his wife. Not the perfection of a true immortal.

I lowered my head and composed my face into a smile.

"Thank you, Your Majesty. For the generous gift. And the generous words."

I wanted him to believe me. To believe that the smell didn't matter to me any more than my plainness mattered to him or

the truth mattered to Cat. But he turned away. I knew that all the other ladies and courtiers noticed. I had the king's favor for an instant and lost it.

Edmund guided me to the trestle laden with culinary delights. It all tasted of soil and smut, and I gagged on the secrets in the back of my throat.

When Cat burst triumphantly into the room, rosy and fresh in her pink gown, her hair a little disheveled, but her face composed, everyone turned and cheered.

"He can't have been looking very hard," Cat told the king. "I was in my rooms the entire time!"

"I couldn't have guessed you would go back to your apartments," Culpepper said coolly. "I searched the most unusual nooks and crannies, delving into the very depths of the palace."

I squeezed my eyes shut, unable to bear the buttery innuendoes issuing from Culpepper's mouth. He was so glib, so smarmy, and so horrible. I didn't know how Cat could stand to be near him.

"Sometimes it is as if my queen is a friend of the fairy folk," King Henry said. "She can be as light as gossamer, ethereal. It is no wonder to me that you could not find her. It has taken my entire life to find one like her."

The courtiers smiled, and the ladies tittered about romance. I wanted to cry.

"But I am real, my lord," Cat said. "Firm flesh and bone. Certainly not transparent."

"No, my love," the king murmured, and held out a hand to

her. She stood by him, and he wrapped a giant arm around her tiny waist. He was almost as tall sitting down as she was standing up. He laid his head upon her breast.

"I am famished, my lord," she said, and extricated herself.

She came to the table and picked delicately at the food laid out there. She glanced up at me, taking no notice of the pain in my face. But she stopped, staring, eyes upon my pendant.

"Where did you get that?"

"From the king," I said. "For the hide-and-seek game."

"What about your reward, Your Majesty?" Alice asked Cat. "Surely yours will be the greatest, as you were the last one found."

"Oh, my prize!" Cat cried.

If she had been anyone else, she would have left it. She would have had the grace to win the game, however dishonestly, and let it go. But not Cat. She returned to the king and perched on his lap, ignoring his wince.

"Your prize, my love, is to be married to me," he said quietly, lovingly.

"The most handsome man in the world," Cat said. She said it as if she had repeated these words a thousand times already.

"I do have a gift for you," the king said. He gestured to a servant who brought forward a plain wooden box, perfectly square, with a hinged lid. It fit perfectly in her lap. Just the right size for a crown. She stared at it, one finger on the catch.

"Open it," the king said.

Cat threw one look out into the room. One minute glance

that hit its mark without question. Culpepper. I felt faint with relief. If Cat got her crown, Culpepper would be history.

The box opened silently, revealing its sumptuous lining of crimson silk. On which sat a wreath fashioned from the blooms of a pink rose.

"My rose without a thorn," the king said. He picked up the wreath and placed it on her still unruly curls.

Cat attempted a smile, her eyes on the lining of the box.

"Kitty got an emerald," she whispered.

"There is more," the king said. "But you shall have to wait for it until we get to York."

"York!" Cat cried. "But that will be forever!"

The king smiled. It didn't seem to bother him that his wife was just a child. And a deceitful one at that.

"But wait you must," he said. His smile faltered as he shifted again in his chair.

"We will leave you now, my lord," Cat said.

"Yes," the king agreed. "We begin our journey as soon as possible."

As one, we turned to look out of the window, expecting to see the rain still churning from the sky. But we saw only white clouds and green hills and just the faintest hint of sunshine.

"We cannot have you tired on the first day of the progress," the king added.

"Of course not," Cat said.

We all knew that the king meant that *he* could not be tired for the first day of the progress. He already looked exhausted. Like he wanted to be alone. I left the room with the rest of the ladies, leaving the king behind with his devious favorites and his uxorious oblivion.

35

WE LOST OURSELVES IN THE CHAOS OF MOVING THE EXTENSIVE HOUSE-hold and all of its contents through the English countryside. Each day's embarkation took the entire morning. By the time the last horses left a place, the king and queen, at the head of the procession, had already stopped for lunch. Which took hours.

We moved from London to Dunstable, Ampthill to Collyweston, stopping at royal residences and the houses of the great and the good along the way. No single palace could contain us all, so additional housing had to be found, tents erected, beasts slaughtered, bread requisitioned, beds made, and every comfort supplied.

I often rode pillion behind Edmund. I told myself it was to enjoy the fresh air. But really I found myself enjoying the feel of my arms around him, the rumble of his voice against me. It ignited something deep inside me that I recognized with acute embarrassment as lust. Cat would be gratified to know that if we ever formed an attachment, it would be driven solely by sex. There seemed little chance we would ever form a bond through conversation, as he didn't say much.

Everywhere we went, the populace thronged to watch our passage. Our entourage clogged the roads and paths, trampled the fields, left trash and excrement in its wake, and yet everyone seemed happy to see us.

"Long live King Henry!" they shouted.

They wore baggy clothing of coarse materials, sometimes patched and torn, their beards untrimmed. They smelled different, too. Like fields and mud, something I found not altogether unpleasant.

They cheered for Cat, too. They called for her blessing. But I don't think I was the only one who saw the determination and concentration it cost her to keep from drawing back from the filthy hands of the toothless peasant women and men cowed by life. She couldn't bear for their want, their need, to be transferred to her. She couldn't stand to be in their presence. And they grew wary and sullen in hers.

I watched her closely, constantly. I watched her work hard to ignore Culpepper.

But I couldn't ignore him. He flirted with all the girls, jested with the king and his men. He and Edmund Standebanke lived in each other's pockets. He went hawking and hunting when we stopped somewhere for more than a few hours. He went nowhere near the queen.

I almost began to believe that Cat had changed her mind. That perhaps one taste was all she needed.

She spent more time in the company of Jane Boleyn, who appeared younger every day. I saw her reach into her pocket

less and less, and wondered if the memory of Anne Boleyn was being erased by the reality of Catherine Howard.

Then we crossed into Lincolnshire, the wellspring of the rebellion five years before. The Lincolnshire Uprising began as a protest of the suppression of the monasteries. But it got out of hand, demanding tax reforms and the repeal of property laws, and lead to riots and the forcible occupation of Lincoln Cathedral. It spurred the Pilgrimage of Grace in Yorkshire and everything ended in a round of bloody executions.

We had a picnic a few miles outside of Lincoln, the region's capital. I fancied I could see the cathedral high on Lincoln Cliff in the distance. We stopped again just outside the city for the king and queen to change their clothes. The king, dressed head to foot in cloth of gold, glowed as if he were Apollo himself. And by his side, Cat was Diana, her gown a tissue of cloth of silver, studded with jewels and embroidered in gold. She wore her hair bound in a caul of white silk studded with sapphires and rode a white horse.

At the gates of the city, the mayor and town gentry approached and made speeches. Groveling supplication for forgiveness. They knelt and cried, "Jesus save your Grace!" And all was forgiven. That easily.

We walked on aching feet through the gates and up to the cathedral. The building shone in the waning summer light, blinding over the brick edifices surrounding it. Inflated on sanctity, it towered over the town and all the people in it. The king claimed it as the tallest building in the world. He

insisted that he and Cat take communion there. I couldn't imagine that Cat had confessed her sins. She was too wary of the wagging tongues of priests. Though truly, entering that great space, the light coming in kaleidoscopically through the stained glass, and the pigeons flying high overhead like angels amongst the ribs, would make anyone want to fall on her knees and confess.

The city was full of exhausted and drunken revelers by the time we exited the cathedral into the darkened streets. I wanted nothing more than to roll onto my pallet and fall asleep. We had a few days in Lincoln. Perhaps we could rest. Really rest.

The Bishops' Palace stood close by the cathedral, renovated and decorated, made warm and comforting by the Duke of Norfolk, who stood at the gate to welcome the king and queen. I carefully avoided looking for William. I didn't need the pain of seeing him look for Alice. I didn't need the pain of seeing him, period. The loss of him still felt like a hole in my chest the size of a fist.

The rooms sat tight on top of each other, accessed by dark stairwells and interconnecting doors. The queen's apartments were surrounded by the rooms of her ladies, separated from the king by the centuries' old west hall, dark and cavernous compared to the gaudy-bright great hall of Hampton Court. Cat kissed the king lightly and he hobbled off to bed, followed by his men.

The city pressed in against the towers of the palace. Torchlight marked revelers in the streets below us, visible from

the squat, narrow windows. Cat turned to her ladies as soon as we reached her bedchamber.

"I require only Mistress Tylney and Lady Rochford," she said "The rest of you should get some sleep."

Groans of appreciation rose, and the room emptied within seconds.

Jane and I helped Cat to take off the glowing silver-white gown. Despite Cat's vow never to wear the same gown twice, I folded it carefully and packed it away. It seemed sacrilege to dispose of it.

I felt toilworn and depleted, and Jane looked like a ghost, her skin pale as thin parchment and her eyes sunken into black sockets. When Cat's hair had been brushed and her nightgown straightened, I removed my slippers and sighed at the freedom of it.

"Do not undress yet," Cat said.

"Why?" I asked, unable to prevent the peevishness in my voice. "Cat, I'm exhausted. We've spent eight days on the road and I've worked my fingers off, and I just want four hours of sleep before you have to get up tomorrow."

"Well, I'm sorry, Kitty, but you'll just have to attend to your queen for a change instead of to your own selfish desires. You are here under my auspices. You are here to do my bidding. You are not here for your own pleasure."

I knew that only too well.

She stared at me for a long moment. Jane stood frozen, her breath held.

"Well?" Cat snapped. "Do you not know how to curtsey? Do you not know how to pay me proper respect?"

Her voice rose ever higher until it became an indignant screech.

I dipped into a curtsey and refused to look at her.

Before she could say more, a knock came at the outer door of her chamber. She looked up, her eyes ringed white and wide with fear. Her expression caused my heart to judder.

"Who is it?" she said. "Kitty, go see."

I stepped tentatively to the door, unsure whether I should expect a cabal of Lincolnshire rebels or the wrath of the king himself. A single guard stood there, the scent of the night and smoke outside still clinging to his garments.

"I wish to tell the queen . . ." he paused as if considering his words. "I would like to make sure she feels protected."

"Oh," I said, my alarm increasing, but he didn't wait for my response.

"I found the back stairs door unlocked and standing open," he reported, his words tumbling over each other. "The stairs lead directly to the queen's apartments. I searched the stairs and the surrounding area, but found no one. I secured the door and locked it myself. She is in no danger."

My mind raced back to the cheering people at the gates of the city that afternoon. The faces all blended in my memory, mouths agape with what I had thought was joy but could easily have been rage. I wondered if the noise and crowds had hidden an assassin. I shuddered at the thought of the hordes still in

the streets, massing beneath the overhanging buildings, drinking and cursing into the night.

"Please, dear lady," the guard said, "be not afraid. I secured the door myself. No one can get in."

"Thank you," I tried to say, but a pebble of fear clogged my throat. I cleared it and said, "Thank you very much. I shall let the queen know."

He bowed.

"I must return to my rounds. You are all safe with me."

"I'm sure," I said, and smiled at him. I did not know the man but had seen him before. His presence was understated and unobtrusive, but ever-present. And indeed, I did feel safe with him on duty.

I returned to the bedchamber and Cat's questioning eyes.

"It was a guard." I wondered how I could tell her without making it sound too terrifying. Danger had been averted. She need not fear for her life.

"What did he want?" Cat said. "What reason could he possibly have for knocking on my door at such a late hour?"

I decided just to tell her straight and hope she could sleep that night.

"He said the back stairs door was left unlocked and hanging open. He said he locked the door and checked the area and believes that there is no danger."

Cat punched a tiny fist into her goose-down mattress.

"Oh, by the Mass, thwarted at every turn!" she cried. "That stupid man!"

I stared.

"Kitty, you must go down the back stairs at once," she said. "Wait there. Listen. Take the key with you."

"But I don't want to, Cat," I whispered. "The guard said there was no danger."

"Danger be damned!" she shouted. "Do as I say!"

Jane scurried to get me a taper.

"And Kitty, when you hear someone outside the door, let him in."

"Let him in?" The guard had just averted one assassination attempt and I was requested to expedite the next?

"Yes!"

"But Cat, are you sure?" I looked at Jane, hoping she would recognize Cat's lunacy. Jane wouldn't meet my eye.

"It is not your job to question me!" Cat said, her voice lowering to that dangerous growl. "It is your job to do as I wish. Now go."

In a daze, I stumbled barefoot down the rough-cut stone stairs, hardly able to see my feet in the weak light of the candle. I was glad I hadn't changed into my linen shift, because the walls exuded the chill of three hundred years of northern winters.

I came to the door and listened against it. The taper guttered, and I prayed I would not be left in that tomblike space in the dark. I thought I heard the whispers of ghosts. I imagined the vagrants and rebels and drunks of the town amassing outside the walls. I envisioned spiders and crawling bugs and the slithering of worms and snakes.

I was so caught up with the terror in my head that a scuffling outside the door made me shriek.

The noise stopped, and even through the thick oak door, I suspected I could hear a man breathing. Or an angry mob quietly discussing how to dissect a maid.

The latch snapped with a metallic echo up the cold dark stairs. I watched it, horrified. The door creaked almost imperceptibly followed by an angry grunt outside when it held fast.

I slipped the key in the lock with trembling fingers and turned it slowly. As soon as it clicked the latch snapped again and the door flew open.

Thomas Culpepper stood before me. In one swift movement, he pinched the flame of my candle out.

"Jesus, Kitty," he hissed. "Do you want everyone to see us?"

He slipped through the door, and in the reflected light of stars, Edmund emerged behind him.

"Stay outside, Standebanke," Culpepper ordered. "If you see anyone, knock, and Kitty here will come and warn us."

"Can I not keep Kitty company?" Edmund asked.

Oh, yes, please, I thought, though I told myself it was because I was afraid of the dark.

"No, you fool. One man standing outside will raise no questions. You're a yeoman of the chamber. You're guarding the queen. If you're with a girl, inside or out, you will be in dereliction of duty."

He pulled the door closed on Edmund's disappointed face,

238

and we were plunged into a blackness so complete I could hardly breathe. I heard the key turn the lock.

"Stay here," Culpepper said, his breath as crepuscular as the vestibule.

"I don't want to." My voice shook.

"Too bad for you," Culpepper replied. He pushed me up against the wall, his body full on mine, hand over my mouth to stifle my scream.

"Stay here in the shadows. Perhaps next time you will cover your light."

He leapt up the stairs, his soft shoes whispering on stone, as if he could see in the dark like a cat. Or a devil.

The darkness clamped itself to my skull, to the backs of my eyes, and I shook with the effort of driving away the memory of Culpepper's touch. I wanted to peel my own skin away to divest myself of the taint of him.

A cough outside the door startled me. Edmund. Reminding me he was there. Signaling me to let him in. He would hold me. Protect me.

I turned the key with shaking fingers and fumbled the latch.

"So soon?" Edmund's voice was hollow in the empty courtyard, but with a grin in it. He knew. Of course he knew.

"It's me, Edmund," I whispered at the crack in the door. "I need you."

He swung the door open farther and seized my face in both of his hands. He lowered his mouth on mine in one swift, taste-

less kiss, hard and anxious, and then he pushed me away.

"Culpepper is right," he said. "I can't be seen with you. Now, stay."

He shut the door.

I locked it.

I sank down and pulled my skirts around my feet to trap the warmth. I wrapped my arms around my knees to stop their trembling. When I closed my eyes, finding comfort in a more familiar darkness, I felt a tear slide down my cheek.

I was aiding and abetting treason. I had allowed a man into the queen's chambers in the middle of the night. Not just any man, but Thomas Culpepper.

The man I chose to protect me was Culpepper's best friend. A man who made my blood race but my heart fail. A man who left me in the darkness that terrified me.

I crushed my palms against my eyes to press the thoughts away, sending shooting sparks through the writhing blackness. I stayed there, huddled beside the door, until I fell asleep against the wall.

36

A BOOT IN MY RIBS STARTLED ME BACK INTO THE WAKING DARKNESS.

"Your queen needs you," came Culpepper's voice. The sound of the key in the lock. A line of charcoal gray as the door opened. Whispers.

I sat up, rubbing my side, my arm and face cold from the damp stone. I didn't want to return to the bedroom. To the tumbled sheets. To the smell of him.

I didn't want to talk to Cat.

My bones creaked when I stood, the rough floor painful beneath my chilled feet. I reached out to close the door, but was stopped by Culpepper's voice.

"Well, now you have no choice, Standebanke."

Edmund was still out there.

"It's not like I had any to begin with," he muttered.

"My thoughts exactly," Culpepper said, and I saw his shadow slap Edmund's on the back. With a laugh, he sauntered away.

"Kitty?" Edmund whispered.

"I'm still here."

Edmund wedged himself through the crack in the door and

put his arms around me. His cloak and doublet carried the cold mist from outside and offered little warmth, but I leaned into him anyway.

"What did he mean?" I asked. "That you had no choice?"

"What does Thomas Culpepper ever mean?" he said. "His way is the only way and the rest of us have no say in the matter."

"Shouldn't we all have a choice?" I asked. Knowing that I didn't. I'd pledged my choice away when I had sworn my loyalty to Cat.

Edmund pulled away and kissed me on the forehead.

"Get to bed, kitten," he said, and then moved his lips closer to my ear. "I wish I could go with you."

But I was glad he couldn't. Despite his tentative sympathy, I couldn't forget his coldness in the dark. When I needed him.

I felt my way back up the stairs and into the blinding light of a single candle in Cat's room. Joan turned at the sound of my footsteps, took in my appearance in one glance, and shook her head. She drew the velvet curtain around the bed.

"Shhhh."

"Is the queen not asleep yet?" I asked.

"Yes, even now," she said. "I hope he was worth it."

She pushed me gently out the door and shut it in my face. Joan thought I was the one having an affair.

Jane Boleyn stood alone in the withdrawing room. Haggard. Pale.

"Good morning, Kitty," she said.

I gazed at her for a long moment. Had she already been through this once? With Anne Boleyn? Or was that all a fabrication to rid Henry of his second queen? And even if Jane hadn't been through it before, why was she doing it now?

"How do you do it, Jane?" I asked her.

"Do what?"

"Do what you're doing? Why do you allow this sort of thing to go on?"

"I'm not sure what you're talking about," Jane said.

"My friend is ruining her life," I said.

Jane moved to the outer door and checked behind it. She pulled me to the far corner of the room. Away from the windows. Away from the fire. Away from anything that could conduct our voices.

"Perhaps not."

"She's killing herself!" I said.

Jane made a *tsk* and I realized how dramatic and hysterical I sounded. Like a little girl throwing a tantrum. I took a breath.

"If word gets out, she could be executed," I said. "So could we."

"So we will not allow word to get out," Jane said. She placed a hand on my shoulder. Like a friend. Like a mother. Dispensing wisdom.

"She can't keep doing this!"

"But she will. No matter what we do or say. Look at it this way, Kitty. It's serving a purpose. One that cannot help but strengthen her position here at court. Strengthen the country as a whole. An heir to the throne, especially one from the conservative, Catholic-leaning Howard faction, would stabilize everything."

"You're letting this happen so she can get *pregnant*?"

"It is my duty to make her path smooth."

"That's not smooth, Jane, that's treason."

"No, Kitty, it's the way of the monarchy. Bastards have come to the throne before and will come to the throne again. The Duke of Richmond would have grown to be king had he not died and Prince Edward not been born. The king himself may be descended from the son of an archer and not the royal line at all. If the king cannot do what is necessary to produce children, then we must pursue other lines of possibility."

"So this is your idea?" I asked. "This doomed, ridiculous romance?"

"No!" Jane looked aghast. "I would never suggest such a thing."

"But you would promote it."

"I will do whatever the queen asks."

"Well, isn't that noble of you."

"It is my duty, Kitty," she said, and fixed me with her feline eyes. "And it is yours. You would do well to remember that."

"My duty is to my friend, not to the monarchy."

"Right now, the needs of both are one and the same, and that is your silence," Jane said. "At court, a word spoken is a word disseminated. Even if you think you are alone, you are not. Trust me on this."

I did. I had to. Because if anyone knew how secrets got out at court, Jane did.

37

We continued slowly through Gainsborough and Scooby and on to Hatfield, where we paused to spend a few days hunting. Every time we had new quarters, Cat sent Jane to search the castle or the house or the outskirts of the tent-laden field for secret hideaways and hidden entrances. I never questioned her. I knew why she sought them.

I watched. I felt that my very observation could somehow prevent Cat from doing anything more. Anything foolish. Anything obvious.

At Hatfield, I saw Jane shake her head after touring the four narrow wings and dim central courtyard. Nowhere to hide. Not enough space. Cat stayed quiet in her chambers, enclosed by the Coven, listening to music and tired gossip.

More than anything, I wanted to leave. I imagined going back to Lambeth, back to my parents, but knew that even there, people were always watching. Always finding fault. I wanted to go somewhere else. Somewhere I could breathe.

I would even marry Lord Poxy if it would get me out.

Jesus, I must be desperate.

I wished I could tell Cat, laugh with her about it. But the Coven, clucking and tutting, surrounded her.

Gossiping that perhaps she was pregnant.

"It must be why she doesn't ride," Cat's stepmother said quietly when the queen moved to look out the window. "What else could it be?"

"It's about time," Cat's sister muttered. "All his other wives were pregnant within three months."

"Not Anne of Cleves," the Countess of Bridgewater reminded them.

I moved restlessly away. I felt confined, all of us piled into the queen's apartments, waiting for the hunt to return. The closed square of the palace allowed contemplation of the surrounding countryside but cut off escape. I couldn't think straight breathing other people's air, their skirts touching mine, every rustle and whisper setting my teeth on edge.

"What are you thinking?"

The voice sounded calm. Comforting. Familiar.

It belonged to Alice Restwold.

"Nothing," I said. I almost wanted to confide in her. To open the circle again to Joan and Alice and Cat, our friendship like a bulwark against the gossip and the scheming. But Alice had William. And I couldn't break that wall.

"Is it true she's pregnant?" she asked.

"Aren't you the one who's supposed to know everything? How should I know if she's pregnant?"

"Or by whom?" Alice asked.

"I didn't say that."

"You didn't have to."

"She's married," I said firmly. "She's the queen of England. Whose child could she possibly have?"

"Whose indeed," Alice murmured. But she had that sly look about her. The look that carried secrets and used them as currency. Used them as weapons.

"Listen to me, Alice Restwold," I said, and gripped her by both arms. I topped her by at least a head and carried more weight on me, too. She was thin and pallid like a sickly child, and my fingers reached right around her upper arms and nearly met my thumbs.

"Listen to what, Katherine Tylney?" she said, her chin tilted to look me in the eye.

"You will not go spreading idle gossip in this place," I hissed. "You are one of the queen's ladies and as such you should be loyal only to her."

"Whoever said I wasn't?"

I itched to clout the smirk off her.

"You and I both know that you are loyal only to yourself," I said. "But if you breathe one word of gossip about Cat to anyone—*anyone*—I will come down on you like the sword of Damocles. I shall be watching you, the sword held by a hair, waiting to drop." A sudden anger lent force to my words and my fingers tightened involuntarily. I wanted to squeeze until

the blood stopped running to her hands. Maybe that would stop her mouth.

For a second, her eyes grew wide with fear. Then she shook me off.

"You can't threaten me, Kitty Tylney," she said. "I know too much about you. About Cat. About Lambeth."

"We all do, Alice," I reminded her.

A ghost of her smirk reappeared, but she leaned back into the shadows and all expression blurred.

"It's not like Cat was ever particularly discreet when she lived there," she said. "After all, she used to meet Francis Dereham in the back of the chapel."

"So we must be discreet for her," I said, panicked at her indifference to the danger we could all be in.

"For the love of God, Kitty," she said. "Grow up. I'm not likely to breathe a word, because I'm quite happy where I am. I'm in this for me, as you said. But Kitty, you should know better than anyone that your loyalty will get you nowhere."

"What do you mean by that?" I asked, taken off guard. My loyalty to Cat got me everything. It saved me from my parents' neglect. It bought my way out of Lambeth. It rescued me from Lord Poxy.

"I mean that you've been friends with Cat Howard for as long as I've known you. She can make all the promises in the world, swear enduring friendship, insist on her virtue and make everyone believe her. But it all comes down to Cat making Cat

happy. Nothing and no one else matters. At the end of the day, your loyalty means little to her, except for what it can make you do. But you're better than that. You're worth more than that. Surely by now you've begun to think for yourself."

"I've always thought for myself, thank you very much," I said, but the sharpness of my words couldn't keep tears of recognition from my eyes.

"Well, you've certainly never shown it."

The words stung. More so because she was right.

I looked over to Cat, staring vacantly out the window, and saw the way the sun played across her face and the blankness in her eyes. The formal garden outside appeared cramped and precise in contrast to the spread of the fields beyond. She didn't seem to notice any of it.

Then she changed. She stood taller, with her shoulders pulled back, and her bosom heaved like that of a balladeer's heroine.

I followed Cat's gaze and caught sight of Culpepper out the window. He sat on his horse, positioned for full view from Cat's window. He threw a glance over his shoulder and she caught it like a kiss on the wind.

I searched the room to see if anyone else had noticed. The Coven stooped over their endless tapestry silks. The other ladies hovered over a tray of delicacies. Jane Boleyn stood stark and brittle as a frozen sapling, her eyes darting from Cat to Culpepper and finally resting on Joan, who stood at Cat's elbow, ready with a selection of jewels for her hair, one hand raised in

immobile supplication. She stared at Cat openmouthed, blue-eyed and bewildered.

And the secret spread, held by another keeper.

I looked again out the window and caught sight of Edmund on a gray charger, his hair as flowing as the horse's mane. He saw me staring and flashed a knowing grin.

"That man could teach a girl a thing or two," Alice said quietly.

Her eyes were on Edmund. But she could very well have meant Culpepper.

"Maybe there are some things I don't want to learn," I said, and walked away. As if she hadn't already stolen the one man I'd ever wanted. As if Alice Restwold, purveyor of secrets, might not be collecting clues to treason.

I felt the sword myself, hanging by a thread above us all. And only our silence could save us.

38

Rumors of Cat's pregnancy hastened and expanded until the entire court, from the king to the cooks, watched her every move and studied every morsel she ate. She never said a word, did nothing to increase or dispel the rumors.

We moved on to Pontefract, the last days of August turning to autumn in the northern climate. In London, it would still be summer. But here in the northern wilds, the wind whipped across the jagged rocks of the hills and in through the shuttered windows. The timeworn castle stood isolated on a hill, proud and solitary, undulating fields and forests splayed below it.

"They say this was the favorite castle of Richard III," Alice told me. A king who, stories said, usurped his crown from his brother and murdered his nephews in the Tower of London.

"And King Richard II died here," she continued. "Imprisoned and starved to death. The local cook said both Richards might haunt the towers."

The wind sounded enough like ghosts as it was.

"Shut up, Alice," I muttered, unwilling to ponder treason and its shades.

Cat swept into the room, a furious bundle of energy, her face pale, hands clenched in fists so tight I could see the white of bone.

"I wish to speak with Mistress Tylney alone," she said.

The ladies moved gracefully, laying aside embroidery, casting lazy, disgruntled glances my way.

"I wish you all to leave me!" Cat shouted. The ladies jumped and scattered, leaving behind the detritus of court life: needles and thread, paper and chess pieces.

"Joan, Alice!" Cat said. "You stay here, also."

The Countess narrowed her eyes and stalked out the door, her lips twitching. Jane Boleyn paused, cast a quick look around the room, suddenly stark and colorless without its occupants, and closed the door behind her.

"What is it?" I asked.

"It's my grandmother."

"Is she not well?" I hadn't seen the duchess that morning, and it seemed a little disingenuous for Cat to be so concerned about her health.

"She wants me to employ a new secretary."

I failed to see the connection between this piece of information and Cat's agitated state.

"But you hate writing," Joan said. "A secretary would be a good thing."

"She wants me to appoint Francis Dereham."

"Francis!" I gasped. The duchess must have gone mad. There was no way a logical person would think placing Francis

253

in Cat's household would be a good idea. The endless odious possibilities flooded my mind.

"What the hell does she think she's doing?" Cat demanded.

"What did she say?"

"That he wants to better himself, the little weasel."

"Maybe he does just want a more advantageous position," I said lamely.

"He wants to take advantage of *my* position," Cat said hotly. "Like the rest of you. Even that horrible Mary Lascelles tried to worm her way in. As if I'd ever let her near me again, the miserable tattletale. But you lot I couldn't keep away."

A shocked silence overtook us. Rain flung itself against the shutters and sputtered in the fire.

"We just wanted to be with you, Cat," Joan said.

"So that's why you wrote me that letter?" Cat sneered. "Because you were in 'utmost misery' without me? Because of your love for me? Because of the 'perfect honesty' you have always found in me?" She said the words *utmost misery* and *perfect honesty* in a simpering mockery of Joan's childish lilt.

Joan gaped, open-mouthed.

"It's true, Cat," she said. "I *was* in misery without you. You'd promised Kitty. Alice had her family connections. And I had nothing."

I felt a quick, tight guilt. I would have left Joan behind. Sure as Cat left Francis when the light of something better shone.

"But you didn't have to resort to blackmail!" Cat wailed.

"I didn't blackmail you, Cat," Joan blubbered. "What are you talking about?"

Perfect honesty?" Cat said. "What else could it mean? That you know the truth about Francis! That perhaps I am not honest, but your own conscience would behoove you to tell the truth if I didn't put you out of your misery."

Joan's rosebud mouth formed a perfect circle and her eyes brimmed with horrified tears.

"Oh!" she gasped, shook her head. "Oh, no!"

Cat stared at her. Narrowed her eyes. Then her face cleared.

"You mean you actually meant just what you said?" she said, still quick with doubt.

"Yes!" Joan protested. "I was miserable! You had promised Kitty. I just thought if I prompted you, I could be included in the promise. You believe me, don't you?"

She looked around at all of us, desperately. Wanting reassurance. I certainly couldn't imagine Joan Bulmer attempting anything so devious.

"Of course, Joan," I said. I snapped a quick smile at Cat.

"And all this time, you thought I would do that to you?" Joan asked, horrified.

Cat shrugged. Mystery solved. Matter forgotten.

"At least having you here has kept you quiet. It might work with Francis, too."

"The duchess is discreet," Alice reasoned. "She knows the

court. She wouldn't bring him here if it weren't safe. And the duke is here to keep an eye on things."

"And you know the duke so well," Cat snapped.

Alice looked taken aback.

"I suppose Francis is harmless," Cat said, waving away any concerns with her beringed hand.

I pictured Francis. The jaunty tilt of his cap when he swept into the maidens' chamber. The hangdog look on his face when Cat had dismissed him. How, when I saw him again at Lambeth, he made a show of appearing more dashing and important than he really was. The spite and jealousy in his voice when he told me about Cat and Culpepper.

"Are you sure?" I asked.

"Silly Kitty," she said. "He's safer here than out there." She flung her arm to the windows and the world beyond. "God only knows what he would say or who he would say it to out there, especially if I turned away his suit. If he's here, he'll know what's at stake. And stay quiet."

So I stayed quiet, too. I suppressed my doubts about Francis. And I suppressed my fears that Cat had brought me to court only to keep me quiet, not to keep me close.

39

FRANCIS STRUTTED INTO THE QUEEN'S CHAMBERS A FEW DAYS LATER, flaunting his chin dimple. His shoulders looked broader, his smile more determined.

"Your Majesty," he said, and bowed low before Cat, just as he had done in the maidens' dormitory.

"Master Dereham," Cat said. She clipped her words. They held as little warmth as that wind-chilled room.

"Lovely to see you again," Francis said, and gazed unflinchingly into her eyes. The Coven, nesting by the fire, rustled and whispered at this flagrant bravado.

"You were in my grandmother's household, were you not?" Cat asked.

I held my breath, willing Francis to play along.

"I was," he said.

I breathed again. He was coy, but perhaps he wouldn't endanger us. Yet.

"You work well with a quill?" Cat asked. "You are discreet?"

Questions that anyone would ask of a new secretary. Discretion was essential. Even if the secretary wasn't your ex-lover.

"I have been told that my handwriting flows like the Thames," Francis said.

I snorted. What a prat.

"And I can be as quiet as a mouse. At sea, we hold many secrets. What are a few more?"

"Well, you will not be keeper to any secrets, sir," Cat said. "My life is an open book. Anyone here can tell you of my love for my husband, my appreciation of music and dance, and my fondness for clothes and jewels and occasional lighthearted mischief. I'm afraid I consist of not much more than that."

"Of course." Francis grinned. "The Queen of Misrule."

"You mistake me, sir," Cat said, and I swore the temperature lowered around her. "And you mistake your place."

"Forgive me." Francis bowed low, eyes closed, face red. Fists clenched.

"I will call you when I have need of you," Cat said.

She leaned close to him and I heard her whisper icily, "Take heed what words you speak."

We processed to York, the center of the Pilgrimage of Grace, where the king bestowed his beneficence on abject city officials, who called out blessings and gratitude. And yet, we did not feel welcomed. The city walls hunched dark and foreboding—resistant to invasion and impending weather. The gates funneled us into the narrow streets, overhung with half-timbered buildings leaning fat and heavy like the rigging of a ship in full sail. The ancient minster perched at the north end of the city like a raven, black and looming against the heavy gray sky.

The people bowed grudgingly when we passed. They didn't care that their city was graced by the presence of the king and queen. All they knew was that the houses and inns and every courtyard were full of strangers who required rich foods, meat, wine, and ale, who would fill the gutters with waste and deplete the surrounding fields of the crops that should sustain the city through the winter and now wouldn't.

In their eyes, I saw that they hated us.

I understood better when I saw the sun-bleached skeleton of

the Abbey of St. Mary. The abbot's house had been renovated and richly furnished for our arrival. But the abbey itself looked beyond repair. Destroyed by the king's reformation.

The weather turned colder, and a miserable, mizzling rain fell. Cat kept me constantly by her side. Me and Joan and often Jane Boleyn. And when Jane wasn't with us, Cat sent me to her with cryptic messages. Promises. Accounts paid. And little gifts. "Two bracelets, to warm the arms." I noticed she didn't say whose arms.

Alice crept around the outskirts of our little quartet, disappearing for hours at a time. To the company of the Duke of Norfolk and his entourage. To William Gibbon. My heart twisted at the thought, so I turned my mind to Edmund instead.

He worked in shifts, guarding the king's chamber, and would find me at odd hours, stealing moments in dark corners and dim courtyards that left me breathless and confused. But wanted.

In September, at the end of a dreary day spent indoors with the Coven, Cat sent me to Jane's rooms at the opposite end of the abbey gardens. I slipped through the deepening shadows of the splintered church on my way back to Cat's apartments, carrying in my mind Jane's cryptic words, "If she sits up for it, I will the next day bring her word myself."

One shadow unhitched itself from the wall and spoke.

"Where have you been?"

"Edmund," I said. My voice betrayed the fact that he had frightened me. "I've been . . . out."

"Alone?" he asked. "Or perhaps sneaking about?"

"I wasn't sneaking," I said. But I couldn't tell him the truth.

"Oh, so it is habitual for you to wander?"

"I needed the air." My excuse sounded lame even to me.

"You needed nothing of the sort," he said, his voice hard. "You planned to meet someone."

"Now who would I be planning to meet?" I asked. My blood fizzled. Edmund's jealousy was shockingly misplaced and unfounded.

"Perhaps a lover?" he said, sinewy and sly. "That's why you shun me, why you play hard to get. There is someone else. A servant? A lord? A married earl?"

"I'm meeting no one," I said. "And I don't shun you." It wasn't as if he had expressed undying devotion.

"Then stop playing games with me, Kitty."

"I don't play games."

"You flirt with me," he said, ticking items off on his fingers. "Kiss me. Arouse me. And yet you make no effort to sleep with me."

I thought back. He always advanced, not I. I didn't want to appear too eager. Too wanton. But there was something else.

"I don't love you."

Edmund threw back his head and laughed.

"Love?" he said. "Who needs love?"

I do, I thought, but knew the answer would elicit more laughter.

"Courtly love is something else entirely," he said, stepping closer. "It's not the treacle of romantic ballads, the knight who dies in defense of his lady."

He put his arms around me.

"Courtly love is a dance," he said, his lips brushing the tender skin just below my ear. "A dance of flirtation. A dance of give . . ." he pushed ever so gently against me . . . "and take." He turned his head and kissed me.

And I let him. Lost myself and my fears in the solid reality of his body.

"I wonder about the appointment of the queen's secretary," he said, casually, breaking away from me. "Dereham. You knew him before, did you not? At Norfolk House."

"He . . . he was in the dowager duchess's employ," I said, my thoughts thrown into disorder by his rapid changes of topic and mood.

"He knew the queen, too, yes? I believe they used to go to chapel together."

"Everyone in Lambeth went to chapel together." Just not the same way Cat and Francis did. Edmund's knowledge struck too close to the truth, and it made me nervous.

"He got into an argument at the dinner table the other night. As a mere secretary, he is not entitled to stay at table with the queen's privy council after everyone else has risen. When Mr. Johns reprimanded him, Dereham replied, 'I was of

the Queen's Council before you knew her and shall be when she has forgotten you.' Now what do you suppose he meant by that?"

Oh, Francis, I thought, *your vanity always did get away with you.*

"He's just a popinjay," I said. "A loud-mouthed braggart. You shouldn't listen to anything that man says." My attempt at a laugh came out a sad bark.

"I could keep him quiet," Edmund said. "I could ensure his bragging goes no further."

"The queen would appreciate her secretary being held accountable."

"But little kitten," Edmund said. "Would you? What would you do to stem the tide of gossip in this court?"

"Gossip is a snake, ready to strike the innocent indiscriminately," I said. "It isn't worth the breath used to vocalize it."

"Then it is probably best to say nothing," he said, his lips against mine. "To seal the lips and speak no more."

He kissed me again. But it wasn't the tenderness I wished for. His hand squeezed the back of my neck, possessive, his lips hot and hard and tasting of charred meat and the malt-and-porridge tang of small beer.

This time, I couldn't kiss him back.

He stepped away.

"Not still thinking of that skinny coxcomb in the duke's employ?"

William. How did this man know everything?

"You didn't really believe he was interested, did you?" he asked. "In you?"

His question bridled me. What else did Edmund know? What did he know that I didn't?

"That creature is out for one thing only," Edmund persisted. "Advancement. He'll get it from the duke. He'll get it from Mistress Restwold. He thought he could get it from you."

"That's not true," I said. I knew it wasn't. But my voice betrayed me.

"The closest companion to the queen," Edmund continued. "That's quite a political connection."

I wanted to strangle him. To stop the words any way I could.

"You'd be foolish to think he'd want you for any other reason."

"Do you mean that I would be foolish to hope that someone would find me attractive? Would care for me?" I asked, my voice shaking. Because I had to hold onto that one piece of truth. That someone had cared about me for me.

"That's exactly what I mean."

The words staggered me backward. He was playing with me. Like a cat with its prey. Pawing at me. Digging in a claw and releasing. Watching the panic rise. Enjoying it.

"And I should think you my savior because you offer to take me to bed?" I managed to spit at him. "What a sacrifice you've made!"

"I've profited from our liaison, as well," he said. "It's not

been unpleasant. And it seemed to me I was giving you exactly what you wanted."

I shuddered at the thought of my own body's betrayal, because in a way, he was right. I tried to find the words to cut him, to make him as small and ashamed as I, but they were obstructed by the tears that threatened to engulf me.

Edmund turned and walked away and let me cry alone.

We waited. For the rain to stop. For the king's nephew, the King of Scotland, to come for a royal confabulation. For an announcement of a coronation or a forthcoming heir for the throne. The buzzing swarm of gossip over Cat's possible pregnancy grew and intensified.

Francis Dereham lurked on the outskirts of Cat's entourage, ever present, like a toothache. Culpepper appeared occasionally, like the stabbing pain of a recurring injury. When they were in a room together, the very air fizzed like the aura of an impending lightning strike.

I told Cat about Edmund. And what he'd said of Francis's indiscretion.

"I can handle Francis Dereham," she said. "Make sure you handle Edmund Standebanke."

She winked suggestively. But where once that suggestion would have made me quiver with anticipation, it now just left me feeling more alone than ever. Isolated and confined by the court, by its occupants and its suffocating requirements.

I wondered if we would stay trapped in York, prisoners of the impending northern winter.

"Why doesn't he crown me and just be done with it?" Cat grumbled one day while Joan and Alice helped her dress, and I tended the fretful little fire in the grate.

"Did he say he would?" Joan asked, lacing Cat's bodice.

"I suppose it's no secret," Cat continued. "He certainly hinted hard enough. Remember our game of hide-and-seek?"

"What about it?" Joan asked.

"Tighter, Joan," Cat said. "Remember the king gave me a crown of roses? And said I should wait for the rest of my prize until we got to York? What else could it have been?"

So what was he waiting for?

"This is just as tight as it was yesterday, Cat," Joan said. "The edges of your bodice overlap."

"So?" Cat said. "Just tie the damned thing and be done with it. I'm sick of you two flapping around me."

"But Cat," Joan said as she knotted the stays, "if you're pregnant, you should be getting bigger."

Cat whirled and slapped Joan across her cheek. Joan reeled backward and tripped over me, sending the pan of ash flying from my hands.

"It doesn't matter if my belly grows yet," Cat snarled. "I'm young and I'm fit and perhaps the baby won't show at all!"

We all stared at her. It was the first time Cat had spoken of a baby. A bubble of foreboding formed in my stomach, thinking of all the things that could go wrong in childbearing. The baby catching its neck in a noose of umbilical cord. The mother bleeding to death minutes after birth. Childbed fever.

Then the dread burst like an abscess when I wondered whose baby it might be.

"Are you really pregnant, Cat?" Joan asked from the floor, a cloud of ash settling upon her.

"I haven't had my monthly courses yet," Cat said.

"When was your last one?" Alice asked.

"As if you don't know, Alice Restwold," Cat said. "You're probably keeping a daily diary of every time I bleed, pee, or fart."

Joan giggled.

"Oh, so a queen can't use rude words?" Cat said, a grin spreading across her face. "Just because I made an oath to be bonny and buxom in bed and at board doesn't mean I've signed away my tongue."

"Ah, but Cat, you wouldn't use those words at the table," Joan said.

"Certainly not!" Cat said. "But I am here with my dearest friends and you have no reason to divulge my secrets. Except for Alice, of course."

"I have no reason . . ." Alice began and then stopped, turning helpless eyes to Cat.

"Go, Alice," Cat said tiredly. "Go and tell the duke that I said 'fart.' Tell him I haven't started my cycle and I was supposed to seven days ago. Go and tell him all. And then tell him to go stuff himself and to stay off my back or I'll never produce an heir, just to spite him. Go and tell him to hang for all I care."

"I—I don't know what you mean," Alice said.

"You've been feeding the duke information about me since the moment you arrived in my apartments."

"No," she said. She stood, small and quiet, by the door. Not looking at any of us. She had always been one of us, but not part of us, and her separation now felt palpable.

"Yes, you have."

"Maybe you have it wrong, Cat," Joan said, "Like with me and my letter."

"Call me Your Majesty!" Cat shouted, and Joan cringed against the hearth. "And I don't have it wrong. What do you think brought her here?"

"Her family connections," I said quietly. Wanting things to stay the same. Wanting to depend on the family of girls. Wanting the circle to remain unbroken.

"Alice's family connection was the duke," Cat said. "You're the one who told me he was looking for a spy, Kitty. He's the one who asked me to take on Alice. I didn't need any great intellect to decipher that puzzle."

"Is it true, Alice?" I asked her. If anything, she appeared smaller than before. About to disappear.

She nodded. Looked up at me, desperately.

"I tell him what he wants to know and nothing more. When she sleeps. When the king visits."

"Intimate details of my life!" Cat shouted.

Joan whimpered.

"This is the royal court!" Alice cried. "The courtiers know the consistency of the king's shit. If the duke didn't hear about

it from me, he would hear it from someone else. He just wanted a reliable source."

"It's still spying, Alice," I said. "No matter how you dress it up."

"It's what got me here," she said. "And Joan got here through blackmail."

"I didn't do it!" Joan said. Tears were streaming down her face.

"It's still why you're here," Alice said. "Without secrets, none of us would be here. Not me, not you. Not Francis."

"You're right, Alice," Cat said in a low growl. "Without secrets, none of us would be here. Not even me."

She approached Alice steadily, primed for an attack.

"I know that, Cat," Alice said. "We all know that. I only tell him what he needs to know. He has to know first, or he'll send me back to my husband. I can't go back, Cat."

"Call me Your Majesty."

"Yes, Your Majesty," Alice whispered.

Cat smiled.

"Go on, then," she said. "Get out. All of you."

Alice was out the door almost before she threw the latch. Joan wiped her face with ash-covered hands, smearing streaks of tears and soot. She looked broken, walking out the door. I picked up the discarded clothes from the floor and stuffed them in an already overflowing chest before turning to leave.

"I'm so tired, Kitty," Cat said, quietly enough that I almost missed it.

"You need to rest," I said.

"Tired of everything," she said. "The gossip and lies and secrets and truth."

"Are you really pregnant, Cat?" I asked, unable to stop myself.

"How should I know? I've never been pregnant before. I don't know what it feels like."

She sounded shrill. Evasive.

"Because," I said, running my words together in my haste to begin the argument so it would be over sooner, "If you are, I think you should stop."

I left *seeing Culpepper* off the end of the sentence. But Cat heard it anyway.

"All we do is talk," she said.

"He's not a good person, Cat."

"This discussion is concluded."

If I told her, maybe she would put an end to it, and it would all be forgotten. No one would ever know how close we came to treason. Even I would never need know the baby's parentage. One more piece of information I could let go. One more secret none of us would have to keep.

"No!" I said. "No, it isn't."

"Kitty," she said, "You don't want to do this."

"I have to tell you. I saw him. I saw him . . ."

I couldn't say it. After so much time, I couldn't say the words.

"I don't want to know," Cat said. She stood, ready to leave.

"But you must." I found my voice. "I saw him raping a girl in the park. In Lambeth."

The words themselves caused me to shake. A blind veil of horror passed down over my eyes as the images flashed back through my mind.

"The King pardoned him," Cat said. "I don't know why you bring it up."

"What?" She knew? I shook my head. She couldn't know.

"He was pardoned. That must mean what he did was pardonable."

"He raped her!"

"That's what she said. She's a peasant! He's a gentleman usher. Emphasis on the word gentleman."

"But he did it, Cat. Don't you hear what I'm telling you? I saw him."

The woman on the ground, her hair tangled in the fallen branches and crumbling leaves. Culpepper's determined smile. The growl of his voice. Telling her she wanted it.

And suddenly it all came clear. That's what he told the king, too. What he told Cat. And they believed him. I had kept the truth hidden for so long it distorted, gave the appearance of falsehood.

"You don't believe me," I said.

"Kitty," she said pleasantly. "You're just jealous."

I could think of no response. No justifiable reaction to the queen of England telling me a deliberate falsehood.

"You should be happy for me," she said. "Because I have

everything I've ever wanted. Everything I need to make me happy. Pretty clothes. Beautiful jewels. And the company of a man my own age who understands *exactly* what I want."

"But do you love him?" I asked.

"No!" she replied. "And the sooner you realize you don't need love, Kitty, the happier you'll be. I'll tell you what you need. You need firm, strong thighs, hot lips, and hands that know what they're doing."

"And all you do is talk."

Her mouth hardened and she twisted one of her many rings.

"It happens in all friendships," she said. "When one girl gets a man. The others feel left out. Abandoned. Left behind.

"And now you've ruined things with your own lover. You've lost him. And you want me to do the same. You're lying to make Thomas Culpepper look bad. And that's just ugly."

She studied me critically. My clothes. My hair. My face.

"It makes you ugly."

Each word landed like a blow. I flinched. And I thought I saw her smile.

I WENT OUT INTO THE RAIN-SLICK COBBLED STREETS OF YORK. Corpulent clouds hung over the inns and merchants' shops. Carcasses dangled from hooks outside the butchers', headless and dripping blood. Living quarters crowded over the shops, open windows allowing waste, words, and laughter to spill out and over me.

I walked blindly. I wanted to walk forever, rain or no rain. I wanted to go home. But I had no home to go to.

"How did I get into this mess?" I asked myself aloud. A woman dressed in an unwashed skirt and tattered cap stepped around me and hurried away.

Not only was I feeling crazy, but I looked crazy, too. Like someone not to be believed.

I listened to Cat, I followed her, because it was easier than standing up to her. I let her tell me what to do. What to think. What to want.

But what did I want? Not this. Not a partial existence of lies and deceit and relationships so hollow they cracked like empty eggshells. I had thought that I wanted to be at court, like the games we played as children. But the reality was a life of doing

Cat's bidding. To her it was still just a game. And all of us Cat's pawns to play as she pleased.

I stumbled to my knees on the cobbles. The blow allowed a sob to escape me. The pain felt good, sharp and distracting.

"Let me help."

William Gibbon leaned over me, a hand outstretched to assist me to my feet. As always, he was dressed in the Duke of Norfolk's livery, his boots shiny beneath the mud spattered there. One eye was hidden by a shock of hair, the other wary. His touch sent a flutter of gooseflesh up my arm. And perhaps he held my hand just a little longer than necessary. But not long enough.

I looked around, like a person waking from a very real dream, and saw that I had walked three quarters of a circle and was now headed back to the queen's lodging.

William thought I was Cat's shadow. Her stooge. William was keeping company with Alice Restwold. But the sight of him felt like the first good thing to happen in this drenched and unhappy city on this long and arduous progress.

"Why so melancholy?" he asked. Then he looked at me. Really looked at me. Not the challenging gaze of Edmund, daring me to give in to him. Not the skeptical gaze of Cat, suspecting that I would turn her in. Not the prying gaze of Alice or the ingenuous gaze of Joan. The searching, concerned gaze of a real friend. A friend I couldn't have.

"I'm afraid I tend to think too much when I'm alone," I said. There was no way I could tell him the truth.

"Ah, but at court, you are never alone."

"So I never think, is that what you're saying?" I asked. I meant to sound flippant, teasing, but the words came out sniping and pinched.

"That isn't what I intended," he said, looking away, twin splotches of pink on his cheeks. "I've always known you could think for yourself."

"But that's not what you said," I blurted. "You said I was Cat's shadow."

"I said too much," he murmured.

So did I.

I didn't know how to tell him. How to fight my way around the lies and the hurt and the secrets and my own betrayal. How to stop the tyrannical compression of emotion in my chest.

"I just never imagined court would make you happy," he said. "Court and all that goes with it."

"Pretty clothes," I said, echoing Cat's words. "Beautiful jewels." The words crumbled and dissolved like wafers on my tongue, with none of the sweetness. Dust.

"Pretty clothes?" he asked. "I believe that is what the queen wants. Or at least that is what she believes she wants. I don't know about every girl."

"You're wrong," I said. "Every girl wants to feel pretty. Every girl wants to *be* pretty."

"I know a girl who used to wear hand-me-down gowns so unbecoming they would make the angels ugly, and yet she wore them with grace and beauty because of who she was."

I couldn't reply. Just over a year ago, that girl had been me. I suddenly, desperately wanted her back. Shabby clothes and all. The livery of the unloved. Except, maybe I had been loved. I wanted to believe that. Despite what Edmund had said.

"What happened, William?" I blurted. "To us?"

"Us?" The look of hope that crossed William's face bordered on desperation.

I wanted to reach for him. But I didn't know how. There was so much in the way. Cat. Edmund. Alice. Me.

"You said . . ." he didn't finish. His hand went to his cheek where I had slapped him, and something crushed the hope from his eyes.

"I didn't mean it," I spoke so quickly my words garbled in my mouth. "You told the truth. About so much."

The crooked smile stoppered me as effectively as a cork in a bottle. A sad smile.

"I was wrong to tell you what to do," he said.

"But since then I've made so many bad choices. I don't know what's right anymore. I hold so many secrets."

"Secrets just get in the way," he said. He'd said it before.

It wasn't by choice. It was by necessity. I waited on the queen. Living the lie that was life as a courtier. Living the dream. That had become a nightmare.

The membrane that held the rain at bay finally snapped and water fell from the sky like a bucket of slops thrown from an overhanging window. It shook us awake and back to reality. Back to the lie.

William tried to shield me from the rain with his cloak. Ever the gentleman. The action brought him close enough for me to feel the warmth of his body and breathe in his fragrance of pine resin and autumn leaves.

"Allow me to escort you," he said. "Before we become as waterlogged as the city of York itself."

We walked together, matching strides on the cobbles, not speaking. I didn't want to break the magic spell that had somehow brought us together under that cloak.

We arrived too soon at the abbey, the unroofed nave and cloister crowded with tents dragged low and heavy by the rain. We stood beneath the arch in the great north wall, sheltered from the worst of the weather.

"I'm glad you came out today," he said, and leaned closer. I thought, for a brilliant, glowing instant, that he might kiss me.

"Well met, Mistress Tylney," he said, the hope in his face masked. And with a quick bow, he was gone. Back to the duke. And his other responsibilities.

And I had to return to mine.

43

THE KING PROWLED THE GALLERIES AND COBBLED STREETS LIKE SOME kind of cornered predator, like the lions he kept in the Tower of London. Dukes and earls and ladies and council ministers fed off his agitated energy and spread it through the entire court like the plague.

I watched Cat's enemies gather in the darkness. The Seymours who had been displaced when the Howards came to power. Elizabeth Cromwell, her father-in-law beheaded the day Cat was married. The families of mistresses past and future.

We spent yet another rainy day endlessly sewing. I wondered at all the shirts we sewed. For the poor. For Cat's husband. How many shirts did he need? Or was it like the fairy tales, and the things unsewed themselves every night? Was she forever sewing the same shirt, like Sisyphus pushing the rock up a mountain for all eternity?

I sat in the corner of the too-hot room, unobtrusive and unnoticed. Weary of the false gaiety of the wall-hangings and draperies brought from London. Knowing that when we left, the dark paneling, the tiny windows, the yawning hearth would echo empty and ugly as the gossip of the Coven.

"The duke will never return to his wife," the countess said shrilly, speaking of her half-brother, the Duke of Norfolk. "She has become too shrill. Too demanding."

I wondered that her own husband didn't desert her.

"But I don't indulge in gossip," she continued, pretending integrity. "It harms the bearer as much as the subject."

The irony was lost on her audience.

Suddenly, Cat cringed and gasped. Everyone stopped mid-stitch and mid-sentence.

"Are you well, Your Majesty?" Jane asked.

"Quite well," Cat said, and sat up straighter, her face pale.

But seconds later she gasped again and curled up into herself.

I knew immediately what it was.

Her courses.

I jumped up to go to her, but she stilled me with a look.

"I have no need of you, Mistress Tylney," she said.

Someone tittered. The others bent their heads over their sewing, but their eyes flickered up to Cat every other heartbeat. Cat bit her lip and poked her needle at the hem of the shirt she worked.

Cat cringed again and a sound escaped her, the kind a wild animal makes when injured and afraid.

"You are not well, Your Majesty," Jane said, rising and going to her. "Let me help you to bed."

Cat said not a word but allowed Jane to assist her to the bedchamber.

"Something warm," Jane said over her shoulder to Joan. "And a cloth, please, Kitty?" she asked. "She will need only her chamberers."

I found the stash of special cloths and bundled one, moving swiftly. Joan pulled a hot stone from beside the fire and wrapped it in fur to place behind Cat's back.

Alice disappeared.

Cat curled up and tears slipped from the corners of her eyes.

"I thought I might be . . ."

She didn't finish. We all knew what she thought.

"God's blood!" A shout and the bang of the door to the outer chamber made us jump. "Where is my niece?"

The cackling of the Coven preceded a heavy knock at the bedchamber door. It flew open before I could reach it. The duke, red in the face, his small body swollen with self-importance and righteous vitriol, pushed past me.

"She is in bed, Your Grace," I said, falling into a curtsey.

"In the middle of the day?" he asked.

"She is unwell, Your Grace." Jane Boleyn stepped in. She, too, curtseyed, and then stood to face him. The duke, in his black velvet doublet with gold piping, looked like something the devil dragged in. Jane, in pale blue and yellow, stood placid and unmoving. He looked as shocked as I felt by her defiance.

"She is not so unwell that she cannot receive her uncle." The duke shouldered his way past Jane. Unable to cow her with his anger, he had to resort to physical bullying.

"It is a ladies' ailment, Your Grace," Jane said.

"I don't care if it's the plague itself."

Cat lay cocooned in crimson velvet. The bed, transported by cart all the way from Greenwich, stood high and wide, but the duke looked ready to drag her from it bodily.

"Do you not bow before your queen?" she said, her voice edged.

"You are menstruating," the duke said by way of reply.

"It is none of your business," Cat snapped.

"I make it my business."

"Then unmake it."

"You stupid girl!" he shouted. As if Cat had any choice to control it.

"Go away, uncle," Cat muttered and turned from him.

"If you don't get yourself with child, we will all be thrown out!" the duke blasted.

"It's not entirely up to me, you know," Cat said.

The duke leaned so close to her face that Cat turned away, corners of her mouth down and nose pinched.

"If you so much as breathe that in less loyal company, we will all lose our heads," he hissed, ignoring her expression. "And you will do what is required of you, or you will not have my loyalty much longer."

Cat laughed to the closed curtains on the other side of the bed.

"I'm a Howard," she said. "The Howards stick together."

"I helped put your cousins' heads on the block," the duke sneered. "If you think I will come to your rescue or welcome

you back to the fold after disgrace, you are very much mistaken. But you will earn the loyalty of every man at court if you put an heir in a royal cradle."

"By any means necessary?" Cat asked.

The duke's head snapped back. He gazed at her for a long moment. And stalked out of the room.

"Go away." Cat waved at us dismissively, as if shooing flies. "Leave me alone. All of you."

Jane followed me from the bedchamber in time to see the Coven still swirling and stirring in the wake of the duke. I took advantage of the confusion to pull her aside.

"She's going to use this as an excuse!" I said. The whole country wanted Cat to get pregnant to provide an heir for the king. I wanted her pregnant to provide protection from Culpepper.

Jane looked at me. She didn't nod or blink or speak. But I heard the faint tremolo of pearls in her pocket.

"How can you of all people just stand by? How can you actively participate?"

"What do you mean, me of all people?" she asked.

She was being purposefully obtuse, and it made me want to hurt her.

"You," I said, allowing my words to come out sharp as a new blade, "who watched your husband and his sister lose their heads over the exact same issue that you now facilitate."

"My husband was accused of incest," Jane said, casting a flickering glance about her. "I see nothing of that sort happening here."

"I thought you were a grown-up," I spat. "I thought you were a mentor."

Jane's expression changed for a fraction of an instant. Sadness. Pain. My words had done their work. Then the courtier was back.

"You have no call to be so blunt, Kitty," she said. "I have done nothing to you."

"No, and you've done nothing for Cat, either," I retorted. "Nothing good, anyway."

Jane stared at me with eyes the color of the withering fields beyond the city walls. The eyes of a woman who had seen great sorrow. Who saw terror and possibly madness in the future. It filled me with remorse.

"I'm sorry, Jane."

"Don't feel sorry for me, Kitty," she said, her voice so cold I almost flinched. "I'm not worth it."

As the ladies of the court nibbled over the gossip that Cat's pregnancy had come to naught, the king and his councilors plotted our journey south.

"Oh, Kitty, we're finally going home!" Joan pulled me into a little dance.

"Home?" I muttered. How could you have a home if all you did was move from place to place? Hampton Court to Windsor to Greenwich to Whitehall to every godforsaken castle in the North. York certainly wasn't home. But neither was London.

Cat recovered from her cramps, and her smile returned.

"There is still time for a coronation," she said. "I always wanted to be crowned in Westminster, anyway, not some hell-hole like York."

A huge final banquet was scheduled to see us off. The Court illustrating extravagance and power with one last hurrah. The people of York celebrating our impending absence.

Cat dithered endlessly over jewelry. She barked at the Coven for wearing hoods that hinted at a peak of gable. She chose and discarded five gowns.

"I've worn that one," she said. "That one has too high a neckline. That color orange makes me look ill."

The ladies clustered and twittered around her, their skirts brushing the floor in a rhythm like waves on a riverbank.

"I shall dress in my most girlish pink," Cat said finally. "All hope and innocence and freshness. He will forget the baby never happened, and remember why he married me."

When she had secured her hair with jeweled pins, she weighted her neck with the diamond collar—the C glittering at her throat.

"You are beautiful, Your Majesty," the members of the Coven cooed, and Joan nodded with eager abasement.

"Attend me," Cat said when she was ready, and the others followed her into the gallery, the flock that moved as one. I closed the door behind them.

I couldn't face the crowd. The press of flesh and fabric. The stink of meat and men. I wanted the scent of ripe apples, and a round, river breeze. Being alone in Cat's chambers would have to do.

I picked up Cat's gowns and folded them carefully, wondering why I bothered. She would just take them out again the next day. Or never wear them at all. But I stroked the soft fabrics and laid them gently to rest.

I cleaned the ash from around the fireplace, my hands stinging from the lye. I washed my hands in the basin and fetched fresh water for Cat to use when she returned.

I picked up Cat's discarded nightdress and hung it on a peg

on the wall near the window. The sunlight shone through the fine linen, bright white as if created from the sky itself. Not like we used to be, in our nightclothes worn ragged, stained yellow by sisters we rarely saw.

I twitched open the bed curtains, chasing dust and ash. I straightened the tangled furs and smoothed the linens. The bed was so large that even I had to stretch to reach the middle of it. I heard the door creak behind me.

"Ah, now that's how I like my ladies," Edmund Standebanke said. "Bent over and exposing the arse."

I spun around and backed up to the bed, wanting to hide the area mentioned. I didn't want him thinking proprietarily of my backside or anything else.

"You have not been invited," I said.

"That looked like an invitation to me."

I held my ground. But the room, with its crowded tapestries and heavy velvet curtains suddenly felt very small and close, and the heavy oak door, shut tight against the empty sitting room, looked very far away.

"Please leave the queen's bedchamber," I said. "It isn't seemly for a man to be in here."

"But I am not the first," he said. "However, I can be discreet. I *have* been discreet, and will continue to be so. Given the right enticements."

"I'm sure the queen could find you a better position," I stalled.

"I am happy where I am," he said.

"You wouldn't say anything." I faked a bravado I didn't feel.

"Not about Culpepper," he said with a grin. "No, he'd kill me. But I've heard that you have a penchant for late nights. For stolen wine and spiced wafers."

Someone had told. Someone had let slip the stories of our midnight revels.

"Who told you that?"

"A little bird."

"What else did you hear?"

"That you were not the only one to share Catherine Howard's bed."

He knew everything. As yet, Edmund Standebanke had kept quiet about his friend and the queen. But would he keep quiet about her past? And this was not only Edmund endangering us. This was someone else. Someone who had already proven to have a loose tongue. I had to dispel the rumor before it grew more legs.

"Did Alice tell you that?"

"No, Mistress Restwold has been too busy with the Duke of Norfolk's entourage, hasn't she?"

"Well," I said, trying to keep my voice from shaking, "gossip isn't the word of God."

"It came from a very reliable source."

"Then it didn't come from any of the girls who lived with us in Lambeth!" I laughed, but had to rub my palms on my skirt to stop them trembling and sweating.

"Oh, a disreputable lot, then?" he leered. "And your reputation as tattered as the rest of them."

"You can say nothing about me that anyone would mind," I said. "I am a mere servant here." I gestured at the room, showing the work I had done.

"It may not be you who needs my protection, but it is you who desires it."

"I don't know what you're talking about."

"The queen has been indiscreet," he stated.

"It is treason to speak ill of the queen," I reminded him, but my warning had little effect.

"Perhaps when Anne Boleyn first came to the throne," Edmund said. "But she proved that a queen can be ruined by injudicious actions and immodest gossip."

A chill ran through me.

"You wouldn't," I whispered.

He stepped closer still, so that I had to bend backward to avoid his barrel chest and prominent codpiece. He smelled of soot and stale sweat.

"What wouldn't I do?" he asked, his voice a purr. "Tell on your little friend? No. Probably not. The court is so boring without a queen and her ladies. But you don't really want to find out."

"You don't care about me. I don't think you even find me attractive." I immediately wanted to snatch back my words. As if I cared what this man thought.

"I never said that."

He just implied it.

"Why are you doing this?" I asked.

"Because I have no choice in the matter." He bent to kiss me.

That was what Culpepper had said, back in Lincoln. Edmund did whatever Thomas Culpepper asked. They were two sides to the same coin.

Repulsed, I wriggled myself backward and away from him, up onto the bed. But he followed, matching my movements. Covering my body with his.

"No!" I cried, my voice cut off as his weight pressed the air from my lungs.

"You cannot refuse," he said quietly, nuzzling me. "Not to save your reputation. Nor to save yourself for your fiancé, for he can give you no pleasure, of that I am sure."

I struggled, but he held me tighter.

"You know you want me," he said and lifted himself to stroke the embroidery where the neck of my bodice met my skin. I had. But I didn't anymore.

When he kissed me, I no longer felt the feverish rush that had overwhelmed my senses. His tongue forced its way between my teeth, wet and abhorrent. I pushed at him, but it only seemed to make him heavier.

So I bit him, the metallic taste of his blood following swift upon the grease of his lips. He cursed and moved to strike, but I rolled out from under him and slid off the bed to my knees, my skirts pulling up to expose my legs.

He reached for me, but seized only my snood, which ripped

at my hair as it came off. I cried out at the pain, the tiny hairs at my temples pulling tears to my eyes. I stumbled to my feet, but his other hand was too quick and snagged me around my waist.

"Let go!" I cried, and reached blindly for the door handle. He pulled me toward him, arms tightening. I laid my fingers upon the latch and pulled with all my might.

The door swung open with a lurch and slammed into the wall behind us. The movement sent us reeling backward, and Edmund dropped me to the floor, panting. Running footsteps approached.

"How dare you use the queen's rooms in such a disrespectful manner?"

Edmund pushed away from me, leaving me quaking at his feet.

"It was not without provocation, sir," he said.

"Hussy," the voice growled. I looked up to see one of the duke's gentleman pensioners. Next to him, Edmund stood nose-to-nose with William Gibbon.

Fear kicked me in the chest.

"It's not what it looks like," I said. Edmund's codpiece was askew. My skirts were hiked above my knees, sleeves coming loose, snood thrown to the floor and my hair tumbling around my face. I stood and tried to straighten the disarray. Miserable tears blinded me.

"She invited me." Edmund smirked.

"I did not!" I cried, anger replacing misery.

"She's been trying it on with me for weeks now," he continued.

I risked another glance at William and his gaze slid off mine like oil from water. If only I could speak to him alone. If only Edmund Standebanke had a modicum of honor.

"I did not invite this man to this room," I insisted.

The other man snorted. But I didn't care if he believed me.

"I stayed behind to tend to the queen's affairs," I said to William, my words tumbling over each other in their haste to be heard. "To tidy the room and straighten the bed."

"You are always at the queen's side," William replied, his voice even. "You would never be left behind."

"She stayed behind for me," Edmund declared. Enjoying himself. No matter what, he came out of the situation looking great. He was a man.

He was believable.

And what could I say? I hadn't told anyone I would stay behind. I doubted that anyone even noticed I was missing. It looked exactly as Edmund made it out.

"I wished to be alone," I admitted, looking William directly in the eye, willing him to believe me.

"With me," Edmund agreed. Smug bastard. I couldn't even look at him. I couldn't let him see the irreparable damage he was doing. He would consider it a triumph.

"A word of advice," the other man said, winking at Edmund. "Keep out of the queen's rooms when you're looking for romance."

I could have screamed with fury.

"And what are you doing here?" Edmund puffed up his chest as if intending to push William over with it.

"We heard a disturbance," William said. "And thought we should investigate."

I risked a glance at him, but his face was as blank as a new piece of parchment. Doing his duty. Blocking me out. Forgetting about me.

"Well, heaven forbid I interfere with the men of the Duke of Norfolk," Edmund said, his voice dripping with sarcasm. He slithered out of the door with a flourish as if bowing to William and the other man, though the move was more show than substance.

"There is obviously nothing for me here," he added, throwing me a look of contempt, and strode away up the gallery to the banquet.

I struggled for breath in relief of his absence, grasping the bedpost for support.

"Are you well, Mistress Tylney?" William asked, hollow courtesy emptying his words of meaning.

"I am innocent." I tried not to sob. But was I? Guilt, like secrets, multiplied at court. I *had* wanted Edmund. Once.

"Any maid who allows a man into her bedchamber cannot be as innocent as you wish us to think," the other man laughed.

William turned scarlet.

"From what I hear, the queen's chamberers are not as pure as Christmas snow," the man continued. His eyes traveled down my bodice.

"Cease, man," William said. I turned to him but he did not acknowledge me. "Let us escort the lady to the banquet."

I didn't want to go to the banquet. I didn't want to have anything to do with the court anymore. I hated the drudgery and the tedium. I hated the people and their superficiality. Most of all, I hated the lies. But I shoved my hair into place and brushed down my skirts. I was not going to let Edmund Standebanke win.

"Lady," the other man muttered under his breath, but I ignored him and left the room. I walked with my head up, looking neither right nor left and they both fell into step behind me. I quailed at the thought of all the eyes that would be upon me when I entered the hall. Eyes that would take in my dishevelment. Ears that would already have heard the rumors of my illicit misdeeds in the queen's chambers.

But when I entered the banqueting hall, all eyes were focused on Cat. And though she pretended to pay them no heed, the attention made her more radiant. She glowed like a candle flame, and all the men in the room were moths drawn to it.

So even Cat didn't notice me as I stood in the grand entranceway. Cat, who had known my thoughts and feelings and secrets for almost ten years. Even Cat didn't know that the man she chose had just forced himself on me in her bed. I stared, my wide eyes dry. Even as my world fell apart, she remained its focus, and that of everyone in the room.

A cough at my elbow reminded me of William and the other

liveried man behind me. I turned and William lowered his eyes. He had been watching me.

And I'd missed it.

"We will leave you now," the other man said and they walked away.

William didn't speak a word.

I was a much more subdued court that followed the rather convoluted path back to London. Autumn clouds hung low in the sky, tinting everything drab. Mud-colored leaves drooped on the trees and the harvested fields looked like the stubble of a man's unshaven face. The people no longer clamored on the roads to see us but kept to their houses, battening down for the winter, as if they knew a storm was coming.

Alice practically lived with the duke's traveling entourage. Cat put up a bright façade, shrouded in jewels. Jane maintained her quiet steadfastness. Joan scampered around the outskirts like a lost lapdog. I did my job and kept my mouth shut. I avoided Edmund. And William. And everyone. I was alone in the middle of the most crowded court in Christendom.

At Hull, Culpepper sported a new jeweled cap. An expensive one.

"What's that for?" I heard Francis growl at him in a corner of the banqueting hall.

"To keep my head warm." Culpepper grinned. "Reward for services rendered."

I had seen Jane with it the day before.

And then one night in early October, in some castle that seemed as much of a blur as the rest—it could have been Ampthill, it could have been Kettleby—Jane came back from one of her reconnaissance missions and cornered me.

"The queen needs help this evening."

"With what?" I asked, unable to control my insolence.

"She needs you."

Cat always needed me. To steal a key for her. Lie for her. Keep her secrets.

"What if I don't want to help?"

"I'm afraid it has nothing to do with what you want, Katherine Tylney," Jane said. "You have no choice in the matter. You are here as the queen's servant, and as her servant you will comply with her wishes. Not your own."

I couldn't walk away from this. Life with the queen was like the marriage I'd always feared. My time, my thoughts, my life were not my own. I was completely beholden to another. A possession.

"Fine."

"You will invite Edmund Standebanke to the outer rooms," Jane began.

The very thought made me want to run. How dare Cat ask this of me? But of course, Cat didn't know. She had never asked. She had never noticed.

"No."

"It is your duty."

"It is my duty to make the queen's bed. It is my duty to take charge of her gowns and shifts and laces. It is my duty to clean up after her and tend to her needs. It is *not* my duty to consort with that man."

"You say it is your duty to tend to the needs of the queen," Jane said reasonably. "This evening she needs someone to provide a distraction."

"No," I said. "And I will talk to Cat about it."

I barged my way into her bedchamber and slammed the door behind me.

"You can't make me do this," I said without preamble. "I won't do it."

Cat looked up. She sat by the fire. Alone, for once.

"I provide a perfectly respectable, devilishly handsome man to you at your disposal and you do nothing," Cat said coolly.

Devilish, indeed. My skin burned with anger at the injustice. But I remained silent. I had no need, no wish for my story to become gossip. Or a weapon to be used against me.

"Why is that?" she asked.

"He is not respectable," I said. "He is not honorable."

"Perhaps you are not that way inclined," Cat said, her face as pinched as her words. "Perhaps you miss the evenings in the maidens' dormitory. Perhaps you miss sharing a bed with me, with Joan. You prefer the company of women. The bodies of

women. Perhaps *that* is why Standebanke hasn't got you into bed yet."

I stared at her. If Cat's words escaped that room, I would be thrown from court, my engagement nullified, my prospects eradicated, my future corrupted.

"You shouldn't say things that aren't true, Cat."

"It doesn't matter if it's true," Cat sneered. "Once it's uttered, people believe it. Just like they believe that Archbishop Cranmer has a wife, or Anne Boleyn had sex with her brother, or Catherine of Aragon consummated her marriage to her first husband. Once it's said, you can never shake it."

She let her words hang in the air. Everything stopped moving, trapped in the amber of fear.

"You never had a boy visit you in the maidens' chamber, did you?" she asked.

She knew I hadn't.

"I never met the right one," I said. Thinking of William. I met him too late.

"The *right* one?" she repeated. "*Any* one would do. I for one didn't want to go into a marriage not knowing what to expect. And finding someone handsome enough, with decent *equipment*, wasn't difficult."

Her statement brought to mind a long-past conversation.

"What about rich?" I asked. "And powerful?"

"That came later," she said. "The maidens' chamber was all about *fun*. I didn't want to die without ever having lived."

I toyed for a moment with the idea of telling everything I knew. Of being the one in power for once. Extricating myself from the web Cat had spun around us. I could go to the king with the information *I* had. Or maybe not the king, for the thought of his towering rage made me shiver. But a priest, perhaps. Or Archbishop Cranmer.

"You couldn't get away with it, Kitty," Cat said confidently. "Once I got through with you, no one would believe a word you said." She still had an uncanny knack for reading my thoughts. When it suited her.

"You and Joan will sleep in my chambers tonight," she instructed, as if knowing I could no longer argue. "The other ladies will be excused. Joan and Jane will be in the withdrawing room. And you will remain with Edmund Standebanke in the outer chamber as a decoy. From what I've heard, you two have already caused quite a commotion. Another public display cannot hurt you too much."

She knew. The entire court knew. Edmund's version. I would never be able to tell the truth. Because it is human nature to believe the first story heard, and not its rebuttal.

"I could pretend to stay up sewing," I said feebly.

"You're meeting your lover," Cat said. "It must appear authentic."

I didn't know why they were creating such an elaborate ruse over this particular meeting. They never had before. It seemed to me that Cat had been positively reckless for previous meetings.

But I followed the plans. I didn't ask how Culpepper would enter the narrow bedchamber, high in the castle wall. I didn't want to know. Cat locked the door behind her and I remained in the fusty antechamber, alone and anxious. I would tolerate Edmund's presence. I would sit with him. It would be the last time.

But when the knock came, I opened the door to Anthony Denny, who stood, fully dressed, in the doorframe. He had the grace to avert his eyes from sight of me in my nightclothes.

"The queen is abed," I said.

"And why aren't you?" he asked.

"I came to answer the door," I stuttered, my blush sure to give everything away.

"She stayed up to meet with me, sir," Edmund said from the gallery behind Denny, and emerged, grinning like a gargoyle into the light.

"Well, the king wishes the queen's company," Denny said with a cough.

"She is asleep," I murmured.

Denny strode through to the withdrawing room door and turned the latch, but it didn't open. I held my breath.

"It is locked," he said quietly, one eyebrow raised. "Does that not seem odd?"

He knocked softly, and not a sound emerged from room beyond. Sweat ran hot and icy down my back and between my breasts.

Then the door opened a pinch, and Jane peeked out. If

she was surprised to see Denny there, her eyes gave nothing away.

"The queen is indisposed," she told him.

"Then I shall wait." Denny went to a stool by the fire and sat down. No one said no to the king. Not even Cat.

"Why don't we give Denny a show while the others sort out the queen?" Edmund whispered in my ear. His words slid down my neck and nipped bitterness down my spine.

"For the sake of this farce, I will tolerate your company." I made sure my tone implied I would tolerate nothing more.

"I promise I won't bite." Edmund reached up to stroke my mouth with his thumb.

"I don't."

His thumb stopped moving as he tried to stare me down, but I somehow found the steel to keep from looking away. He moved his hand to my waist.

"Still," he said, "I suppose we should act as friends."

"Acting is a skill every courtier learns early."

"Why have you become so harsh?" he asked. "Why are you no longer the pliable little girl I met when you first arrived? The one overwhelmed by the gaudiness of the dresses and the extravagance of flirtation?"

"I have lived at court for a year," I answered. "And now know that the doublets and bodices hide moral disfigurement. That flirtation is merely a warped sense of possessiveness. That love and truth have no place here. You and your friend have taught me well."

"Perhaps," he said with a little smile, his hand on my waist pulling me to him. "But you still have more to learn. Come closer."

His eyes left mine to check on Denny. Looking for an audience.

"Get off," I said, sickened by it all. By being forced to spend time with Edmund. By having it be a show for the entertainment and titillation of others. By losing William. I pushed on Edmund's chest and he rocked backward, nearly losing his balance.

"Feisty," he said, with an unctuous grin at Denny.

I hit him again. I suddenly didn't care for duty, for friendship.

"Shut up!" I shouted. "Why can you not see that my desire to be rid of you has nothing to do with feistiness or women's problems or fear of being caught, but has everything to do with you!"

Denny stifled a laugh in the corner, turning it into a discreet courtier's cough.

At that moment, the bedchamber door opened, and Jane stepped out.

"The queen," she announced, and the men bowed low.

"Are you to escort me to my husband?" Cat asked Denny.

"At your service," Denny said. "Standebanke, leave your paramour, we have an important duty to perform."

I smiled at Denny gratefully, and he nodded in return. A real gentleman. Probably the only one I'd met at court.

After they left, Jane rushed back into the bedchamber and threw open the door to the garderobe.

"Get out!" she hissed. "Get out and leave this place at once."

Culpepper slunk like a hound from the little room. Not with his tail between his legs, but like a dog who had just picked a choice bone from the table.

"I cannot leave now," he remarked. "Surely there are guards at the door who will note my departure."

"Then you shall have to exit through the only available portal," Jane said, and indicated the garderobe.

"Far too mucky," Culpepper sniffed. "I could hide beneath the bed until my lady returns."

"No, Master Culpepper," Jane declared. "You must leave at once. I insist."

"Oh, you insist, do you, Lady Rochford?" Culpepper swaggered up to her. "And what will you do if I don't comply? Call the guards? How will you explain my presence to them? In the queen's bedroom, smelling of the queen?" He smiled wolfishly—hungry, lean, and carnivorous.

"Yes, she insists," I said, surprising myself as much as the others. Joy and horror rose within me in equal measure. I stilled my quaking limbs and felt a surge of strength.

"Ah, the whipped kitten speaks," Culpepper scoffed.

"The kitten has grown claws," I said, and stepped between him and Jane. We stood eye-to-eye, exactly the same height, though his build was much more masculine, heavy and tight

in the shoulders. I was no match for him, but I didn't care. I was tired of being bullied.

"I quake in my boots."

"So you should," I replied. "You've made my life hell, from the very first second I laid eyes on you. But no more. Get out."

He shrugged noncommittally and threw a conspicuous grin at Joan, who stood in the corner. She smiled hesitantly, and he turned back to me.

"Edmund told me you were a servile mollycoddle," he said. "He said you may not be beautiful but would make a nice auxiliary, available as necessary."

Each word stung but didn't surprise. I stood still as stone and didn't react. I couldn't let him see that he hurt me. I couldn't back down.

"But I think, on closer inspection," he continued, salivating for the kill, "that perhaps he was wrong. You have not the queen's vivacity or elegance, but you certainly have her spark. And therein lies passion. Perhaps not beautiful, but hardly frigid."

He stepped closer. One hand reached up, and I willed myself not to recoil. He rested it on the back of my head, firm and unyielding as a wall.

"And those eyes," he said. "That see all and judge accordingly."

I held my breath, unable to bear the carrion stink of his words. But I stared him down, letting him see my judgment of him.

"Perhaps you should be *my* auxiliary." He brought his face so close to mine his features blurred and shadowed, and all I saw were his hooded eyes. His lips moved on mine like the feathers of a vulture. "For when the queen is unavailable."

I blinked, and a malicious glee entered his eyes. Suddenly, he stepped away, and I nearly fell, like a tree on an undercut riverbank, my footing lost and nothing before me but rushing water.

"But then again," Culpepper announced to the room. "Perhaps you'd rather *watch*."

He strode to Joan in the corner, pulled her whimpering into his arms and mashed his mouth to hers.

He knew that I saw. Edmund must have told him what I'd seen. He knew I'd done nothing. That I would continue to do nothing. He kneaded Joan's bodice and her hands fluttered weakly, her face screwed up in revulsion and shame.

"Stop," I pleaded weakly.

"Yes," Culpepper dropped Joan unceremoniously on the floor amongst the rushes. "Perhaps I will. The company grows wearing, and I think I shall seek more stimulating acquaintances."

He disappeared into the garderobe, and with a thunk, he was gone.

"Back with his own kind," Jane said. "The shit."

Joan began to cry, and I sat down beside her. She put her

head in my lap and I leaned back against the bed that smelled of the ancients, and I stroked her hair.

"Why does she do it?" Joan asked. "How can she?"

Allow Culpepper to touch her. Commit treason. Put us all in danger. Treat us as though we're worthless.

"I don't know."

WE RETURNED TO HAMPTON COURT AT THE END OF OCTOBER, exhausted and out of sorts. It wasn't home. I wasn't even sure what home felt like. Or if I'd ever had one. But after weeks of sleeping in other people's rooms, returning to the palace by the Thames felt almost comfortable. The chambers had been scrubbed in our absence, the windows opened to let the river breezes through. New rushes were scattered on the floors, and the bed linens all smelled of rosewater and lavender.

Everything felt fresh. There were no secret passageways to the queen's apartments. There were no reasons for Edmund to visit. Even the HA HA in Anne Boleyn's gateway looked more scarred and worn. The past was past.

On the first of November, King Henry demanded that a prayer of thanksgiving be said in the churches throughout the country. We heard it in the chapel royal near the king's apartments. The rising sun slanted through the stained glass window, the ghostly figures of Katherine of Aragon and Cardinal Wolsey pale beside the golden glassy monarch in his early years. And the present king himself spoke words of benediction that rang off the vaulted ceiling, painted blue and studded with gold stars.

I render thanks to Thee, O Lord, that after so many strange acci-
dents have befallen my marriages, Thou hast been pleased to give me a
wife so entirely conformed to my inclinations as her I now have.

He turned to smile at her, the light from the window reflecting dramatically off the silver that striated his hair. She kissed
her wedding ring and beamed at him.

I stood against the wall, wedged between Alice and Joan.
By craning my neck, I could just see the king in the royal pew,
elevated above us all. I watched him throughout the ceremony.
An old man, the excesses of his youth catching up to him. But
totally assured that everything would always go his way. In
that, at least, he and Cat were a perfect match.

The service ended and the king rose slowly, lifting himself with his arms, shoulders straining with the weight. He
stumbled and dropped his prayer book, which an usher
retrieved for him, as well as the piece of parchment that had
fallen from its leaves. The king scoured the room to see if anyone acknowledged his weakness. I looked away and watched
the tide of courtiers hustling through the doors below the bal-
cony, all of them eager to catch the king as he exited through
his private door.

Above them, the king hadn't moved. He stood in the same
place, one hand on the back of his chair, reading a letter, his
face the same color as the parchment. His eyes, wild with
some unconcealed emotion, looked up and this time caught
me. For an instant, he searched my face as if looking for an
answer to a desperate question, but I lowered my gaze as any
courtier would. And when I raised my eyes again, he was gone.

A week went by, the palace surprisingly quiet. Everyone was exhausted from the progress. The Coven picked up where they had left off, sewing and gossiping, though the gossip remained tired and stale, tongues as idle as our hands.

"There is word of the Protestants in Germany," Lady Howard began.

"Don't make me yawn." Cat rolled her eyes. "Next!"

"There are accusations of piracy in Ireland," Isabel Baynton said.

"Piracy?" Cat asked. "Sounds daring."

"You have an interest in pirates, Your Majesty?" Elizabeth Seymour, Lady Cromwell, said quietly.

"Only on an intellectual level," Cat explained. "What drives a man to do such a thing?"

"The dowager duchess might know," Lady Cromwell said. "I believe one of her gentlemen pensioners left her service to try his hand at it."

Francis.

Cat and I exchanged a look, and she shook her head ever so slightly.

"Actually, I think pirates are dull, too," she said. "What else is there to talk about? Perhaps we should plan a banquet. A celebration."

"The king may not be up for any festivities," Jane Wriothesley said. She was normally quiet—or absent—so her words came as a bit of a shock.

"Why?" Cat said. "Is he ill?"

The ladies all shook their heads, but none of them spoke. Most of their husbands or lovers were in the constant presence of the king. If anyone knew, they would.

Their silence was worse than their words.

"Kitty," Cat said, turning to me, her face pale, "would you please go down to the king's apartments and ask after his health?"

I stepped out into the long gallery. Courtiers studded the room at intervals, some clustered by the windows, others huddled in shadows. Whispering stopped as I passed.

I moved between the knots of people, skirts swishing against me, swords knocking in their scabbards. I had just cleared a thicket of clergymen when I encountered William. We stood so close we almost touched.

"What are you doing here?" I asked.

The courtier's mask fell away and I easily read the expression that replaced it. Hurt. Betrayal.

"Business of the duke's," he said, securing the mask firmly back in place.

"I thought the duke was at home." He had left us during the progress back to London. Alice had been moping. I had felt a mixture of pain at William's absence and relief that I didn't have to relive that night in York on a daily basis.

"He was recalled to London," William said. "On . . . important business."

His manner stopped me. Businesslike, dissembling, his every emotion obscured. It was so unlike him that my heart

311

broke for what felt to be the thousandth time. Clearly he didn't want to have anything to do with me.

"You come only for the duke's business."

"I work for him."

"And I serve the queen," I said. "So it is my duty to go to the king's apartments."

He moved to allow me safe passage between him and a group of pages. My stomach twisted.

"You might reconsider your misplaced loyalty," he said quietly. So quietly no one around us could have heard.

"Misplaced?" I said. "Who are you to be telling me my loyalty is misplaced? You who live in the pocket of the most self-serving man at court?"

He looked as if I had slapped him again.

"I'm just saying," he murmured, his voice broken and pitched so low I had to lean close to hear him, his breath on my cheek, "take care of yourself, Kitty."

He laid a hand on my shoulder. He looked directly into my eyes, his own pleading, not hidden, for once, behind the shock of sandy hair.

"I have to," I said, suddenly angry. "No one else will."

William hadn't taken my side with Edmund. He'd assumed the worst.

I hurried away, seething, and didn't look back. Take care, indeed.

The gallery ended in the king's apartments, and another stretched away to the chapel royal. Clusters of petitioners and

hangers-on crowded the processional gallery the king would take to his evening prayers. Anthony Denny answered the outer door and gave me a tight smile.

"I've come to inquire about the king's health," I said.

"The king is indisposed."

"The queen is concerned," I said. "She has not seen him these four days."

"The king will send word."

He wouldn't even look at me.

"What should I tell the queen?" I asked.

"Tell her . . . to be patient."

He looked at me finally. Into my eyes.

"The king," he said, "will leave Hampton Court shortly."

He waited a beat, nodded, and then shut the door in my face.

A cold, thick feeling came over me like quicksilver in my veins. I wanted desperately to run away. Everyone was acting so strangely: the most indiscreet ladies silent; the most silent, speaking; the duke recalled on important business; William speaking of my "misplaced loyalty"; the king departing without even a word to Cat.

My heart raced, but I ignored its pounding. I couldn't give in to the fear that had lain dormant for so many months. I couldn't make a slip, because the very thing I had been afraid of might be coming true.

I tried to affect Jane's smooth, gliding walk back to the queen's rooms. I tried to remain calm. But as I wove my way between cardinals and cupbearers, I became aware that I

passed through the rooms no longer unnoticed. Rather, I felt everyone's eyes upon me.

I hastened to the queen's withdrawing room and sketched a halfhearted curtsey, causing the Coven to twitter and cluck. I didn't care.

"Sir Anthony says to be patient," I told Cat, knowing every ear waited to twist my words.

I willed her to understand, to read my mind as she always had, but she just nodded. I waited, gripping my own fingers with knuckles so pale they yellowed. She looked up.

"He leaves this afternoon," I said.

"The king?" Dawning understanding drained her face of color. I nodded helplessly.

"Where is he going?" she asked the room. The ladies appeared not to listen, intent on their stilled needles and silent gossip.

"I want to know what's going on!" Cat shouted. "I want to know when I can expect things to get back to normal!"

She pushed past me and out the door. The Coven all stood, staring. Lady Howard rocked from one foot to the other, looking for all the world like a heron feeling along the bottom of a muddy pond. I followed Cat to the door.

"Your Majesty," one of the guards said, standing in her way.

"I go to see my husband." She stepped around him.

The guard reached out and laid a hand on her arm.

"How dare you?" She rounded on him.

The guard's visage opened wide. He couldn't speak, but he

didn't let go. The room fell silent, all its occupants shuffling against the walls like drifts from the river.

Cat wrenched her arm from his grasp and turned to run down the gallery.

"Henry!" she cried, a note of hysteria rising like waves of heat in summer. "Henry!"

Her voice broke as two of the guards began to run after her. She turned her head, her hair streaming across her face. She stumbled.

"Cat!" I cried and started forward. Another guard pushed me back.

"Henry!"

The shriek raised the hackles on my neck. Two guards had her by the arms, pulling her backward. She struggled, kicking, looking like a prisoner, not a queen. No one moved to help her. Gawkers and gossipers melted into the sharply carved paneling.

The guards dragged her to the apartments, the ladies shrinking back as though retreating from contagion.

Jane Boleyn stood rigid by the bedchamber door, eyes wide like those of a mouse about to be pounced upon.

"Kitty?" she gasped, grabbing my arm, paper-thin skin covering a vise-like hand. The other clicked the pearls in her pocket.

"Lady Rochford," I said. "See if you can get the kitchen to send up a posset. The queen is unwell."

She nodded, the bland courtier's façade restored, and hus-

tled the rest of the ladies out of the bedchamber. I closed the door behind them.

Cat curled up into a ball at the foot of the bed, knees to chest and elbows to ankles. Her body shook with sobs. I sat down near her and watched her cry. There was nothing I could say.

"Oh, Kitty!" she cried. "Why doesn't he give me a crown? Why doesn't he visit? What have I done?"

I could think of several things, but she looked so small in that big bed, like a child hiding from a thunderstorm. I couldn't say them.

"Cat?" I whispered.

"I never wanted to be queen," she sobbed.

I almost laughed. Cat had always wanted to be queen. Queen of the maidens' chamber. Queen of Misrule. But she hadn't wanted this.

I let her cry until no more tears came.

"I couldn't stop," she finally whispered. "He wouldn't let me."

Her words hung in the silence that followed them like spiders suspended from the ceiling. They could creep away unobserved or continue down their silken strings and bite the unwary.

"Culpepper?" I asked, inviting the spiders down.

She turned away from me and curled up again. I waited for her to tell me that Culpepper had seduced her once and black-mailed her into further meetings. I waited for her to say she

wanted to extricate herself from him, but that he forced her, held her prisoner.

"He didn't force me," she said. "But I couldn't say no."

Trapped. By herself. Not by blackmail.

"Don't tell," she said, so quietly the words could have come from the very air around us. "Deception is my only defense."

"I won't."

"It was all him," Cat said, and paused. "And Jane."

"Jane Boleyn?" I asked, incredulous. The woman who did nothing but what was asked of her?

"Yes," Cat said slowly. "Yes, see, she pushed me into it. She suggested it. To get me pregnant. She carried messages for us."

"No, Cat," I said.

"But she did," Cat said. "Even you saw. She carried messages. She found hiding places."

"She did it because you *asked*." A shudder of revulsion ran through me. Cat couldn't really be thinking of blaming Jane for all of it.

"No one has to know that."

"*You* know it!" I cried. "How could you do something like that to another person?"

"Because she didn't stop him. She could have stopped him."

"It wasn't *him* she couldn't stop, Cat, it was *you*. You were so set on this doomed romance that you wouldn't listen to reason. I tried to stop you. Maybe Jane did, too."

"She didn't," Cat interrupted. But I wasn't finished.

"So because she couldn't stop you it's her fault? That is the ultimate injustice!"

Cat bolted up from the bed, a tiny tower of fury and self-aggrandizement.

"You know what injustice is, Kitty? It's a seventeen-year-old girl being bound to a fifty-year-old dying man!"

"We knew that all along, Cat."

"That didn't make it any easier," she said, desperate tears clinging to her eyelashes. "I can't die for this."

But we both knew she could.

"We don't know what it is yet," I assured her hollowly. "We don't know why the king is leaving. Perhaps he *is* ill."

"He's not ill, Kitty," Cat said. "And we're dead."

THE PALACE TOOK ON AN AIR OF SILENT EXPECTANCY FOR THE NEXT twenty-four hours.

The king left with his entourage for dinner. In Westminster. The entire Privy Council went with him. And stayed all night.

Francis Dereham was missing. Rumors of his involvement in Irish piracy continued to circulate. Culpepper disappeared as well. Someone said he had gone hawking. But I didn't know if I dared believe it.

Cat's apartments quietly emptied as well. Lady Cromwell grew ill. Some of the others were called away on urgent business.

The Coven stayed.

"The Howards stick together," Cat said with a tight smile, nodding her head in the direction of the older ladies in the corner. Sitting like statues. Not sewing. Not gossiping. Just staring into the fire.

"The rest are like rats," I muttered.

"This ship is not sinking!" Cat shouted, causing everyone to jump. "Kitty, Joan, Jane. Come with me."

I searched the room for Alice—the last piece of the circle—but she was missing.

Cat led us into the more public receiving room. It was usually crowded with councilors and servants but now disturbingly empty, as if we had woken in the middle of the night.

"Dance!" Cat commanded.

"There isn't any music, Cat," Joan said, bemused.

Cat made a strangled shriek of frustration.

"When will you stop calling me by that name?" she cried, making Joan wince and stammer an apology.

"We never had music in the maidens' chamber," Cat said. "And we danced all the time."

Her voice fell to a whisper. As if the effort to speak was too great. The weight of memories too much.

I took Jane's hands.

"Something lively, yes?" I asked.

Jane nodded. I started a country dance. One that didn't involve intricate foot work or careful interaction. One that didn't require courtly etiquette. Jane tried to keep up, but her face remained vacant, as if something had pulled away inside her.

Cat grabbed Joan and kept pace. Joan began to hum, off-key as always, stomping her right foot to keep time, the tune growing breathy as they whirled about the empty room.

I turned once more, skirts swinging, and there before me stood Archbishop Cranmer.

He filled the door, tall and wide. The white sleeves of his cassock billowed from his shoulders. His face was bottom-heavy, with small eyes holding little humor. The dust settled around

us as the others froze. I thought I heard Jane whimper.

Behind the Archbishop stood the Duke of Norfolk, more menacing than I had ever seen him. The duke wasn't shouting. He wasn't purple in the face or sweating anger. He was silent, his forehead creased with choler.

Trouble had arrived at our door.

"We have come with some questions to put to the queen," Cranmer said.

Behind him, the duke rolled his eyes up to the ceiling and then closed them tightly, as if sending a silent prayer to the heavens.

"You may enter, Archbishop," Cat replied. Her voice raised a notch in pitch. "We were just dancing."

The men stepped in, and Cranmer motioned for me to close the door behind them. I did so, and stood against the crack, feeling the whistle of wind from the cold gallery up my back.

"The time for dancing is over," said Cranmer.

The duke made a strangled sound like a dog choking on a fish bone.

"I have some questions about your secretary," Cranmer continued.

Cat looked up at him, her expression betraying nothing. Cranmer went on.

"One Francis Dereham, I am told?"

"Is he in some sort of trouble?" Cat asked. "I have not seen him for a number of days."

"He is in London."

"Well if you have any communication with him, I should like you to tell him I resent his disappearance and neglect of his duty."

"Yes," Cranmer said, more cough than speech.

The duke clenched his fists.

"It has come to my attention," said Cranmer, "that perhaps you knew Master Dereham prior to his post here."

The duke shuffled his feet. The rest of us remained as still and silent as the furniture.

"Yes." Cat lifted her chin and smiled engagingly. "He was a retainer in my grandmother's employ. At Norfolk House." The last words pointed. Directed at her uncle. Claiming kinship. Claiming support.

The duke ignored her.

"Is that all?" Cranmer asked.

"Yes, of course," said Cat. "Though I believe he went to sea before I came to court."

"You knew him in no other capacity?"

"How many times do I have to say it?" Cat snapped. "I didn't know the man well. My grandmother employed him. My grandmother asked me to find him a place in my household." She paused. "The Dowager Duchess of Norfolk asked for my patronage as queen." Playing her trump card.

"My source says you knew him quite well," Cranmer's face showed not an inkling of suspicion, not a symptom of sympathy. Not a fragment of consideration for Cat's rank and influence.

"And who is this source?" Cat said imperiously. "Have you spoken with the man in question?"

"At length."

Those two words knocked the life out of her. She disappeared into herself; her eyes remained open and clear, but completely absent of any human intelligence or emotion.

"I see," she breathed.

And then she collapsed. Her skirts flumed around her in a cloud of silk. Her hood tilted to one side, pulling with it streamers of auburn hair. Jane knelt down beside her and drew Cat into her lap. Cat clung to her like a sailor to a piece of wreckage.

The Archbishop stared, horrified, at the cluster of human arms and legs on the floor before him. The duke cringed and then arranged his face to a look of horror and surprise. I couldn't move. Not out the door, nor to the knot of loyalty on the floor.

Cranmer waited for an eternity before turning and approaching me.

"The queen may keep her privy keys," he said.

A candle of hope lit the back of my mind.

"Her ladies are dismissed," he said, extinguishing it. "I suggest she keep to her rooms. I shall send some men to inventory and remove all her jewels."

At this, Cat set to sobbing and wailing more loudly still, her voice high and keening, as if at the death of a loved one.

Cranmer didn't move.

"Please allow me to exit," he said quietly.

I realized I still stood at the gap where the door met the wall. The handle pressed into the small of my back, my hand gripping it so tightly I could no longer feel my fingers.

"Get out of the way, you stupid girl," the duke blustered, and pushed me aside. He ripped the door open himself and swept from the room in a lather of petulance and fear. Cranmer nodded once to me and followed.

The Coven went quickly. The ship was obviously sinking now. They must have heard everything through the withdrawing chamber door. They gathered nothing but their skirts and fled Cat's rooms for their own.

"Oh, mercy," I heard the duchess mutter. "There will be a divorce and she will be sent back to me."

Cat remained on the floor, buffeted by the ebbing tide of retreat, half hidden in Jane's skirts. Joan watched the others leave, panic corroding her soft features. But then resolve hardened them, and she turned back to stroke Cat's hair.

"What did he say?" Cat said after I had closed the door.

"Cranmer?" I asked.

"No, you idiot, Francis. What could he tell them?"

We stared at her. The remnants of her tears still streaked her face. Her hood still lay askew on her head, giving her the look of a demented patient of Bedlam. But her eyes were hard and calculating.

"Well?"

"I guess he could tell them everything," Joan said slowly.

"Everything?" Cat shouted. She pushed Joan away and stood up.

Francis knew a great deal. Knew Cat's past. Knew of her prior interest in Culpepper. How much more did he know?

"Well, he could, Cat," Joan protested.

"But would he?" asked Cat. She turned to me. "Kitty, would he tell them everything?"

"He has to, Cat," I replied. "They are the king's men."

"No, he doesn't *have* to, Kitty Tylney," she mocked me. "He could *lie*, inconceivable as that may seem to you."

"How will you ever know?"

"They'll ask me to confirm what he's said."

"No, they're smarter than that." Jane spoke for the first time since the men had left. "They will ask open-ended questions that require specific answers." Her voice shook. "They will ask them again. And again. And again. Until you answer."

"They can't be that smart," Cat muttered. "They didn't ask me anything before."

"They had no reason to," Jane pointed out. "You were brought to the king as a virgin. Why should they ask any questions? The dowager duchess vouched for you. They had no reason to be suspicious. Now they do."

"We need to find out what they know," Cat declared. "Where is Alice? Alice hears everything. Go find her, Kitty. The queen requires her presence."

I hurried from the room, retracing my steps from the day before. All I'd needed to do then was ask after the king's health. Now, our lives hung in the balance.

I hurried through the eerily quiet palace in search of the

Duke of Norfolk's rooms. I had no desire to see him again; his anger would impale me. But I went, through the galleries, the Great Watching Chamber, Anne Boleyn's gate, the HA HA mocking me. All emptier than I had ever seen them, deserted by those loyal to the king.

William stood outside the duke's door.

"William!" I said. "I need to find Alice."

"Alice left for Kenninghall this morning."

The duke's estate in Norfolk. The duke must have wrung as much information out of her as he could in return for safe passage. Alice got out. I slumped back against the wall.

"Kitty?" William asked. "Are you well?"

"No, William," I said. "I am not well at all."

"Do you need a place to go?" he whispered.

I looked at him. The mask was gone, his features mobile with concern. His eyes flashed over my face, checked the gallery, and returned to me.

"My family's house in Cheapside is rundown and crowded," he explained. "But with a message from me, you would be welcome. And you wouldn't be found."

The implication of this struck me hard in the center of my chest. Leave court. Leave Cat. Save myself.

"Go into hiding?" I asked. "Is it really that bad?"

He nodded. "They're questioning everyone about the queen's activities before she married. Any secrets . . . could be damning."

"Secrets just get in the way."

"And worse."

We stood in the empty gallery, listening to the bustle of the duke's servants packing his things, preparing for flight.

I could leave Cat and all of her secrets behind. Go where no one knew me. Where no one told me what to do or what I wanted. The question was, what did I want?

William stood before me, waiting for an answer, and only one came to mind. *Him.* I only wanted him. The one thing I couldn't have.

Alice was out already. William would surely soon make his way to Kenninghall to be with her. And I, who knew the most, but also knew how to say nothing, was indentured to the queen. Her sister of the soul.

I couldn't abandon her.

"Thank you, William," I said, "for the offer. But I can't take it."

Those words appeared to hurt him more than anything had before. He closed his eyes and let go a great shuddering sigh.

"Go well, Mistress Tylney."

I returned to the queen's rooms. Three men in the scarlet and gold of the king's livery busied themselves, taking stock of all the jewels and valuables in the apartments. They packed everything away in boxes lined with velvet. Pearls. Brooches. An enameled coronet garnished with rubies. The diamond collar.

Cat sat silently weeping by the fire while the men moved about the room.

"My lady," one of the men said to Cat. "Could you please remove your rings?"

"My rings?" she asked, her voice hollow as if traveling a great distance.

"Yes."

Three from the left hand and five from the right. She handed them to him one by one. When finished, she sank back, defeated.

"And the last one," he pressed.

"But that's my wedding ring."

"We were told to take everything." His voice betrayed a perverted joy in her sorrow.

Cat handed him the ring and removed her jeweled hood. Her hair tumbled down her back and she buried her face in her pale, naked hands.

But as soon as the men had left and the door closed behind them, she lifted her face and wiped it with her sleeve.

"Where is Alice?"

"Gone," I said. "To Kenninghall."

"The duke's protection," Cat muttered. "Damn that girl. She knew I would need her, and she only saved herself."

I felt a sudden desire to justify Alice's actions. They so closely resembled what could have been my own. But I stayed silent.

"We're here for you," Joan said, kneeling down to put an arm around Cat. "Aren't we, Kitty?"

"And a damn lot of good you'll do me."

Joan looked stricken.

"And Jane," she attempted.

"Jane?" Cat cried and looked around. Caught Jane by the window. "Jane Boleyn? The woman who has served five queens and survived them all?"

I thought of Jane's fingers on Anne Boleyn's pearls, the beads tapping quietly. The darkness in her eyes as she spoke of Cranmer's questions. And I wondered if that survival was worth the cost.

"No, four," Cat said. "Because Jane won't survive this queen. No one will."

"Don't talk like that, Your Majesty," Joan argued.

"You've finally remembered to call me by my title," said Cat, patting Joan's hand.

I shivered at the coldness, the blankness in her voice.

"We'll all survive," Joan said. "Together. We're family. Right?"

49

CRANMER RETURNED THE NEXT DAY, ARMED WITH QUESTIONS, PEN AND ink. He sat down at Cat's little writing desk and looked at her inquisitively.

Cat sat mute by the fire. Joan sat next to her. I waited by the door, still fighting the urge to flee. Jane stood by the window, still and silent. The perfect, invisible courtier.

"My lady," Cranmer pronounced, "We can do this one of two ways. Based on the extensive information I have already gathered, I could give a full account of the punishment you will reap for your past misconduct. Or you could tell me your side of the story, and I will be content to listen and draw my conclusions."

Judge and jury, all in one cassock.

He sat back and waited. If there was one thing Cat couldn't stand, it was silence when she was expected to fill it. She tried valiantly. I watched her jaw moving as she chewed her lower lip. She stared into the fire with what I'm sure she hoped was a tragic expression for a good five minutes and then she broke down.

"I knew Francis Dereham when I lived with my grandmother in Lambeth," she began.

"In what way?" Cranmer inquired.

"As a friend."

Cranmer waited. Again, Cat failed to wait him out. She began to sob.

"More than a friend."

"So you knew him . . ." Cranmer let his question trail off, obviously expecting her to continue.

"We kissed in the gallery," Cat said with an impatient shrug. "And in chapel. You can ask any of my friends." And with a single gesture, implicated all of us with an airy insouciance that took my breath away.

"Was there no talk of marriage?" Cranmer asked.

"No."

"Surely, in a household of girls, there would be some mention of marriage?" he pursued.

"No."

Cat met his eye and held firm.

"You never talked to your friends about it. Forgive me if I do not understand, but don't girls discuss these things? Carry locks of hair like holy artifacts?" His mouth turned down in a sneer of distaste. "There was no gossip? No girlish, fanciful discussions of dresses and flowers and the future?"

"No," Cat insisted. "None. We never spoke of those sorts of things because we knew our families would find the best husbands for us."

Her attempt at ingenuousness failed and she just looked desperate.

"All of you?" Cranmer asked. "You, Mistress Tylney? Did you trust your parents to find you a husband?"

"Of course," I forced myself to say. "And I am betrothed to Lord Graves."

Cranmer made a note.

"None of you attempted to make a match on your own?" Cranmer pursued. He sounded so mild, so kindly, like a priest. A father confessor. None of us responded.

"But you, my lady," he turned back to Cat, "chose your own husband in the end. Or he chose you. It wasn't your family's doing at all. It was a love match, is that right?"

Cat swallowed. I saw her Adam's apple swell delicately at her throat.

Cat didn't believe in love. Her match with the king had nothing to do with it. And everybody knew it.

"Yes," she said.

"So I can infer that perhaps it was always in the back of your mind to do so. Then what did you think of this dalliance with Francis Dereham?"

"I thought nothing!" Cat cried and broke into fresh sobs. "I was young, impressionable. He was older and I thought him handsome. I thought he would know better than I. I had been brought up to trust my elders, to listen and obey."

"Listen and obey," Cranmer repeated, making a note.

"My will is not my own," Cat said.

"So you believed that Dereham would think of your best interests."

"He said he would."

"It is my information that he shared your bed." Cranmer fixed Cat with a beady eye. No longer grandfatherly, he now looked like a hawk going in for a kill.

Cat crumpled like the sail of a ship that has turned against the wind. She lost her voice in her skirts. Cranmer leaned forward to catch a whisper of confession. But the fabric muted Cat so thoroughly that the sounds she made could just have been sobs. I couldn't bear it. I couldn't stand to see Catherine Howard debased. Despite her treatment of me, she was still my friend.

"Can't you ask her later?" I pleaded. "She isn't well."

"Fine," Cranmer made a note. Turned to me.

"Did he share your bed, Mistress Tylney? The one you occupied with Mistress Howard?"

I could have cried, too. My intention was for him to leave, not turn his interrogation on me. But he posed the question in such a way that I could tell the truth and yet not all of it. Yes, Francis Dereham shared my bed. It just so happened that he also shared it with Cat. I didn't have to distinguish with whom he *chose* to share it.

"He did," I said.

I thought that perhaps Cat had stopped breathing, as the sounds coming from her skirt suddenly diminished. But she looked up at me, a flash of hate in her eyes. She thought I con-

demned her. A stab of guilt rent through me, though my intention hadn't been to indict her. She dissolved again in pathetic tears.

Cranmer calmly made a note.

"Did you ever share a bed with Francis Dereham when he was naked?" he asked.

Yes. Though I wished to forget that particular night.

"No."

"Did Mistress Howard?"

The room fell silent.

"No," I whispered.

"No, no more did I!" Cat sobbed. "He came to our rooms and . . . and . . ."

"He used to grab my breast beneath the covers," I said over the noise of Cat's renewed sobbing. It had been an accident. The last time I'd tried to pretend he wasn't there. After that, I'd always found another place to sleep. Cat let up slightly, to be better able to hear my confession.

"Dereham?"

"Yes."

"Was he naked at the time? Were you?"

"No!" Cat cried. "Never! How can you keep asking?"

"Because he said he was. He said he came to your bed without his doublet. Without his hose."

We stared. At Cranmer. At Cat. As if watching a silent, frozen tennis game.

"Sometimes he came without his doublet," Cat admitted.

"And once . . . maybe twice, he came without his hose. But not fully naked. Never like that."

"And you never called him husband. He never called you wife."

"No," Cat said in a throaty whisper. "He forced me."

I could have throttled her. Because that one question could be her salvation. Perhaps salvation for all of us. Commitment, consent, and consummation amounted to a legal marriage. It would make her marriage to the king invalid. Give him a reason to divorce her, like the duchess said. To let her go. To let her live. But if Cat had not been betrothed to Francis, then she was a slut and possibly an adulterer. A calculating, manipulative harlot who used her wiles and abilities to dupe the aging, romantic King and then bring her lover into her household, committing high treason just like her cousin, Anne Boleyn. Bigamy was preferable to the alternative.

"But how?" Cranmer asked. "The doors to the maidens' dormitory were locked, were they not?"

"Not in the beginning," Cat said, casting a fleeting look my way. I held my breath. It was one thing knowing about Cat's affairs. It was something else entirely to facilitate them. I looked at Cranmer, who flicked his glance back to his notes.

"I see."

Cranmer packed up his pen and ink and stood.

"You would be best advised to stay in your rooms," he declared, pointedly scanning each face in turn. "All of you."

We bowed our heads in assent. What else could we do?

Cranmer paused at the door.

"Don't think this is the end of the matter," he said. "The truth will out. In the end. And the end is nigh, my lady."

And he didn't know the half of it. Yet.

50

"THAT BASTARD!" CAT SHRIEKED WHEN CRANMER WAS OUT OF EARSHOT.

"Your Majesty!" Joan gasped.

"Not Cranmer," Cat said scornfully. "No, not the perfect image of God on earth. Dereham! The bloody waste of a pirate!"

She slammed the door to her bedchamber and started throwing everything that came to hand. A half-sewn shirt. A wooden box full of embroidery silks. A small mirror of Venetian glass that shattered, sending fragments like raindrops all over the hearth.

Joan ducked out of the way and tried to hide behind the bed. I leaned back up against the door.

"It wasn't my fault!" Cat screamed. "He forced me! And now he's ruined me!"

I was staggered by the strength of her adherence to a falsehood that would be her ruin.

Cat picked up an inkpot from the desk and made to hurl it into the fire. Jane stepped smartly up to her, grabbed her wrist and held the inkpot still.

"Oh, no you don't," Jane said.

"How dare you manhandle me!" Cat roared. "As if I were a common wench!"

"Did you not hear Cranmer?" Jane demanded. "You *are* a common wench, Mistress Howard."

"Until the king says otherwise, I am queen," Cat said imperiously.

"Fine," said Jane, letting go. "But you throw that ink to your own hazard."

Cat set it down carefully.

"Why do you say so, Lady Rochford?" she asked.

"Because now is the time to write your letter of confession to the king. Beg his mercy. You have said more than once that the king loves you, perhaps to the point of delusion. If he still loves you—and he must still love you—then you can appeal to his feelings. Tell him everything."

"Everything?"

Jane paused. "Perhaps not. But everything about Dereham." She made a moue of distaste.

"You judge me, Lady Rochford?" Cat said. "You, who sent your husband to the gallows without a breath of hesitation? You, who let it be believed that he and Queen Anne committed the unnatural sin of incest? You dare judge me for a childish infatuation?"

"No," Jane muttered. I saw her fingers close around the pocket that hung from her waist.

The room lapsed into silence.

"So what do you think?" Cat turned to me. "When I give it

to him, should I go down on my knees and kiss the hem of his cloak?"

"Cranmer?" I asked. "He doesn't strike me as the sort of man who would respond well to such a thing."

"The king," she scoffed, as if I were the stupid one.

"The king has left Hampton Court, Cat. I don't think he's coming back."

"He must come back," Cat said. "I have to see him. Make my confession. Beg for his mercy. He'll come back."

"No, he won't," Jane assured her. "He let Catherine of Aragon suffer illness and death alone in Kimbolton. He left Anne Boleyn at a tournament, and never saw her again. He sent Anne of Cleves to Richmond, only allowing her to return when she was his beloved sister and no longer his wife. He will not see you again."

"But he has to," Cat insisted.

"He won't." Jane's voice sliced like a sword through the still room. "You must make your confession and beg for mercy on paper."

"But that's not fair!" Cat cried. "My writing is chaos! I need to see him in person. I need to practice. I must see him."

"You won't."

"But I've done nothing wrong."

Her brazen denial stupefied me. Despite knowing her, sleeping with her, being her mirror for most of my life, I couldn't understand her now.

"I'll just have to beg forgiveness of Archbishop Cranmer,"

she said. "Kitty, come here and pretend to be him. Should I face him with my head bowed? Or clasp him around the knees?"

She knelt before me and reached for my skirts.

I stepped aside, disgusted by her desire to practice. To find a way to tug the heartstrings of Archbishop Cranmer instead of face up to the truth. Terror rose within me. If Cat didn't clutch at the one possibility that might save her—that she was betrothed before she married the king—she could face worse than the loss of her throne.

"You should tell him to his face that you were married to Francis."

"I wasn't," Cat replied stonily. "He forced me."

"It would render your marriage to the king invalid," Jane interjected.

"It would render me a nobody! Mistress Dereham instead of Queen Catherine! I will not consider it. I will not even participate in a conversation about it."

She turned her back on us, arms folded across her chest. I knew there would be no way to persuade her, and the tiny hope I had harbored died.

"Then you should find a way to explain why you brought Francis Dereham into your household."

"Because the dowager duchess told me to."

"Which she may deny!" I cried. "Besides, you're the queen. You don't have to do what she says anymore."

"You mean people will think I brought him here because I

loved him?" Cat asked, incredulous. "People will think that I would actually prefer *him* to the king? I care *nothing* for Francis. I never did."

I almost laughed, but choked on a sob instead.

"It doesn't matter," I said. "Once a rumor gets started, everyone believes it. You of all people should realize that."

It was what she had threatened me with: a rumor that would ruin my life. But now it was the truth that would ruin us all.

"Francis will tell the truth," Cat predicted, ignoring all that I implied. Ignoring the fact that Francis had already told the truth.

"It only takes a little torture to make a man say only what his inquisitors wish to hear," Jane said, her eyes glittering dangerously. No doubt she was remembering the musician Mark Smeaton, tortured to confession of adultery with Anne Boleyn.

We paused to consider this. Francis on the rack, his bones popping, chin dimple receding into his screams.

"Very well," Cat sniffed. "So what should I say in this letter? God, I hate writing! Can't someone else do it for me?"

"Who?" I asked, finally giving in to my frustration. "Your secretary? Oh, maybe not, as he's locked up in the Tower spilling his guts to the king's men."

"You watch your step, Kitty Tylney," Cat growled. "I can still take you down."

"But you already are!" I cried. I wanted to force some sense

into her. To make her see that her games and diversions and petty preferences were no longer of any use to her.

"You show no regard for others and none for the future!" I exploded, each word a catharsis.

"You dare to attack me?" Cat gaped.

"I do! You wasted every moment at court on clothes and baubles and silly games. You wasted your friendships on petty rivalries and manipulation. You've wasted your own life and you've wasted ours, and you will have to suffer that for the rest of your days, however few they might be!"

I stopped when the tears sprang to my eyes, a searing pain rising just beneath my ribs.

Cat stared at me. The others hardly seemed to breathe.

"You *wanted* to be here," she accused. "You wanted the baubles and silly games. You wanted it as much as I."

It was true. I had wanted to be at court. Because it was what Cat wanted. I hadn't thought for myself since I was eight years old. And when I did, I spoke too late. Too late to change her, or to accomplish anything but the infliction of pain.

We might have stood there for eternity, but for another knock at the door and the entrance of Sir Thomas Wriothesley, one of the king's secretaries and most trusted servants. The one Jane had warned me to stay away from on my first day at court.

He wore unfashionable clothes, but well-fitted and startlingly white against his thick neck and russet beard. His face might once have been genial, but had long been marred by antipathy.

"You will pack your things," he said, addressing the room.

"You're taking my ladies in waiting?" Cat asked, looking even more shocked than she had after my outburst.

"Just these particular ones," Wriothesley explained. "You shall have others. Of my choosing. Your days with your clan of friends are over. From now on, none of you shall hear what the others have to say. You will tell only the truth. There will be no connivance."

Joan and I looked at each other, at Cat, unable to move. We might never see each other again. I might never get a chance to tell Cat that I loved her as much as I hated her.

"Come now," Wriothesley snapped. "I have other places to be."

"Can we not say good-bye?" Cat asked, batting wet eyelashes.

Wriothesley hesitated. For the first time, he looked remotely human.

Cat took advantage of this and turned to Joan and hugged her. Tears streamed down Joan's face. Cat hugged me, too, a tight, strangling embrace, her fists balled into the knobs of my spine. I sensed a reprieve in that embrace—a truce in our war of words. "Don't forget your family, girls," Cat said tightly, then added in a whisper, "Do not betray me."

I got the message. Without each other, we were nothing. Without Cat, I was nothing. Our fates were inextricably tied. Cat would still need me. And I would continue to do her bidding.

I saw Jane, over Cat's shoulder, face so white as to be translucent, arms gripped to her sides. Left out of the circle.

"Come now," Wriothesley said again.

"Are we being arrested?" I asked.

"Not yet," Wriothesley said, then narrowed his eyes. "But undoubtedly you will be."

That's when Jane Boleyn began to scream.

I SAT ALONE FOR FIVE DAYS IN A ROOM AT THE FAR END OF THE PALACE. A room with bare walls and a shuttered window that let in little light but all the reek of the river at low tide. A room I filled with too many memories and a fear that smelled far worse than anything outside.

Wriothesley came daily. He assaulted me with the same questions, as if he hoped I would crack and he could pull me apart, layer by layer. But on the sixth day, he brought news.

"You are to be taken to the Tower of London."

I willed myself not to show a reaction while he waited for me to digest the information. It eddied in my stomach like Thames-water.

"The king may be convinced to be merciful," he advised. "He must be given good reason. I don't suspect he will be so toward Mistress Howard. When the facts were presented to him, he grabbed the sword of the nearest usher and shouted, *I'll kill her myself!'* But you are no one. He can afford to be merciful to you. If you help us."

I remained silent.

"Your family has responded to none of our attempts to elicit information from them," he told me. "They say they have had little contact with you since you moved to the dowager duchess's household."

"That is true." I ignored the pinpricks of hurt that came from hearing of their indifference from a stranger.

"And the man to whom you were betrothed?"

"I have not heard from him."

"He tells me the betrothal has been broken," Wriothesley reported. "That your actions in the queen's household—and before—are enough to break any promise he may have made to you."

Abandoned by my parents. Abandoned by Lord Poxy. I really had nothing but my family of girls.

"How fares the queen?"

Wriothesley looked askance at my question.

"Mistress Howard is cheerful," he said. "And demanding. And peevish when her demands are not met, despite the fact she does not deserve to ask for anything."

That sounded like Cat. Still thinking only of herself.

"And Jane?" I asked, afraid of the answer. I didn't know if the screams in my nightmares were real or imagined.

"Lady Rochford is no business of yours."

"What of the others?" I persisted. "They're my friends!" They were the only family I'd ever known.

"Not anymore." Wriothesley's legs creaked in their leather as he leaned closer to intimidate me. He succeeded, despite the fact that he was shorter than I.

"What can you tell us of your life at Norfolk House?" he asked yet again. "How well did the duchess keep an eye on you?"

"Oh, the duchess had an eagle eye, sir," I told him, neglecting to mention the duchess's eye was also blind to what didn't affect her personally.

"So how then did Mistress Howard manage an affair with a servant in her household?"

"Francis Dereham wasn't a servant."

Wriothesley took a deep breath, beard quivering, leaned back and changed tactics.

"What happened when the duchess locked the door?"

"Locked the door?"

"We have it on good authority that when the duchess found out about Francis Dereham, she ordered that the door to the maidens' dormitory be locked. What happened then?" He sounded irritable.

"Francis tried to come in a window."

"And failed. We know this, too."

I shrugged.

"Did the queen steal the key?"

"She wasn't the queen then," I said.

"You equivocate to avoid the question," Wriothesley retorted. "You have truly learned the art of being a courtier. But your answer is clearer than you think. She may not have been queen, but you did not say she didn't do it.

"And you have told me" he continued, "that Dereham could

not have forced his attentions on a girl who went to such lengths to be with him."

Oh, God. I had just told him that Cat stole the key. If she stuck with her story of *not* being engaged to Francis, to the story of him forcing her, my response would prove her a liar. Because no girl would steal a key to unlock the door to unwanted advances.

"I see by your face that you understand," Wriothesley said with a slender, knowing grin.

One more lie, throbbing like a sliver beneath a fingernail.

"Mistress Howard stole the key," Wriothesley declared and waited for affirmation. Again the smile that made his lips disappear beneath the fur of his beard.

I couldn't let him condemn Cat for my misbegotten cleverness. My attempts to say nothing, to give away nothing, only served Wriothesley's purposes. Not mine.

"No, she didn't," I admitted. "I did. I replaced it with a chess piece wrapped in lace."

The truth swung between us, glinting in the light from the windows. It hung by a single thread. Ready to set me free or send me to the gallows.

"To unlock the door of the maidens' chamber," Wriothesley said, the smile so thin he could hardly speak. "To allow entrance to the young men of the house. To encourage relations between your friends and the men they admired. Because that was what you wanted. You wanted to be the arbiter of that affair."

My stomach roiled. I dropped my head into my hands, my

mouth filling with the foretaste of vomit. I would be blamed. The madam of the maidens' chamber.

"And when Catherine Howard married and became queen, she brought you and your friends and Francis Dereham with her because she saw no reason to give up her wicked ways."

"What?" I lifted my head, my hair sticking to the sweat that coated my brow.

"A den of iniquity." He stood and sneered. "Right under the *eagle eye* of the dowager duchess herself. A seething mass of corruption and falsehood. Brought whole to court by the queen herself like a festering wound. Did she think the stench would not give her away?"

I stared at him.

"You cannot prove that," I breathed. He was using me not as a scapegoat but as surety.

"You are the proof," he said, pointing a bony finger at my face. "You are all the evidence I need."

52

I WAS TAKEN FROM HAMPTON COURT BY BOAT, FORCED TO WALK IN CAP-
tivity around London Bridge to avoid shooting the wickedly fast
water flowing between the piers. The skulls of traitors, stripped
of titles, names, and faces, dangled from pikes above the bridge
gatehouse. Thomas Cromwell's must have been there, but was
indistinguishable from the rest.

I could see the White Tower—the castle keep—glowing
eerily from the river as we rowed the second leg of the journey.
Around it, double-walled and multi-turreted, huddled the
battlements. A single crescent broke the wall at water level,
dark and dripping like a dragon's mouth. The Water Gate.
Traitor's Gate.

The portcullis raised and I stumbled up the stairs behind
my guard, across a cobbled alley and up a spiral staircase to my
cell. I hid behind my hair to avoid the curious glances of the
people who populated the castle. The people who were free to
come and go.

I was locked in a room with a tiny window that overlooked
the Tower Green, where Anne Boleyn had lost her head. I had
a hard wooden bench, a straw pallet, and a pathetic excuse for

a fire that sputtered and singed. I lay awake at night, listening to the ghosts of the many prisoners who had lost their lives to Henry VIII's reign. Thomas More. Anne and George Boleyn. Thomas Cromwell. Margaret Pole.

I couldn't bring myself to look long out the window. The scaffold stood there, stained dark by the rain. People laughed and walked, and once I saw a stolen kiss against the wall to the inmost ward. But what hurt most was the tiny portion of sky, cut close between window and wall, crowded by towers.

December arrived on feet waterlogged by rain. The light faded from the lowering sky and the castle walls took on the dampness of winter. But Wriothesley arrived looking positively cheerful.

"I wonder what you know about a certain member of the king's privy chamber of the name Thomas Culpepper."

I sucked in a whistle of air and then ducked my eyes to avoid the shot of Wriothesley's glance.

"Culpepper?" I asked, looking at my slippers.

"Yes. The prisoner, Dereham, said that he is completely innocent of any carnal knowledge of the queen since her marriage to the king. He said that he had been replaced in her affections by one Thomas Culpepper."

"I believe he danced with the queen on occasion," I said.

"Anything else?"

"No," I said, and this time looked him right in the eye. Daring him to believe me.

He gazed back, implacable.

"I will find the truth, Mistress Tylney. No matter how deeply it is buried. You can trust me on that."

I did. I trusted that this man with his leather breeches and his whip-smart questioning could find any truth he wished. But I was set on another course of lies.

"Were you aware of Mistress Howard's activities in the evening while the court was on progress to the north?" Wriothesley asked.

"Of course," I said. "I was her chamberer. It was my duty to know what she was doing, when she went to bed, and to ensure her comfort."

"Did her comfort include Culpepper?"

"No."

"What happened in Lincoln?"

"Lincoln?" How did he know these things?

"Yes. It's a cathedral city on the River Witham in Lincolnshire. The King's progress spent some days in the Bishops' Palace there."

I nodded, pondering, hoping I looked as if I was struggling to place the city amongst the many we visited.

"The guard said he had to lock the back stairs to the queen's apartments that night. That anyone might have entered."

I allowed my face to lighten.

"I remember!" I said. "I answered the door. He told me and I thanked him for keeping us safe."

"Yes," Wriothesley coughed.

"The queen." I hesitated. "She sent me down the stairs to check. I was afraid."

His dark eyes glowed keen with interest.

"And when I returned, I remember asking Joan Bulmer, 'Is the queen asleep yet?' And she answered, 'Yes, even now.'"

The absolute truth.

Wriothesley stood up and moved behind my chair. He gripped my shoulder with one hand, and my hair beneath my hood with the other. He tugged, the tension pulling my head back and to the side so that I looked up at the ceiling. His pallid and heavy eyelids appeared in the corner of my vision.

"Don't play games with me, Mistress Tylney," he said, his wine-soaked breath slippery on my cheek. "I know more games than you have ever considered. I know the games of the king's master inquisitors. I know how to get answers."

I didn't doubt him.

"But are those answers the truth, my lord?" I asked, feeling the fear convulse in my throat. "Because answers called forth by torture are expedient, but often false."

He pulled harder, my neck wrenched painfully, and stars burst across the ceiling.

"You know better than that, Kitty," he said, and let go.

I rubbed my neck. I had no script, no way of knowing what I would say or when. Perhaps the closeness and sureness of death really did addle a person's judgment.

"Did you ever carry messages to Culpepper from the queen?"

"No."

"Between the queen and Lady Rochford?"

I hesitated.

"I often relayed messages between the queen and her ladies," I said carefully. "I was her chamberer. It was my duty."

"Do you remember any in particular?"

"She once asked Lady Rochford for something that was promised her," I said. "That's all I know."

"You never sought out secret hiding places."

"No."

"Not even for a game?" he asked, a slyness to his question.

Hide-and-seek.

"Only for myself."

"Did Lady Rochford?"

"Have you asked her?" I regretted the question as soon as I asked it, and shrank from the fury on his thin lips.

"Jane Boleyn is not in a fit state to answer questions at the moment. In fact, she appears to be quite mad. You may have heard her screaming from the Wakefield Tower."

I thought it was only my dreams. But if she was insane, she could not be executed. It was the king's law.

"It may be real. She may be pretending," he said. It was as if he, too, could read my mind. "The king's own physicians are attending her. And his councilors are attending to the law.

"Thomas Culpepper says the affair was Jane Boleyn's idea," he continued. "Mistress Howard confirms this."

Oh, Cat. I sagged, no longer able to fight the implications of his words.

"For this, Jane Boleyn faces the scaffold. And she knows it. It is her guilt that sends her into madness. But you don't face the same fate.

"At *best*, Mistress Tylney," he said, reverting to my last name and striding across the floor to the tiny window, "you will be charged with misprision of treason." He turned, practically snapping his heels together. "Do you know what that means?"

I shook my head.

"It means that you had knowledge of treason in the form of the queen's former relationship with Francis Dereham. You didn't bring it to the king's attention, when he thought he was marrying an innocent girl with no marital entanglements."

He had had annulments from three of his wives for "marital entanglements." Only Queen Jane escaped that by dying before he was ready to get rid of her.

"You had no part in the act of concealment," he went on. "You were not present when the king was courting. This is a feeble way of saying that you knew and did nothing, and you walked away from responsibility.

"However," he continued, "at worst you will be convicted of treason. You had knowledge of the affair with Dereham and promoted it. You had knowledge of the affair with Culpepper and purposefully concealed it."

I stayed silent. He waited for me to admit to one or the other. But I could do neither. Did he expect the young to be stupid as well?

"Would you like to know what sentence you may expect?" he asked with the air of a man asking which sweet I would like from the tray at a banquet. "In both cases, you will be attainted and stripped any titles, land, or money you possess or stand to inherit. I gather that none of this applies to you?"

He looked at me from under his eyelashes, a cunning smile splaying his lips. He knew very well that being attainted would have no effect on my status.

"Misprision can garner a sentence of death or perpetual imprisonment. Treason is punishable by death, unless the king extends his mercy. Either way, you're looking at the end of your career at court, the end of your youth, and the end of your life as you know it."

He waited for this information to register in my mind and trigger an emotional outburst or tearful confession. I struggled with the tears, but kept them at bay. I wanted nothing to do with his manipulation.

"Thank you for telling me," I managed.

"My pleasure."

I'm sure it was.

"Culpepper and Dereham have confessed. They have already been tried and found guilty of high treason. Sentenced to death. Do you know what this means?"

I couldn't move. Not to speak. Not even to nod my head.

"It means that unless the king grants their pleas for clemency, they will be hanged by the neck, cut down alive, their members removed."

My body found its ability for motion and shuddered violently. Wriothesley stepped closer and whispered in my ear like a lover.

"Their members will be removed before their very eyes," he said softly. "Their bowels will be removed as well. They will still be alive when this happens. They will see their innards trailing on the ground and burned before them."

I couldn't beg him to stop. My tongue cleaved to the roof of my mouth.

"Their still beating hearts will be removed. Their heads will be stricken off, their bodies cut into quarters and the pieces hung high on the London Bridge so all may see the fate of traitors to the king. They will be left there until the gulls and ravens have feasted on every morsel of flesh. And there, their bones shall remain, bleached by the sun, buffeted by the wind, until they fall into the Thames or into the road and are trampled to dust and forgotten."

I wanted to cover my ears. I pictured Francis, his cocky swagger, faced with the gallows. I saw Culpepper, his blond good looks shrouded in blood. Even after all he had done, I could not wish such a fate on him, or anyone.

"Their only hope is for the king's leniency," Wriothesley murmured. "To be merely decapitated. I imagine the king's past

358

fondness for Culpepper may lead him to mercy, but Dereham? Dereham has no hope.

"Women, however, do not attract such a punishment." Wriothesley spoke casually, as if discussing the difference between boning a goose and roasting it whole.

"Queens and nobility like Jane Boleyn are dispatched by the ax. Common women convicted of treason are burned at the stake. Their skirts erupt into flames around them. On a windy day, it could take hours to die as the flames lick and char the delicate skin only to be teased away by the breeze carrying ash throughout the city."

I feared I would remain mute until that day, when at last I would find my voice as it screamed over the cheering of the bloodthirsty crowd. And the tears finally won.

Wriothesley smiled again.

"I shall leave you now."

53

In the next few weeks the Tower grew gluttonous on the incarceration of traitors.

They brought in the dowager duchess after she burned a coffer full of papers said to belong to Francis Dereham. The rest of the Coven came, too. The number of prisoners soon exceeded Tower capacity. Lower-ranking and obviously innocent members of the duchess's household were shipped off to other prisons. But not I.

The duke stood outside the Tower gates, outside the prison, outside the very law itself and exclaimed loudly and constantly that he knew nothing of his slatternly niece's dubious conduct. He vilified her. Condemned her. Stood free upon the back of her guilt.

The Howard men groveled at the feet of the king, swearing loyalty. And were allowed to go free.

And Edmund Standebanke continued in the king's service.

Men, I thought. *Even guilt can't shackle them.*

But then Francis and Culpepper were executed. Pulled from the Tower by an ox-drawn cart, met with the jeers and silent judgment of Londoners. Culpepper's sentence was commuted to decapitation. Francis was not so lucky.

1542

54

With Culpepper's death, my horrifying dreams ended. But the long winter nights loomed black and empty. I woke each morning, my muscles cramped from cold, shocked anew at my situation. At the mistakes and betrayals that got me there.

Gossip moved even faster in the Tower than it had at Norfolk House. I got snippets of news from the guards, from the charwoman, from the gardener who fixed a loose stone in the corner outside my door. Cat was imprisoned in Syon House, a monastery suppressed by the reformation, the nuns dispersed and the property relinquished to the crown. Joan languished somewhere in the Tower, far distant from me. Alice remained outside the prison, a star witness. Traitor to our family of girls. The circle broken.

We saw each other briefly at our indictment. Each of us was brought singly through the crowded room, through the press of bodies to the bar. Each of us pled guilty. Lady Margaret Howard. Edward Waldegrave. Alice. Joan. Me. Condemned to perpetual imprisonment. Goods and titles forfeit. The room rocked with weeping—from grief for a future behind stone walls or relief for keeping our heads, I knew not which. I sat on the bench, my head bent, and looked at no one. Utterly isolated in a place where the walls dripped with the moisture of collective breath. Alone.

Christmas came and went, bringing with it nothing but more rain and endless dark days. It seemed nobody kept Christmas that year. The king, they said, too heartbroken for festivities, brooded and wept, and the entire country followed suit.

My family sent me no word, no message, no hope. I was nothing, no one, forgotten in a world so dark that even the shadows got lost. I suffered no longer from the fear of my fate but from the knowledge that nobody cared, not even me.

Early in the New Year, a knock at my door admitted the guard, followed by a tall, thin man with shorn hair and a velvet cap. He wore the king's livery. I retreated involuntarily. Even without the mane of golden hair, without the air of snide superiority, I recognized Edmund Standebanke. My movement brought a flicker of emotion across his face. Understanding? Or humility?

"What do you want?" I asked.

"To help."

I almost laughed. "Nothing can help me."

"I am still the king's yeoman of the chamber," he said.

"And how did you manage that?" I asked. "How did you come to know every contemptible aspect of our lives and still remain employed by the very man you sought to dupe?"

He didn't move. Just stood there in that tiny room, looking

lost. Like he didn't know how he had got there, or how he had escaped.

"They believed me," he said finally.

As I once had. I believed he spoke the truth. I believed he might have cared for me.

"Well, aren't you just the lucky one?"

"Don't, Kitty," he said. "I feel horrible."

"*You* feel horrible?" Bitterness laced my words with poison and I wanted to press them into his flesh. To make him suffer. "You, who stand there, well-dressed and well-fed, not cowering beneath the sword of execution? How *dare* you?"

"He was my friend."

"Cat is my friend! And Joan and Jane and all the rest. Oh, boo hoo, Edmund, one of your friends cheated and despoiled everyone and suffered for it. You helped him! You are free. And here you stand trying to elicit sympathy."

"Just so you know, I have not been well-fed. I cannot eat."

It looked to be true. He was thin. His broad chest collapsed in upon itself. I willed myself to feel nothing.

"And I am not free," he continued. "I am imprisoned by my own remorse. I do feel horrible. I wish things were different."

"Then you will have to learn to live with your guilt," I told him. "Do not bring it to me. Wishing is a pointless exercise. There can be no other outcome to this."

I stood and stared him down. At last, I was stronger than he, because I had nothing to lose.

"I could save you," he said.

With those four words he crushed me. I wanted to be saved. To be protected. From pain. From fear. From heartache. I wanted someone to wipe away the past. To wrap me in something sane and normal and safe.

"Come," he said, "You cannot stay here. You cannot survive on your own. Be mine. Let me . . . Let me make amends."

His words struck bone. *You cannot survive* and *be mine*. He wanted to own me. He did not think I could own myself.

"There is nothing to mend," I said. "There was no structure to begin with."

"But kitten, listen. I can . . . we could marry."

Marriage. My parents, Lord Poxy, everyone had abandoned me. Except Edmund. I turned to the smudged window. To the green where Anne Boleyn had lost her head. Where private executions took place. I would not be so lucky, should it come to that. As it was, it seemed I would sit forgotten in this cell while life and death took place without me.

"Why?" I asked, before I could stop myself. I turned to face him. I wanted to know his answer.

Edmund rubbed his forehead, priming a crease between his brows.

"I could lose my position," he said. "Tying myself to you. The king has no desire to be reminded of . . . her."

"That's not much of a reason," I said. In fact, it sounded like a good reason for him to leave me to rot.

"I'm trying to do the right thing, Kitty," he said, an edge

creeping into his voice. The same edge that told me I was stupid. The same edge that told me I was ugly. "Come, I know you want to."

An echo from far away. From the miserable, aching past. Culpepper's low growl in the park that day, *I know you want this.*

And I saw very clearly that saying yes to Edmund was as sure a prison as saying no.

"Don't presume to tell me what I want."

"Now is not the time for semantics, Kitty. Come with me."

He held out his hand. Reached for me. I jerked away from him.

"No."

"I don't want to live with your death on my conscience."

I flinched. But I couldn't retreat. The room was too small. The past and his part in it were too great.

"Then consider your conscience relieved by my choice. But I do not relieve you of the burden that should be there from the pain you inflicted.

"If you want to make amends, Edmund, go and find that girl from the woods. Find a way to help *her*. Tell her it wasn't her fault. It wasn't her choice. It wasn't what she wanted. No matter what Culpepper said."

"I did nothing wrong," he said, and took a step away, as if to distance himself.

"No, Edmund," I said. "You did *nothing*. And that's not the same thing. It was your fault and it was mine. For not telling the truth. You enabled him to ruin the lives of so many. You

assisted him with a firm grip here, a saucy word there, a little manipulation. You *helped* him rape that woman in the park. And I think you would have done the same to me."

"No, Kitty," he said.

"You assumed, like he did, that you knew what I wanted."

"Because you never said."

"And you never asked."

"I never would have started this if I knew it would hurt you," he said.

"Forgive me if I don't believe you," I replied. "Our entire association was built on lies."

"I never lied to you."

He never told me he cared about me. He never said I was beautiful. He just said he wouldn't let me be until he'd had me.

And that he'd kept my secret.

"You told Culpepper you saw me. That I was in the park that day. Watching."

"I never told him." Edmund looked stricken. Those wide brown eyes smudged and haunted. "I never told anyone I saw you there."

"Then who did?" I asked.

But suddenly I knew. I knew that in this, he wasn't lying. It wasn't Edmund who told Culpepper I had seen him in the woods.

It was Cat.

The betrayal pushed me to the stone floor and pinned me there.

"I am sorry, Kitty," Edmund said quietly.

"Good."

When he left, wordless and wraithlike, I couldn't stop trembling. My chances of survival had slipped from slim to nil. Edmund wasn't much of a savior, but I knew his was the only offer I'd get.

55

Parliament passed a bill of attainder against Cat in February. It stripped her of her worldly goods, her title, her claims to land and property.

And then they stripped her of her right to live. She was condemned to death, without hearing or trial, unable to defend herself or entreat anyone else to do so for her. Her fall brought mine, for a shadow ever falls with its mistress.

And Jane fell, too. Blamed for corrupting the young queen, for abetting the traitorous lovers, for doing her duty, Jane would face the ax as well, one already bloodied by the neck of her young charge. Insanity would not save her. The King reversed that law.

And a new law was created. It declared that if any woman presumed to marry the king without first admitting if she had been unchaste, she would be guilty of high treason, punishable by death. Cat would leave a legacy.

The day they brought Cat to the Tower, I heard weeping. It was cold, the sky heavy and thick as curdled cream. I smelled the river from my room. Not the bright, green scent of a river cleaned by rains and rushes, but the corrupt stench of a river stagnant with blood and offal, death and decay.

Cat came by barge from Syon House, shooting the rapids under London Bridge, where the heads of Francis and Culpepper still hung, impaled on the weather-bleached pikes. She came through Traitor's Gate, just opposite my own cell, out of my line of sight. But I heard her crying.

Silence accompanied her. Not a cheer of support or an offer of prayers. Anne Boleyn had had her supporters. Catherine of Aragon had most of the country behind her. Even poor Anne of Cleves had people who defended her right to remain queen.

Not Cat.

An expectant hush hung over the Tower for two full days, waiting for the ax to fall. The nights were agony.

Then the guard brought me a gown of rich green brocade. I recognized it immediately.

"The queen . . . I mean, Mistress Howard, entreated the king to give her gowns to her waiting women. Being attainted, she had nothing else to give."

I took it and held it up. It looked out of place in that bare room, against my pale skin and frayed slippers. But it felt warm and comforting beneath my chapped hands. It smelled of cedar and better times. I hugged it to me.

"Thank you," I whispered.

"I have also come to escort you . . ." he trailed off. Fear froze me. It was late. Dark. Surely they didn't burn people at night.

An image of a bonfire, shooting sparks into the gloom, blurred my vision.

"But . . ." I gestured helplessly with the gown. How cruel to give a girl such a piece of luxury to burn her in it.

"Leave it here," he said. "You will return to it." His eyes rolled in disdain. He thought I couldn't leave the gown. He thought a scrap of fabric made me stutter and weep. He was right.

I followed him down the spiral staircase and along a muddy track to the queen's rooms. The apartments had been built and renovated for Anne Boleyn's coronation, where she stayed before her day of triumph, carried into the cheering streets of London. They were also where she stayed the night before her execution.

Two guards, dressed in the king's livery, stood before a locked door. They stared straight at the wall opposite them, not even glancing at me or my escort.

"This is the one," my guard said.

I followed him into a dark gallery. At the end, more guards opened another door to a blaze of light and a rush of heat. I stepped into a room furnished with a trestle table and two chairs with velvet cushions. Two goblets sat on the table, a jug of wine beside them. I nearly wept with the relief my hands felt from the constant, cracking cold.

"Kitty!"

Dressed all in black velvet fitted to each curve, Cat looked as beautiful as ever, with her pale skin and dark eyes, her mahogany hair tied up in a simple black hood. She looked sober, quiet.

"Cat," I whispered.

"I can't believe they let me see you," Cat said. "I've been so lonely. So bored. No music. No dancing. No one to talk to. No one to commiserate with. No one to make me laugh."

She didn't offer apologies for landing me and Joan and all of her ladies and family in waters infested by sharks intent to kill. But her eyes retreated into sockets smudged by fear and sleeplessness.

"I heard you had servants," I said stiffly.

"The most boring girls you can imagine. Dull as ditchwater. And so tiresome." She put on a pewling, high-pitched whine. "Don't you want to pray now, my lady? You should ask for God's forgiveness. I pray for your soul every minute of every day."

Cat made vomiting noises and mimed putting her finger down her throat.

"I'm sure they do pray for me constantly," she said. "They certainly do nothing of interest." She walked to the table and picked up the jug.

"Wine?" she asked, waving it over the goblets.

"And the gossip they pass on is frightful," she went on, pouring. "Apparently the king has been seen flirting with Elizabeth Brooke. Thomas Wyatt's wife, the one he left because of her adultery. At least the king knows in advance that she has been *unchaste.*"

I nodded, dumbly. Cat was about to die and she was acting like . . . Cat.

"Come and sit," she said, patting a chair. I sank onto it.

Stretched my toes to the fire. It conjured a visceral memory of the duchess's private room in Lambeth. The first time I'd ever dared to sit in a chair with a velvet cushion.

Cat handed me a goblet of wine. Catherine Howard—Queen of England—served me.

"I need your help," she said. "I have to ask you a favor. Something only a sister could do for me. It will take a stout heart. And more than a modicum of affection for me."

I searched my heart for affection and found that I came up lacking. Cat had used me my entire life. Made me do things I didn't want to do—lie, steal, spend time in the company of Edmund Standebanke. She had taken away the things I loved. Convinced me to do things I knew were wrong. But I always came back for more. So who was at fault?

Cat stood up and walked toward a leaded window that overlooked the green. Before it, on the floor, about the height of a stool, was a massive piece of wood, supported on two sides, with a shallow indent hewn from the center.

"Is that . . . ?" I couldn't ask.

"The block," Cat sounded cheerful. "My block. I had them bring it to me. Tomorrow morning, I will lay my neck here," she touched the depression, worn smooth by scrubbing the blood from it, "and the executioner will swing his ax."

"Don't, Cat," I said. The fire did nothing to warm the cold lump of lead that filled my chest.

"I need you, Kitty," she said. "I want to make sure I do this properly."

She wanted me to help her practice. She wanted me to watch her put her head on the block. My every sinew and muscle ached to run away. To pound on the door and be returned to my cold, lonely cell.

Cat knelt down. She untied the hood from her hair, the mass of curls frothing down her back. She swung it once, a full, sweeping motion to clear every strand from her neck, and laid her head upon the wood.

"Is this right?" she asked.

"I don't know," I said. It wasn't like practicing a curtsey or a flirtatious look. All I could see was the ax beginning to fall. I had to look away.

"Then come over here," she said.

Despite my muscles' desire to escape, I found that I could not stand.

"Kitty," she said in the voice that brooked no argument. "Come. Over. Here."

I moved stiffly like a knight in heavy armor with the joints rusted shut. I hated myself for going. I hated her more for asking.

I could see each hair delineated, the thin, vulnerable swirl of down at the nape of her neck. Her great sweep of curls tumbled toward me like a red tide. The curve of her cheek hid her eyes from me. Her jaw tightened.

"They say my cousin laughed before her execution," she said so quietly she could have been speaking love whispers to the block itself. "She said, 'I only have a little neck.' As do I."

377

I looked at her neck, stretched like that of a swan.

"But that could not stop it from hurting," she continued. "Do you think it hurts, Kitty? When the blow comes? The slice of the blade? When the lips continue to pray or the fingers to twitch? When the blood spurts and the staring eyes lose their vision? Does it hurt?"

"I don't know."

"I think it does," she whispered, and clambered again to her feet, this time her limbs shaking. "I think it hurts a great deal. How could it not?"

I shook my head.

"Why me, Kitty?" she asked. "Why did he choose me? Why not any of the other girls who filled the maidens' chamber or the apartments of Anne of Cleves?"

I thought of all the forces that came together to create Henry's fifth queen: ambition, family advancement, lost youth, vanity, lust. Again I said nothing.

"*Why?*" The scream tore from her throat. Her hands clenched beneath her elbows, her body rigid. For one quavering moment she appeared to hold herself together by sheer force of will.

"Because you're Catherine Howard," I said finally. It could have been no one else.

She turned around and stalked back to the wooden block below the window.

Again, Cat flung her hair to one side. She used to do that when she laughed. Her hair would hit me in the face if I stood

too close. Its trajectory used to catch the eye of the nearest man. But his gaze never followed it to me. It always followed the hair back to her.

She let her head rest as if she could no longer hold it up, and a single tear stained the wood.

"That's not right," I said.

She sat back on her heels. I took in her tiny face, the low-slung collar of her gown exposing her throat, her hands in her lap, clutching at the fabric of her skirts. She looked up at me like a child waiting for a whipping. Like when we were eight and the duchess caught us drinking wine from her golden goblets, Cat with a daisy-chain crown upon her head.

"You should use a hand to pull your hair to one side," I found myself saying. "Gently. It's not so impetuous. So . . . shameless."

Cat nodded, taking my criticism.

"Like this?"

Carefully, she gathered all of her curls in one hand. She bent down and pulled the hair to the left, exposing the tiny bones at the top of her spine.

My breath caught in my throat. Cat, who gave in to her emotions on every whim, wouldn't die a traitor's death, but the death of a queen. I gave in, wanting to mourn for her.

"Yes," I whispered.

Cat put her hands in her lap. She moved them behind her back. They fluttered like lost birds.

"Hold onto the block," I said, kneeling down next to her.

I took her right hand and stretched the arm so she held the rough wood at the side. She did the same with her left. Almost hugging it.

"That's good," she said, her voice muffled. Her fingers tightened, her knuckles white. "I don't have to work so hard to keep them still."

She sat up and stroked the wood.

"Do you think this is the same block they used for my cousin?" she asked. "The king allowed her a swordsman. Brought from Calais. He loved her that much."

Thinking of the heads that had rolled from that block—by ax or by sword—made me want to be sick into the fireplace. More than that, it made me fear the fire, which still might be my own fate. Then guilt enveloped me, as Cat faced her fate so much sooner.

"It looks to have seen a lot of use," she said, as if in conversation about a dish or a goblet. "Perhaps they used it for Margaret Pole. Her executioner didn't know what he was doing. They say he trembled with each swing of the ax."

My stomach began to ferment like old wine, strong and sour.

"I don't want that kind of death," Cat said. "That's why I'm practicing. I have practiced my speech already; would you like to hear it?"

I shook my head.

"No, I suppose not. But I can practice all I want, and I still have no control over the man with the ax. I hope he's practicing tonight."

I fervently hoped the same.

"I wonder what he practices on?" Cat mused. "A cabbage perhaps? Or maybe something more mobile, like a pig. I wonder what happens after it's killed. Perhaps his wife cooks it. If he can afford it. I'd be happy to provide the man with a decent meal if he gets my head with one blow."

I walked blindly to the door. I couldn't listen anymore. I couldn't comfort her. I wished Cat could find the words that would make me love her again. That would make me feel for her, and not just feel sorry for her. But she didn't say another word. It was like I had ceased to exist. As I had told Edmund, wishing was a pointless exercise.

I knocked softly on the door and it was opened into the empty space beyond. I stepped through, fighting the panic that threatened tears. Fighting the anguish of losing my best friend, not to the ax but to the actions that led to its fall.

"Kitty?"

The voice was so quiet I almost didn't hear. Like she wanted me not to hear. I stopped.

"Will you watch?"

"No," I turned. "God. No."

She nodded but didn't look at me, still curled up before the block like a pilgrim at an altar.

"I understand," she said and her voice shook. "Truly, I do. But I would like to know . . . I would like to think that at least one person with a little bit of sympathy watched me die. Wishing me peace. I fear that everyone else will be wishing me ill."

"Why me?" I asked, unable to stop the question.

She faced me then, pale and serene, her eyes untarnished by artifice.

"Because I know you will forgive me."

I nodded.

56

The sun had not yet risen when they took Cat to the scaffold. But there was enough light for me to see the people gathered there. Henry Howard, the duke's son, his face like granite, stood shoulder-to-shoulder with the French ambassador. The small crowd huddled against the drizzling and freezing rain.

Cat walked between two guards, followed by three ladies, one her own sister, Isabel Baynton, their faces emotionless. Women of Wriothesley's choosing.

Cat stumbled at the first stair of the scaffold and the guards had to seize her arms. She collapsed into them, her tiny body tugging them off-balance, as if the knowledge of death added an emotional weight that could wrestle them to the earth. They waited and then, when it became obvious she couldn't do it herself, pulled her to her feet.

They carried her up the stairs, her limbs appearing useless. But when they reached the block, she shrugged them off, and they stepped back.

She stood, alone. I heard nothing of the voice that had shaped my childhood. Every word was pressed down to the earth by the rain, and none reached me, so far from the green, in my icy little tower room.

I watched as she removed her hood and handed it to one of the ladies. She smoothed her dress and then knelt. She pulled her hair to one side, just as she had practiced.

When the executioner raised his ax, I had to look away. I forgave Cat. I wished her peace. But I couldn't watch. In the end, I couldn't do her bidding.

It seemed to take the ax forever to fall. The thump of steel on wood came muffled to my window. Just once. I sank to the floor, wrapped myself in green brocade.

I heard no cheers. I heard no weeping.

An age passed during which I knew Jane went to the scaffold and gave her speech. I covered my head with my arms, unable to offer to Jane Boleyn even half of what I had done for Cat.

But still I heard the second thunk of heavy metal meeting little resistance before burying itself firmly in the block.

57

AND THEN ALL WENT QUIET. THE GUARDS DELIVERED FOOD AND DRINK, but little news. The king seemed to have forgotten me. Forgotten all of us. Or perhaps he was just trying to forget. My eighteenth birthday approached, and I finally wept. For myself. Without Cat, no one remembered my birthday. And I wept for Cat, who would never see hers.

In the end, Cat kept our secrets. She blamed Culpepper. She blamed Jane. But she didn't blame me. She protected me. Enough to keep me in prison for the rest of my life, the shadow of a shadow.

I watched the sun rise earlier and set later. I watched the light of day fade and vanish. I watched the little corner of sky that pierced my window and made my life unbearable. I watched as the scaffold was dismembered piece by piece and finally taken away, leaving the spot where it stood an empty hole of memory.

Spring approached, visible only in the reappearance of the grass on the green and the winking blue eye of the sky from my window. One bitter cold morning a knock woke me from my

Stygian sleep. The room was dark, but the window frame was lit by a slant of the rising sun.

The door opened and there the guard stood. With Alice Restwold.

She hesitated in the doorway, searching my face, my demeanor, for welcome or disgust.

"Visitor," the guard said.

Another shade from my past, again wanting something from me. Did they not know I had nothing to give?

"Hello, Kitty," Alice said.

"Alice."

"You look . . . well."

"Considering I'm in prison. Considering I've been abandoned by my family. Considering my best friend is dead."

"It wasn't my fault."

"No," I said. "I suppose it wasn't. You just stood by and let it happen. You just told whatever was asked of you and got away with it."

"I was imprisoned, too!" she cried.

"You?"

"Yes, they held me against my will."

"Not very tightly." I indicated her apparent liberty.

"I've been pardoned."

"Good for you. What did you give them for that?"

"I have little freedom. I've gained nothing."

"Oh?" I climbed to my feet, limbs creaking in dissention.

386

"Did *you* watch your best friend get beheaded from your chamber window? Did you have to watch her practice putting her head on the block the night before?"

"No, Kitty," she said, a thin line of tears against her lashes. We lapsed into a silence so profound I heard the guard shuffle his feet outside the door.

"Why have you come here?"

"Because you have no one else."

"Thank you for reminding me."

"It's true. Joan has been pardoned as well. She swears she'll never speak to any of us again. She's left for the country already."

"Lucky Joan."

"Cat always said that we only have each other."

I looked at her. She appeared to mean it. I nodded.

"I know you don't like me."

I nodded again. It felt good to acknowledge it.

"I know you don't trust me," she added.

"You've never given me reason to."

"Except that I never said a word about your connection," she said. "Or Joan's."

"You told on Cat, but not on the rest of us? Bully for you."

"Only after they found her out."

"So who told, Alice?" I asked. "I've had plenty of time to think about this and I can figure no one else. None of us but you escaped." I wanted so badly for her to confess. I wanted someone to blame.

"You really think that of me?"

"Who else could it be?"

"Mary Lascelles," Alice said, and waited for it to sink in.

Mary Lascelles. The girl who slept in the corner of the maidens' chamber. The one who suffered when Cat raged over being cut off from Francis. The one who hated us from the beginning.

"How?"

"She told her brother. He told his reformist friends. Friends who resented the Howards. They took the information to Archbishop Cranmer."

Cranmer, who always acted on his conscience.

"Lord Maltravers made sure my husband told me every detail. About how the archbishop left a note for the king in his prayer book. About the investigations that took place before we even knew what was happening."

"But you knew," I challenged her. "Because of the duke. Because of William."

"They sent me away before I could warn you."

"I see," I said, and then turned the full weight of my accusing, judgmental eyes on Alice Restwold. "But Mary Lascelles didn't know about Culpepper."

"It was impossible to hide, Kitty," Alice said. "I knew. You and Joan and Jane Boleyn knew. Francis knew. The true miracle was that no one said a word beforehand. Even Cat knew she was living on borrowed time."

Borrowed time. Isn't that what we all lived on? Every moment

we breathed was borrowed from the person who took the fall.

"They knew that they would be found guilty. We all did. They had no escape when the rumors got out."

"But Jane . . ."

"Will always be blamed."

She hid behind madness and made it that much easier for them. After that, no one would believe a word she said.

I nodded. There was no escape. They were dead.

Alice took a deep breath.

"Kitty, the king wants to forget the past. He wants the whole episode with Cat put from memory. He wants all the prisoners gone, and for no one to remind him of what once was."

"So I'm not even wanted in prison," I said bitterly.

As bad as prison was, the thought of getting out was even more frightening. I had nowhere to go. No one to go to. I could step out of the gates of the Tower onto the London streets and into a life of squalor and pain and premature death. No one in my class wanted me and no one else knew me. A woman alone was a woman fallen. And there was only one thing for a fallen woman to do.

"You're released, Kitty," Alice said, smiling tentatively. "You're free."

I could see that she wanted me to be happy, but all I felt was the cold clench of fear. Fear that turned quickly into anger.

"So you've come here to gloat?" I asked. "You have a position with some household somewhere, you have an understanding

with William Gibbon, you have it all. And you've come to let me know I have nothing?"

"No, Kitty," she said, stepping away from my vitriol. "It's nothing like that. It's just that Joan has decided to cut us off completely. And with Cat gone . . ."

"What?" I raged. "You think we can be friends? Why would you want that? I can't give you anything. All I can do is bring you down."

I turned away from her. Avoided looking out the window. The cell grew so silent I wondered if she had left.

"You're lucky, you know."

Alice's voice came from the far side of the room. I wheeled on her.

"Lucky? Oh yes, being friendless, without family or money, trained for nothing and proficient at little is really an enviable position."

"Yes," Alice said, the word a finality. "You are lucky. You have no ties. I'm stuck. Dependent. My husband was questioned. They thought he knew about my involvement. And now . . . he keeps very tight reins. We are both indebted to Lord Maltravers. I cannot leave. I have nowhere to go. I'm nineteen years old and I am little better than a slave.

"You, Kitty, have freedom. You can walk out of this room and disappear into London. No one will admonish you for being part of Cat's household. No one will tell you every day that you are *nothing* because of who you knew. You could change your name. You could live a real life."

"But Alice, all I'm fit for is life in a whorehouse." I nearly wept at how little she understood. "The streets of the city are dangerous. I have nowhere to live and nowhere to go. At least you have a roof over your head."

"I would trade with you in an instant."

I snorted bitter laughter.

"The grass is always greener, I suppose." I replied.

"I wish you all the best," said Alice quietly. She stepped forward and grabbed my hand, tightly enough that I couldn't pull away, though I tried. She glanced once over her shoulder to the firmly closed door.

"I saved this for you," she whispered. She pulled something out of her pocket and pressed it into my hand. I tried to drop it, but she wrapped my fingers around it and held firm. I felt the soft nubbins of embroidered cutwork.

"Lace?" I asked her, my hand still in hers. "Do you mock me, Alice?"

"No," she said, looking a little shocked.

"Lace is where this all started," I reminded her. "The lace wrapped around the key to the dormitory."

"The lace *you made*."

"So?" I asked. "It means nothing."

"No, Kitty," she said, letting go of me, "it means everything." She walked back to the door, and turned.

"I'm still married, Kitty," she said, almost as an afterthought. "My husband doesn't love me. But I am still married. I have no understanding. Definitely not with William Gibbon."

"Alice," I began, but didn't know where my words would lead. I didn't want her to continue. And I wanted to hear everything.

"He was ordered by the duke to keep company with me, so I could send messages. He would have lost his job, his reputation, if he didn't. I hate to admit that I enjoyed it, even though it wasn't real. Even though it hurt you. William Gibbon is kind and generous, even to a talebearer like me. In the end, he couldn't take the duke's orders anymore, and he left. I believe he's somewhere in London. He had eyes for only one of the queen's ladies. He always spoke only of you."

She knocked and when the door opened, she turned.

"Good-bye, Kitty."

"Word just came," the guard said, allowing her just enough room to pass. "You've received the king's pardon. You're to be released."

Alice always had the news before anyone else.

The guard opened the door wider and it yawned significantly. I could step through. I could go.

"Give me a moment," I said, turning away to hide the panic on my face.

The guard nodded and allowed the door to close, giving me the privacy I might need to use the chamber pot or straighten my skirts.

I opened my hand and looked at the roll of lace. I wondered if I could sell it, make enough money to afford something to eat and drink. It was worn, browned with age and use. It could have been the same piece used to wrap that fateful key,

three years before. Alice was like a squirrel, hiding things away after they'd been discarded. Giving them significance. Keeping things as well as secrets. It felt heavy. Full of memory. Too heavy to be just lace.

I unrolled it slowly, half expecting the key to fall out. I wanted to cry, because Alice had done this to spite me after all. She had a place and a marriage and I had nothing. All because of a foolish childhood friendship and the stupid need to belong. And that bloody, wretched key.

The lace began to spin and an object fell from it, into my left hand. It glowed dully.

The emerald. Set in gold. The one given to me by the king after the game of hide-and-seek, when he asked me to remain her friend. At the very least I had managed to keep that promise.

Alice had rescued the jewel before the men came to take Cat's. I hadn't even looked for it, knowing that my claim to anything precious would come to naught. But Alice, with her forethought and understanding of the importance of objects, had saved it.

And given it back. A river of forgiveness swept through me.

"Alice!" I cried, running through the door, clinging to the stone, the piece of lace trailing behind me like a banner. I passed the stunned guard, stumbled down the spiral stair-case and slipped out the door to the forecourt, but Alice was nowhere to be found.

I ran around the tower in which I had been housed, avoid-

ing the sight of the green. I barreled down the small slope to the gate that opened onto the Water Lane and out to Traitor's Gate, now closed to the river by the heavy portcullis.

"Stop!" One of the king's yeomen stepped in front of me.

"You're a prisoner, aren't you?" he said gruffly, gripping my shoulders.

"I've been released," I panted, the short sprint having taken my breath away. I had not moved more than five feet at a time for four months. My words came out as tiny clouds in the cold air.

He looked over my shoulder. I glanced back in time to see the guard from my cell nod.

"Very well," the yeoman said, letting go of me and standing aside. "But a little more dignity, if you please. There's no rush. You have your whole life ahead of you still."

I looked at him. He was shorter than I, though his hat gave the appearance of height. He was old, maybe as old as the king, the gray hair curling on his temples, wrinkles cornering his eyes. He had seen many prisoners in his time.

"Shall I accompany you to the gate?" he asked, as if concerned that I would bolt before someone announced that a mistake had been made.

I nodded, still breathless.

"A friend visited me," I gasped. "I'm looking for her. Did she pass this way?"

He looked at me sideways, walking down the Water Lane. The battlement walls rose on either side of us, creating a can-

yon of shadow, though the sun brightened the octagonal Bell Tower ahead of us.

"A girl?" he asked.

"Yes. Short, blonde, quite thin. She wore . . ." I couldn't think of what Alice wore. All I could picture was the russet gown Cat had given her.

"I have seen few ladies in the Water Lane today," the yeoman told me. Alice, with her ability to slip in and out of a place unnoticed, had disappeared. "Could she be in the household of someone who resides here?"

"I don't know," I said. "She didn't say. May I look for her?"

"I should think you'd want to be out of the Tower quickly," he said with a grin. "I thought that was why you were running."

"I want to find Alice," I said, stopping to look back over my shoulder. We stood on the bridge that crossed the stagnant moat, the water gleaming and oily around us. Could I have passed her? But there were no ladies to be seen. A milkmaid. A laundry maid. And men. Crowding the bridge, the gates, the Water Lane.

"You won't find her," he said. "The Tower is the size of a village. More people come in and out of these gates than I could count. Visitors. Victuallers. And if you don't know who she's with, the chances are slim."

"The Duke of Norfolk, perhaps?" I tried.

"Not likely," the yeoman laughed. "He hasn't set foot in the Tower. Afraid he'll be forced to stay."

True. The duke wouldn't come near the Tower ever again.

A roar interrupted my thoughts. We passed the animal dens in the Lion Tower, where the road turned sharply to the right to cross the moat one last time. I was leaving. I was walking out. I faced Tower Hill, outside the Tower proper, where George Boleyn and Thomas Cromwell and dozens of others who didn't merit a "private" execution had been put to death. The posts of the scaffold were clearly visible. London lay beyond them.

I stopped walking. "I can't."

"You must," the yeoman said. He must have seen it all before. Prisoners who tried to escape. Prisoners who were executed on Tower Hill. Prisoners released after thirty-five years. Prisoners who had nowhere to go.

He walked me across the bridge. Past the lions' cages where the animals paced in cells smaller than mine, looking balefully through the bars. The lions would never be set free. They would die in the Tower.

I didn't want to do that. Die in the Tower. Even though the thought of being alone on the streets of London terrified me, the thought of dying slowly in that tiny room frightened me more.

"That's the girl," the yeoman murmured.

"Pardon?" I asked.

"You're ready," he said as we came to the Bulwark Gate, the portal to the chaos of the city. "It shows in the tilt of the head, the set of the shoulders. I can see it in your eyes."

He smiled at me again.

"That's a lovely bit of lace," he said, indicating the piece that still fluttered from my hand. "If you cleaned it up, it might fetch a price."

"Thank you," I said. He was being nice. Trying to help me. Giving me possibilities.

"I think the embroiderer's guild makes its home in Cheapside."

Cheapside. William's family once owned a house there.

"My cousin is there. They'll know where to send you. But keep to this side of the river and stay away from Southwark," he added. "Someone might get the wrong impression."

Someone might think me a whore.

"Thank you," I said again, and stepped away from the bridge.

"Good luck," he said. "Keep the spire of St. Paul's in sight, and you'll make your way."

The cathedral jabbed at the sky, clearly visible. Not far. I smiled at him and dipped a tiny curtsey. That made him blush. Though I was no better than he. And thankfully, no worse. No longer a prisoner, I could hold my head a little higher.

He turned and walked back across the bridge. He didn't look back.

I gripped the emerald in my hand and said one more thank you to Alice. She had not only given me a gift, she had given me a push. I didn't need to sell the lace. That I would keep, and I would keep it with me always. It would remind me of who I

used to be. But the emerald I didn't need. I could sell it with no remorse. And for much more money. It represented the secrets I had been forced to keep. The silence.

With the money, I could purchase the materials to make more lace. Make my own way. My own choices. My own life.

The walls of London rose around me, the crushing weight of alleys and crowds. The assaulting odors of hundreds of strangers. The liberating painlessness of anonymity. And above it all, the finger of St. Paul's, beckoning me to my future.

Author's Note

Ask anyone and they'll tell you I'm a little obsessed with English history—particularly Henry VIII and his six wives. Dates and statistics create a framework but to me aren't the appeal of history—the characters are, their motivations, strengths, weaknesses, loves, and beliefs. And the places— Hampton Court, Windsor, the Tower of London. I have always been able to picture the scenes and characters in my mind, the gowns and jewels, the crowded rooms and even the smells (though I'm sure my imagination doesn't come close to the reality).

Because I find history riveting in its own right, I'm dedicated to maintaining historical accuracy in my novels. I spend hours reading histories and biographies. I visit castles and houses and even fields and street corners where palaces once stood, just to get a sense of place. But I have to admit I've taken poetic license when it suits the story.

The facts are these: Catherine Howard was born sometime

between 1521 and 1525. For my purposes, I settled on 1524 for her birth year, her age suiting the character I envisioned.

Little is known about Katherine Tylney. I couldn't discover where she came from or where she went. I don't even know how old she was. I invented her age, her character, her family. I gave her the same birthday as my father.

Wherever possible, I used Katherine Tylney's documented testimony to illustrate her role in Catherine Howard's life—they shared a bed in the maidens' chamber, she carried messages between the queen and Jane Boleyn, she admitted that one night on the progress she came into the queen's chamber and blurted, "Jesu, is the queen not abed yet?" She appeared to be a witness and not a participant. I chose to make her appear more.

Because we know so little about Kitty, we don't know anything about her romantic life. I discovered a T. Gibbon in the Duke of Norfolk's entourage, but changed his name to William because of the multitude of other Thomas names in the story (Culpepper, Wriothesley, Cromwell, Howard). And Ed. Standebanke is mentioned once as a member of the king's guard. I dubbed him Edmund and chose to make him young and handsome, as well.

The two boys are the only fictional characters in the novel. Others are fictionalized—we don't know if Alice Restwold was a "spy" for the Duke of Norfolk or why Jane Boleyn chose to facilitate the queen's affair. Part of the joy of writing historical

fiction is the license to take what we do know and ignite it with the question *what if?*

One historical figure I chose to cut entirely. Henry Manox was the music teacher in the dowager duchess's household, and Catherine Howard's love interest before Francis Dereham. History tells us that it was he who informed the duchess of the midnight revels in the maidens' chamber. But to avoid complicating the story further, and in an effort to shorten the first third of the book, I took him out of the picture. Because Mary Lascelles tattled about Catherine Howard's affair with Manox, I chose to make her the informant on Francis and just cut out the middleman. It tied neatly into the plot because Mary actually did start the snowball of information that eventually brought Catherine Howard down.

There are a couple of other instances where I fudged the truth. Joan Bulmer was in Yorkshire when she wrote the "blackmail" letter to the queen, yet I keep her placed firmly in Norfolk House. I neglect to mention that after the king's illness, the court went on a mini-progress around the south of England before stopping in Greenwich for three weeks—I made it look like they were in Greenwich the entire time. I did this to avoid tangents and explanations that got in the way of the story itself.

While researching this novel, I read the related works of Julia Fox, Antonia Fraser, Karen Lindsey, Lacey Baldwin Smith, David Starkey, and Alison Weir, amongst others. They

write brilliantly and their ability to express the minutiae of historical detail in a profound and engrossing way never ceases to astound me. I am also forever in debt to the encyclopedic knowledge and dedication to detail of my copyeditor, Janet Pascal. Any historical mistakes and all poetic license are entirely down to me.

Acknowledgments

Like Cat, I wouldn't be anywhere without my friends and mentors. I just hope I have made better use of their advice and am able to show the extent of my gratitude.

My brilliant agent, Catherine Drayton, saw the potential in me and in Kitty and launched us further than I ever imagined. Thank you for believing. And my thanks to the rest of the InkWell team who are behind this book: Richard Pine, Lyndsey Blessing, Alexis Hurley, and Nathaniel Jacks.

I couldn't have asked for a more honest or sympathetic editor, but more than that, Kendra Levin's comments and suggestions are always spot on, and for that I am more than grateful. I am also indebted to Regina Hayes for ensuring the book lived up to the title and vice versa. I am eternally beholden to Irene Vandervoort for adoring this book with a sumptuous cover and to Kate Renner for equally embellishing the interior.

From the beginning, I've had the YA Muses to help keep me

sane, to keep me on track, and to keep me going. Novels are not written in a vacuum, and I am thankful for the insight and friendship of Bret Ballou, Donna Cooner, Veronica Rossi, and Talia Vance.

I have also enjoyed the support and encouragement of writers and illustrators I have met personally and those I've only met online. My local critique group, the Apocalypsies, the Class of 2k12, and countless members of the SCBWI, were all kind enough to share their thoughts and wisdom on this rollercoaster, especially Susan Hart Lindquist, who gave me the tools I needed to write this book.

I wouldn't have made it through my crazy life without the friends who populated my childhood and shaped my adolescence, and those I've encountered along my journey through adulthood. You are too many to name, the greatest riches a girl could want. But for this particular book, I must mention Mona Dougherty specifically, because she reads everything I send her.

Lastly, all the words in the world can't express my thanks to my family: Graham Neate, my father-in-law, who never fails to ask how the writing is going; Judy and John Longshore, my parents, who let me find my way; Martha Longshore, my sister and sister of my soul, my first reader and biggest role model; my sons, Freddie and Charlie, who help me believe that anything is possible.

And Gary, who lifts me up and keeps me grounded.